50
Greatest
Stories
from East
and West

50
Greatest Stories from East and West

RUPA

Published by
Rupa Publications India Pvt. Ltd 2023
7/16, Ansari Road, Daryaganj
New Delhi 110002

Sales centres:
Bengaluru Chennai
Hyderabad Jaipur Kathmandu
Kolkata Mumbai Prayagraj

P-ISBN: 978-93-5702-792-2
E-ISBN: 978-93-5702-647-5

Third impression 2024

10 9 8 7 6 5 4 3

Printed in India

CONTENTS

INTRODUCTION

In the enchanting realm of literature, stories have the power to transcend time and space, weaving together the rich tapestry of human experience. They have the unique ability to connect us with cultures and minds far removed from our own, and in doing so, they expand our horizons, broaden our empathy and ignite our imagination. *50 Greatest Stories from East and West* embarks on a literary odyssey to bring you an exquisite collection of timeless narratives from some of the most brilliant minds in both Eastern and Western literature. As you delve into these stories penned by luminaries like Mark Twain, Guy de Maupassant, Franz Kafka, Rudyard Kipling, Virginia Woolf, Saki, Fyodor Dostoevsky, Rabindranath Tagore and many others, you will journey through worlds as diverse as the human spirit itself.

The merging of East and West, both geographically and intellectually, is a celebration of the universality of storytelling. For as long as humans have existed, stories have been a means of expression, education and entertainment, drawing people together regardless of the boundaries of time and space. By bringing together the voices of the East and West, this collection seeks to explore the common threads that unite us all as well as the unique characteristics that make each story an intricate work of art in its own right.

As we journey through these tales, we will discover that while cultures and landscapes may differ, the human condition remains remarkably consistent.

While in Virginia Woolf's stories, the profound exploration of human consciousness and the intricate interplay of inner thoughts and external reality offer a striking and deeply introspective portrayal of the human experience, Mark Twain's stories are a masterclass in the art of wit and social commentary, using humour and satire to expose the absurdities and hypocrisies of the society of his time. In the stories of Guy de Maupassant and Saki, the brilliant blend of dark humour and a keen observation of human nature creates a narrative world where the ordinary becomes extraordinary, often with a twist of irony that leaves readers both amused and contemplative. On the other hand are Anton Chekhov's stories, where in a subtle way the human condition is explored and the complex interplay of emotions reveals a profound empathy for the ordinary lives of his characters. Fyodor Dostoevsky's narratives, too, plunge into the depths of the human soul, wrestling with moral dilemmas and existential questions, leaving an indelible mark on the understanding of the human psyche.

50 Greatest Stories from East and West is more than just a collection of stories; it is a testament to the human capacity for imagination, creativity and the unyielding pursuit of truth, beauty and meaning. These stories serve as a bridge between East and West, highlighting the common themes that resonate across cultures, from the pursuit of love and happiness to the struggle with inner demons and the quest for self-discovery.

In a rapidly globalizing world, the need for cross-cultural understanding and empathy has never been more crucial. These stories provide a unique opportunity to explore the shared experiences, values and emotions that bind humanity together. They invite us to embrace the diversity of thought and expression found in the East and the West and to appreciate the subtle nuances that make each story a masterpiece in its own right.

The collection curated here is an invitation to embark on a literary voyage through time and space, transcending the boundaries of geography and culture. As you delve into the following pages, you will find stories that will entertain, enlighten and challenge you. Each narrative is a gem, a reflection of the wisdom and creativity of the human spirit, and a testament to the enduring power of storytelling.

So, dear reader, prepare to embark on a captivating journey through the 50 greatest stories from East and West. May these tales enrich your life, broaden your horizons and connect you with the hearts and minds of authors who have left an indelible mark on the world of literature. Whether you are well-acquainted with these classic tales or encountering them for the first time, *50 Greatest Stories from East and West* promises to be a literary adventure like no other, a celebration of the timeless art of storytelling, and a bridge that connects the East and West in the shared language of human experience.

THE SELFISH GIANT

Oscar Wilde

Every afternoon, as they were coming from school, the children used to go and play in the Giant's garden.

It was a large lovely garden, with soft green grass. Here and there over the grass stood beautiful flowers like stars, and there were twelve peach-trees that in the spring-time broke out into delicate blossoms of pink and pearl, and in the autumn bore rich fruit. The birds sat on the trees and sang so sweetly that the children used to stop their games in order to listen to them. 'How happy we are here!' they cried to each other.

One day the Giant came back. He had been to visit his friend the Cornish ogre, and had stayed with him for seven years. After the seven years were over he had said all that he had to say, for his conversation was limited, and he determined to return to his own castle. When he arrived he saw the children playing in the garden.

'What are you doing here?' he cried in a very gruff voice, and the children ran away.

'My own garden is my own garden,' said the Giant; 'any one can understand that, and I will allow nobody to play in it but myself.' So he built a high wall all round it, and put up a notice-board.

TRESPASSERS WILL
BE PROSECUTED

He was a very selfish Giant.

The poor children had now nowhere to play. They tried to

play on the road, but the road was very dusty and full of hard stones, and they did not like it. They used to wander round the high wall when their lessons were over, and talk about the beautiful garden inside. 'How happy we were there,' they said to each other.

Then the Spring came, and all over the country there were little blossoms and little birds. Only in the garden of the Selfish Giant it was still winter. The birds did not care to sing in it as there were no children, and the trees forgot to blossom. Once a beautiful flower put its head out from the grass, but when it saw the notice-board it was so sorry for the children that it slipped back into the ground again, and went off to sleep. The only people who were pleased were the Snow and the Frost. 'Spring has forgotten this garden,' they cried, 'so we will live here all the year round.' The Snow covered up the grass with her great white cloak, and the Frost painted all the trees silver. Then they invited the North Wind to stay with them, and he came. He was wrapped in furs, and he roared all day about the garden, and blew the chimney-pots down. 'This is a delightful spot,' he said, 'we must ask the Hail on a visit.' So the Hail came. Every day for three hours he rattled on the roof of the castle till he broke most of the slates, and then he ran round and round the garden as fast as he could go. He was dressed in grey, and his breath was like ice.

'I cannot understand why the Spring is so late in coming,' said the Selfish Giant, as he sat at the window and looked out at his cold white garden; 'I hope there will be a change in the weather.'

But the Spring never came, nor the Summer. The Autumn gave golden fruit to every garden, but to the Giant's garden she gave none. 'He is too selfish,' she said. So it was always Winter there, and the North Wind, and the Hail, and the Frost, and the Snow danced about through the trees.

One morning the Giant was lying awake in bed when he heard some lovely music. It sounded so sweet to his ears that he thought it must be the King's musicians passing by. It was really only a little linnet singing outside his window, but it was so long since he had heard a bird sing in his garden that it seemed to him to be the most beautiful music in the world. Then the Hail stopped dancing over his head, and the North Wind ceased roaring, and a delicious perfume came to him through the open casement. 'I believe the Spring has come at last,' said the Giant; and he jumped out of bed and looked out.

What did he see?

He saw a most wonderful sight. Through a little hole in the wall the children had crept in, and they were sitting in the branches of the trees. In every tree that he could see there was a little child. And the trees were so glad to have the children back again that they had covered themselves with blossoms, and were waving their arms gently above the children's heads. The birds were flying about and twittering with delight, and the flowers were looking up through the green grass and laughing. It was a lovely scene, only in one corner it was still winter. It was the farthest corner of the garden, and in it was standing a little boy. He was so small that he could not reach up to the branches of the tree, and he was wandering all round it, crying bitterly. The poor tree was still quite covered with frost and snow, and the North Wind was blowing and roaring above it. 'Climb up! little boy,' said the Tree, and it bent its branches down as low as it could; but the boy was too tiny.

And the Giant's heart melted as he looked out. 'How selfish I have been!' he said; 'now I know why the Spring would not come here. I will put that poor little boy on the top of the tree, and then I will knock down the wall, and my garden shall be the children's playground for ever and ever.' He was really very sorry for what he had done.

So he crept downstairs and opened the front door quite softly, and went out into the garden. But when the children saw him they were so frightened that they all ran away, and the garden became winter again. Only the little boy did not run, for his eyes were so full of tears that he did not see the Giant coming. And the Giant stole up behind him and took him gently in his hand, and put him up into the tree. And the tree broke at once into blossom, and the birds came and sang on it, and the little boy stretched out his two arms and flung them round the Giant's neck, and kissed him. And the other children, when they saw that the Giant was not wicked any longer, came running back, and with them came the Spring. 'It is your garden now, little children,' said the Giant, and he took a great axe and knocked down the wall. And when the people were going to market at twelve o'clock they found the Giant playing with the children in the most beautiful garden they had ever seen.

All day long they played, and in the evening they came to the Giant to bid him good-bye.

'But where is your little companion?' he said: 'the boy I put into the tree.' The Giant loved him the best because he had kissed him.

'We don't know,' answered the children; 'he has gone away.'

'You must tell him to be sure and come here to-morrow,' said the Giant. But the children said that they did not know where he lived, and had never seen him before; and the Giant felt very sad.

Every afternoon, when school was over, the children came and played with the Giant. But the little boy whom the Giant loved was never seen again. The Giant was very kind to all the children, yet he longed for his first little friend, and often spoke of him. 'How I would like to see him!' he used to say.

Years went over, and the Giant grew very old and feeble. He could not play about any more, so he sat in a huge armchair, and watched the children at their games, and admired his garden. 'I have many beautiful flowers,' he said; 'but the children are the most beautiful flowers of all.'

One winter morning he looked out of his window as he was dressing. He did not hate the Winter now, for he knew that it was merely the Spring asleep, and that the flowers were resting.

Suddenly he rubbed his eyes in wonder, and looked and looked. It certainly was a marvellous sight. In the farthest corner of the garden was a tree quite covered with lovely white blossoms. Its branches were all golden, and silver fruit hung down from them, and underneath it stood the little boy he had loved.

Downstairs ran the Giant in great joy, and out into the garden. He hastened across the grass, and came near to the child. And when he came quite close his face grew red with anger, and he said, 'Who hath dared to wound thee?' For on the palms of the child's hands were the prints of two nails, and the prints of two nails were on the little feet.

'Who hath dared to wound thee?' cried the Giant; 'tell me, that I may take my big sword and slay him.'

'Nay!' answered the child; 'but these are the wounds of Love.'

'Who art thou?' said the Giant, and a strange awe fell on him, and he knelt before the little child.

And the child smiled on the Giant, and said to him, 'You let me play once in your garden, to-day you shall come with me to my garden, which is Paradise.'

And when the children ran in that afternoon, they found the Giant lying dead under the tree, all covered with white blossoms.

THE FATHER

Bjørnstjerne Bjørnson

The man whose story is here to be told was the wealthiest and most influential person in his parish; his name was Thord Överaas. He appeared in the priest's study one day, tall and earnest.

'I have gotten a son,' said he, 'and I wish to present him for baptism.'

'What shall his name be?'

'Finn,—after my father.'

'And the sponsors?'

They were mentioned, and proved to be the best men and women of Thord's relations in the parish.

'Is there anything else?' inquired the priest, and looked up. The peasant hesitated a little.

'I should like very much to have him baptized by himself,' said he, finally.

'That is to say on a week-day?'

'Next Saturday, at twelve o'clock noon.'

'Is there anything else?' inquired the priest,

'There is nothing else;' and the peasant twirled his cap, as though he were about to go.

Then the priest rose. 'There is yet this, however.' said he, and walking toward Thord, he took him by the hand and looked gravely into his eyes: 'God grant that the child may become a blessing to you!'

One day sixteen years later, Thord stood once more in the priest's study.

'Really, you carry your age astonishingly well, Thord,' said the priest; for he saw no change whatever in the man.

'That is because I have no troubles,' replied Thord. To this the priest said nothing, but after a while he asked: 'What is your pleasure this evening?'

'I have come this evening about that son of mine who is to be confirmed to-morrow.'

'He is a bright boy.'

'I did not wish to pay the priest until I heard what number the boy would have when he takes his place in the church to-morrow.'

'He will stand number one.'

'So I have heard; and here are ten dollars for the priest.'

'Is there anything else I can do for you?' inquired the priest, fixing his eyes on Thord.

'There is nothing else.'

Thord went out.

Eight years more rolled by, and then one day a noise was heard outside of the priest's study, for many men were approaching, and at their head was Thord, who entered first.

The priest looked up and recognized him.

'You come well attended this evening, Thord,' said he.

'I am here to request that the banns may be published for my son: he is about to marry Karen Storliden, daughter of Gudmund, who stands here beside me.'

'Why, that is the richest girl in the parish.'

'So they say,' replied the peasant, stroking back his hair with one hand.

The priest sat a while as if in deep thought, then entered the names in his book, without making any comments, and the men wrote their signatures underneath. Thord laid three dollars on the table.

'One is all I am to have,' said the priest.

'I know that very well; but he is my only child; I want to do it handsomely.'

The priest took the money.

'This is now the third time, Thord, that you have come here on your son's account.'

'But now I am through with him,' said Thord, and folding up his pocket-book he said farewell and walked away.

The men slowly followed him.

A fortnight later, the father and son were rowing across the lake, one calm, still day, to Storliden to make arrangements for the wedding.

'This thwart is not secure,' said the son, and stood up to straighten the seat on which he was sitting.

At the same moment the board he was standing on slipped from under him; he threw out his arms, uttered a shriek, and fell overboard.

'Take hold of the oar!' shouted the father, springing to his feet, and holding out the oar.

But when the son had made a couple of efforts he grew stiff.

'Wait a moment!' cried the father, and began to row toward his son.

Then the son rolled over on his back, gave his father one long look, and sank.

Thord could scarcely believe it; he held the boat still, and stared at the spot where his son had gone down, as though he must surely come to the surface again. There rose some bubbles, then some more, and finally one large one that burst; and the lake lay there as smooth and bright as a mirror again.

For three days and three nights people saw the father rowing round and round the spot, without taking either food or sleep; he was dragging the lake for the body of his son. And toward morning of the third day he found it, and carried it in his arms up over the hills to his gard.

It might have been about a year from that day, when the priest, late one autumn evening, heard some one in the passage outside of the door, carefully trying to find the latch. The priest opened the door, and in walked a tall, thin man, with bowed form and white hair. The priest looked long at him before he recognized him. It was Thord.

'Are you out walking so late?' said the priest, and stood still in front of him.

'Ah, yes! it is late,' said Thord, and took a seat.

The priest sat down also, as though waiting. A long, long silence followed. At last Thord said,—

'I have something with me that I should like to give to the poor; I want it to be invested as a legacy in my son's name.'

He rose, laid some money on the table, and sat down again. The priest counted it.

'It is a great deal of money,' said he.

'It is half the price of my gard. I sold it to-day.'

The priest sat long in silence. At last he asked, but gently,—

'What do you propose to do now, Thord?'

'Something better.'

They sat there for a while, Thord with downcast eyes, the priest with his eyes fixed on Thord. Presently the priest said, slowly and softly,—

'I think your son has at last brought you a true blessing.'

'Yes, I think so myself,' said Thord, looking up, while two big tears coursed slowly down his cheeks.

THE PIECE OF STRING

Guy de Maupassant

On all the roads about Goderville the peasants and their wives were coming toward the town, for it was market day. The men walked at an easy gait, the whole body thrown forward with every movement of their long, crooked legs, misshapen by hard work, by the bearing down on the plough which at the same time causes the left shoulder to rise and the figure to slant; by the mowing of the grain, which makes one hold his knees apart in order to obtain a firm footing; by all the slow and laborious tasks of the fields. Their starched blue blouses, glossy as if varnished, adorned at the neck and wrists with a bit of white stitchwork, puffed out about their bony chests like balloons on the point of taking flight, from which protrude a head, two arms, and two feet.

Some of them led a cow or a calf at the end of a rope. And their wives, walking behind the beast, lashed it with a branch still covered with leaves, to hasten its pace. They carried on their arms great baskets, from which heads of chickens or of ducks were thrust forth. And they walked with a shorter and quicker step than their men, their stiff, lean figures wrapped in scanty shawls pinned over their flat breasts, their heads enveloped in a white linen cloth close to the hair, with a cap over all.

Then a *char-à-bancs* passed, drawn by a jerky-paced nag, with two men seated side by side shaking like jelly, and a woman behind, who clung to the side of the vehicle to lessen the rough jolting.

On the square at Goderville there was a crowd, a medley of men and beasts. The horns of the cattle, the high hats, with a long, hairy nap, of the wealthy peasants, and the head dresses of the peasant women, appeared on the surface of the throng. And the sharp, shrill, high-pitched voices formed an incessant, uncivilized uproar, over which soared at times a roar of laughter from the powerful chest of a sturdy yokel, or the prolonged bellow of a cow fastened to the wall of a house.

There was an all-pervading smell of the stable, of milk, of the dunghill, of hay, and of perspiration—that acrid, disgusting odour of man and beast peculiar to country people.

Master Hauchecorne, of Bréauté, had just arrived at Goderville, and was walking toward the square, when he saw a bit of string on the ground. Master Hauchecorne, economical like every true Norman, thought that it was well to pick up everything that might be of use; and he stooped painfully, for he suffered with rheumatism. He took the piece of slender cord from the ground, and was about to roll it up carefully, when he saw Master Malandain, the harness-maker, standing in his doorway and looking at him. They had formerly had trouble on the subject of a halter, and had remained at odds, being both inclined to bear malice. Master Hauchecorne felt a sort of shame at being seen thus by his enemy, fumbling in the mud for a bit of string. He hurriedly concealed his treasure in his blouse, then in his breeches pocket; then he pretended to look on the ground for something else, which he did not find; and finally he went on toward the market, his head thrust forward, bent double by his pains.

He lost himself at once in the slow-moving, shouting crowd, kept in a state of excitement by the interminable bargaining. The peasants felt of the cows, went away, returned, sorely perplexed, always afraid of being cheated, never daring to make up their minds, watching the vendor's eye, striving incessantly to detect the tricks of the man and the defect in the beast.

The women, having placed their great baskets at their feet,

took out their fowls, which lay on the ground, their legs tied together, with frightened eyes and scarlet combs.

They listened to offers, adhered to their prices, short of speech and impassive of face; or else, suddenly deciding to accept the lower price offered, they would call out to the customer as he walked slowly away:—

'All right, Mast' Anthime. You can have it.'

Then, little by little, the square became empty, and when the Angelus struck midday those who lived too far away to go home betook themselves to the various inns.

At Jourdain's the common room was full of customers, as the great yard was full of vehicles of every sort—carts, cabriolets, *char-à-bancs*, tilburys, unnamable carriages, shapeless, patched, with, their shafts reaching heavenward like arms, or with their noses in the ground and their tails in the air.

The vast fireplace, full of clear flame, cast an intense heat against the backs of the row on the right of the table. Three spits were revolving, laden with chickens, pigeons, and legs of mutton; and a delectable odour of roast meat, and of gravy dripping from the browned skin, came forth from the hearth, stirred the guests to merriment, and made their mouths water.

All the aristocracy of the plough ate there, at Mast' Jourdain's, the innkeeper and horse trader—a shrewd rascal who had money.

The dishes passed and were soon emptied, like the jugs of yellow cider. Every one told of his affairs, his sales and his purchases. They inquired about the crops. The weather was good for green stuffs, but a little wet for wheat.

Suddenly a drum rolled in the yard, in front of the house. In an instant everybody was on his feet, save a few indifferent ones; and they all ran to the door and windows with their mouths still full and napkins in hand.

Having finished his long tattoo, the public crier shouted in a jerky voice, making his pauses in the wrong places:—

'The people of Goderville, and all those present at the market are informed that between—nine and ten o'clock this morning on the Beuzeville—road, a black leather wallet was lost, containing five hundred—francs, and business papers. The finder is requested to carry it to—the mayor's at once, or to Master Fortuné Huelbrèque of Manneville. A reward of twenty francs will be paid.'

Then he went away. They heard once more in the distance the muffled roll of the drum and the indistinct voice of the crier.

Then they began to talk about the incident, reckoning Master Houlbrèque's chance of finding or not finding his wallet.

And the meal went on.

They were finishing their coffee when the corporal of gendarmes appeared in the doorway.

He inquired:—

'Is Master Hauchecorne of Bréauté here?'

Master Hauchecorne, who was seated at the farther end of the table, answered:—

'Here I am.'

And the corporal added:—

'Master Hauchecorne, will you be kind enough to go to the mayor's office with me? Monsieur the mayor would like to speak to you.'

The peasant, surprised and disturbed, drank his *petit verre* at one swallow, rose, and even more bent than in the morning, for the first steps after each rest were particularly painful, he started off, repeating:—

'Here I am, here I am.'

And he followed the brigadier.

The mayor was waiting for him, seated in his arm-chair. He was the local notary, a stout, solemn-faced man, given to pompous speeches.

'Master Hauchecorne,' he said, 'you were seen this morning,

on the Beuzeville road, to pick up the wallet lost by Master Huelbrèque of Manneville.'

The rustic, dumfounded, stared at the mayor, already alarmed by this suspicion which had fallen upon him, although he failed to understand it.

'I, I—I picked up that wallet?'

'Yes, you.'

'On my word of honour, I didn't even so much as see it.'

'You were seen.'

'They saw me, me? Who was it saw me?'

'Monsieur Malandain, the harness-maker.'

Thereupon the old man remembered and understood; and flushing with anger, he cried:—

'Ah! he saw me, did he, that sneak? He saw me pick up this string, look, m'sieu' mayor.'

And fumbling in the depths of his pocket, he produced the little piece of cord.

But the mayor was incredulous and shook his head.

'You won't make me believe, Master Hauchecorne, that Monsieur Malandain, who is a man deserving of credit, mistook this string for a wallet.'

The peasant, in a rage, raised his hand, spit to one side to pledge his honour, and said:—

'It's God's own truth, the sacred truth, all the same, m'sieu' mayor. I say it again, by my soul and my salvation.'

'After picking it up,' rejoined the mayor, 'you hunted a long while in the mud, to see if some piece of money hadn't fallen out.'

The good man was suffocated with wrath and fear.

'If any one can tell—if any one can tell lies like that to ruin an honest man! If any one can say—'

To no purpose did he protest; he was not believed.

He was confronted with Monsieur Malandain, who repeated and maintained his declaration. They insulted each other for a whole hour. At his own request, Master Hauchecorne was searched. They found nothing on him. At last the mayor, being sorely perplexed, discharged him, but warned him that he proposed to inform the prosecuting attorney's office and to ask for orders.

The news had spread. On leaving the mayor's office, the old man was surrounded and questioned with serious or bantering curiosity, in which, however, there was no trace of indignation. And he began to tell the story of the string. They did not believe him. They laughed.

He went his way, stopping his acquaintances, repeating again and again his story and his protestations, showing his pockets turned inside out, to prove that he had nothing.

They said to him:—

'You old rogue, *va!*'

And he lost his temper, lashing himself into a rage, feverish with excitement, desperate because he was not believed, at a loss what to do, and still telling his story. Night came. He must needs go home. He started with three neighbours, to whom he pointed out the place where he had picked up the bit of string: and all the way he talked of his misadventure.

During the evening he made a circuit of the village of Bréauté, in order to tell everybody about it. He found none but incredulous listeners.

He was ill over it all night.

The next afternoon, about one o'clock, Marius Paumelle, a farmhand employed by Master Breton, a farmer of Ymauville, restored the wallet and its contents to Master Huelbrèque of Manneville.

The man claimed that he had found it on the road; but, being unable to read, had carried it home and given it to his employer.

The news soon became known in the neighbourhood; Master Hauchecorne was informed of it. He started out again at once, and began to tell his story, now made complete by the dénouement.

He was triumphant.

'What made me feel bad,' he said, 'wasn't so much the thing itself, you understand, but the lying. There's nothing hurts you so much as being blamed for lying.'

All day long he talked of his adventure; he told it on the roads to people who passed; at the wine-shop to people who were drinking; and after church on the following Sunday. He even stopped strangers to tell them about it. His mind was at rest now, and yet something embarrassed him, although he could not say just what it was. People seemed to laugh while they listened to him. They did not seem convinced. He felt as if remarks were made behind his back.

On Tuesday of the next week, he went to market at Goderville, impelled solely by the longing to tell his story.

Malandain, standing in his doorway, began to laugh when he saw him coming. Why?

He accosted a farmer from Criquetot, who did not let him finish, but poked him in the pit of his stomach, and shouted in his face: 'Go on, you old fox!' Then he turned on his heel.

Master Hauchecorne was speechless, and more and more disturbed. Why did he call him 'old fox'?

When he was seated at the table, in Jourdain's Inn, he set about explaining the affair once more.

A horse-trader from Montvilliers called out to him:—

'Nonsense, nonsense, you old dodger! I know all about your string!'

'But they've found the wallet!' faltered Hauchecorne.

'None of that, old boy; there's one who finds it, and there's one who carries it back. I don't know just how you did it, but I understand you.'

The peasant was fairly stunned. He understood at last. He was accused of having sent the wallet back by a confederate, an accomplice.

He tried to protest. The whole table began to laugh.

He could not finish his dinner, but left the inn amid a chorus of jeers.

He returned home, shamefaced and indignant, suffocated by wrath, by confusion, and all the more cast down because, with his Norman cunning, he was quite capable of doing the thing with which he was charged, and even of boasting of it as a shrewd trick. He had a confused idea that his innocence was impossible to establish, his craftiness being so well known. And he was cut to the heart by the injustice of the suspicion.

Thereupon he began once more to tell of the adventure, making the story longer each day, adding each time new arguments, more forcible protestations, more solemn oaths, which he devised and prepared in his hours of solitude, his mind being wholly engrossed by the story of the string. The more complicated his defence and the more subtle his reasoning, the less he was believed.

'Those are a liar's reasons,' people said behind his back.

He realized it: he gnawed his nails, and exhausted himself in vain efforts.

He grew perceptibly thinner.

Now the jokers asked him to tell the story of 'The Piece of String' for their amusement, as a soldier who has seen service is asked to tell about his battles. His mind, attacked at its source, grew feebler.

Late in December he took to his bed.

In the first days of January he died, and in his delirium, of the death agony, he protested his innocence, repeating:

'A little piece of string—a little piece of string—see, here it is, m'sieu' mayor.'

BEFORE THE LAW

Franz Kafka

Before the law sits a gatekeeper. To this gatekeeper comes a man from the country who asks to gain entry into the law. But the gatekeeper says that he cannot grant him entry at the moment. The man thinks about it and then asks if he will be allowed to come in later on. 'It is possible,' says the gatekeeper, 'but not now.' At the moment the gate to the law stands open, as always, and the gatekeeper walks to the side, so the man bends over in order to see through the gate into the inside. When the gatekeeper notices that, he laughs and says: 'If it tempts you so much, try it in spite of my prohibition. But take note: I am powerful. And I am only the most lowly gatekeeper. But from room to room stand gatekeepers, each more powerful than the other. I can't endure even one glimpse of the third.' The man from the country has not expected such difficulties: the law should always be accessible for everyone, he thinks, but as he now looks more closely at the gatekeeper in his fur coat, at his large pointed nose and his long, thin, black Tartar's beard, he decides that it would be better to wait until he gets permission to go inside. The gatekeeper gives him a stool and allows him to sit down at the side in front of the gate. There he sits for days and years. He makes many attempts to be let in, and he wears the gatekeeper out with his requests. The gatekeeper often interrogates him briefly, questioning him about his homeland and many other things, but they are indifferent questions, the kind great men put, and at the end he always tells him once more that he cannot let him inside yet. The man, who has equipped himself with many things for his journey, spends everything, no matter how valuable, to win over the gatekeeper. The latter takes it all but, as he does so, says, 'I am taking this only so that you do not think you have failed to do anything.' During the many years the man observes the gatekeeper almost continuously. He forgets the other gatekeepers, and this one seems to him the only obstacle for entry into the law. He curses the unlucky circumstance, in the first years thoughtlessly and out loud, later, as he grows old, he still mumbles to himself. He becomes childish and, since in the long years studying the gatekeeper he has come to know the fleas in his fur collar, he even asks the fleas to help him persuade the gatekeeper. Finally his eyesight grows weak, and he does not know whether things are really darker around him or whether his eyes are merely deceiving him. But he recognizes now in the darkness an illumination which breaks inextinguishably out of the gateway to the law. Now he no longer has much time to live. Before his death he gathers in his head all his experiences of the entire time up into one question which he has not yet put to the gatekeeper. He waves to him, since he can no longer lift up his stiffening body. The gatekeeper has to bend way down to him, for the great difference has changed things to the disadvantage of the man. 'What do you still want to know, then?' asks the gatekeeper. 'You are insatiable.' 'Everyone strives after the law,' says the man, 'so how is that in these many years no one except me has requested entry?' The gatekeeper sees that the man is already dying and, in order to reach his diminishing sense of hearing, he shouts at him, 'Here no one else can gain entry, since this entrance was assigned only to you. I'm going now to close it.'

A BUSH DANCE

Henry Lawson

'Tap, tap, tap, tap.'

The little schoolhouse and residence in the scrub was lighted brightly in the midst of the 'close', solid blackness of that moonless December night, when the sky and stars were smothered and suffocated by drought haze.

It was the evening of the school children's 'Feast'. That is to say that the children had been sent, and 'let go', and the younger ones 'fetched' through the blazing heat to the school, one day early in the holidays, and raced—sometimes in couples tied together by the legs—and caked, and bunned, and finally improved upon by the local Chadband, and got rid of. The schoolroom had been cleared for dancing, the maps rolled and tied, the desks and blackboards stacked against the wall outside. Tea was over, and the trestles and boards, whereon had been spread better things than had been provided for the unfortunate youngsters, had been taken outside to keep the desks and blackboards company.

On stools running end to end along one side of the room sat about twenty more or less blooming country girls of from fifteen to twenty odd.

On the rest of the stools, running end to end along the other wall, sat about twenty more or less blooming chaps.

It was evident that something was seriously wrong. None of the girls spoke above a hushed whisper. None of the men spoke above a hushed oath. Now and again two or three sidled out, and if you had followed them you would have found that they went outside to listen hard into the darkness and to swear.

'Tap, tap, tap.'

The rows moved uneasily, and some of the girls turned pale faces nervously towards the side-door, in the direction of the sound.

'Tap—tap.'

The tapping came from the kitchen at the rear of the teacher's residence, and was uncomfortably suggestive of a coffin being made: it was also accompanied by a sickly, indescribable odour—more like that of warm cheap glue than anything else.

In the schoolroom was a painful scene of strained listening. Whenever one of the men returned from outside, or put his head in at the door, all eyes were fastened on him in the flash of a single eye, and then withdrawn hopelessly. At the sound of a horse's step all eyes and ears were on the door, till some one muttered, 'It's only the horses in the paddock.'

Some of the girls' eyes began to glisten suspiciously, and at last the belle of the party—a great, dark-haired, pink-and-white Blue Mountain girl, who had been sitting for a full minute staring before her, with blue eyes unnaturally bright, suddenly covered her face with her hands, rose, and started blindly from the room, from which she was steered in a hurry by two sympathetic and rather 'upset' girl friends, and as she passed out she was heard sobbing hysterically—

'Oh, I can't help it! I did want to dance! It's a sh-shame! I can't help it! I—I want to dance! I rode twenty miles to dance—and—and I want to dance!'

A tall, strapping young Bushman rose, without disguise, and followed the girl out. The rest began to talk loudly of stock, dogs, and horses, and other Bush things; but above their voices rang out that of the girl from the outside—being man comforted—

'I can't help it, Jack! I did want to dance! I—I had such—such—a job—to get mother—and—and father to let me come—and—and now!'

The two girl friends came back. 'He sez to leave her to him,' they whispered, in reply to an interrogatory glance from the schoolmistress.

'It's—it's no use, Jack!' came the voice of grief. 'You don't know what—what father and mother—is. I—I won't—be able—to ge-get away—again—for—for—not till I'm married, perhaps.'

The schoolmistress glanced uneasily along the row of girls. 'I'll take her into my room and make her lie down,' she whispered to her sister, who was staying with her. 'She'll start some of the other girls presently—it's just the weather for it,' and she passed out quietly. That schoolmistress was a woman of penetration.

A final 'tap-tap' from the kitchen; then a sound like the squawk of a hurt or frightened child, and the faces in the room turned quickly in that direction and brightened. But there came a bang and a sound like 'damn!' and hopelessness settled down.

A shout from the outer darkness, and most of the men and some of the girls rose and hurried out. Fragments of conversation heard in the darkness—

'It's two horses, I tell you!'

'It's three, you—!'

'Lay you—!'

'Put the stuff up!'

A clack of gate thrown open.

'Who is it, Tom?'

Voices from gatewards, yelling, 'Johnny Mears! They've got Johnny Mears!'

Then rose yells, and a cheer such as is seldom heard in scrublands.

Out in the kitchen long Dave Regan grabbed, from the far side of the table, where he had thrown it, a burst and battered concertina, which he had been for the last hour vainly trying to patch and make air-tight; and, holding it out towards the back-door, between his palms, as a football is held, he let it drop, and fetched it neatly on the toe of his riding-boot. It was a beautiful kick, the concertina shot out into the blackness, from which was projected, in return, first a short, sudden howl, then a face with one eye glaring and the other covered by an enormous brick-coloured hand, and a voice that wanted to know who shot 'that lurid loaf of bread?'

But from the schoolroom was heard the loud, free voice of Joe Matthews, M.C.,—

'Take yer partners! Hurry up! Take yer partners! They've got Johnny Mears with his fiddle!'

CANDLES

Margery Verner Reed

BEFORE a statue of Joan of Arc, in a little country church, a child knelt in prayer.

OH protect my papa—the little one prayed.

SHE lighted a candle—offered it to the Maid of France.

◆

A YOUNG girl prayed at the feet of the Saint. She burned a candle.

FOR ANDRÈ—for his safety.

THE invaders entered the village,—heeding neither church nor ground of the dead.

THEY ripped open shallow graves to show the living they had power—even over those who had gone. They killed the priest. And the nuns, even, from the school.

THEY damaged.

DESTROYED—

THE church caught fire. The candles, burning before the Saint of Domremy, blazed into one huge flame. It shot up to the roof. And seemed to cry—

O JOAN OF ARC—come back—France needs you.

◆

THE child—

AN Angel of Heaven

THE young girl who had prayed for André—two officers had taken her.

SHE struggled—

A SWORD—

THE flames of the burning village had revealed it.

MONSIEUR L'ABBÈ had said suicide was sin—but surely God would forgive—

SHE pierced the sword into her white flesh—blood flowed to the ground.

LITTLE FOOL muttered the maddened officer.

HE went back to the village—for more destroying.

A STONE from a burning house—

HE died with an oath.

BUT André, weeks before, had died with prayer upon his lips—a thought for his sweet betrothed.

THE CAT AND THE FIDDLE

L. Frank Baum

Hey, diddle, diddle,
The cat and the fiddle,
The cow jumped over the moon!
The little dog laughed
To see such sport,
And the dish ran off with the spoon!

Perhaps you think this verse is all nonsense, and that the things it mentions could never have happened; but they did happen, as you will understand when I have explained them all to you clearly.

Little Bobby was the only son of a small farmer who lived out of town upon a country road. Bobby's mother looked after the house and Bobby's father took care of the farm, and Bobby himself, who was not very big, helped them both as much as he was able.

It was lonely upon the farm, especially when his father and mother were both busy at work, but the boy had one way to amuse himself that served to pass many an hour when he would not otherwise have known what to do. He was very fond of music, and his father one day brought him from the town a small fiddle, or violin, which he soon learned to play upon. I don't suppose he was a very fine musician, but the tunes he played pleased himself; as well as his father and mother, and Bobby's fiddle soon became his constant companion.

One day in the warm summer the farmer and his wife determined to drive to the town to sell their butter and eggs and bring back some groceries in exchange for them, and while they were gone Bobby was to be left alone.

'We shall not be back until late in the evening,' said his mother, 'for the weather is too warm to drive very fast. But I have left you a dish of bread and milk for your supper, and you must be a good boy and amuse yourself with your fiddle until we return.'

Bobby promised to be good and look after the house, and then his father and mother climbed into the wagon and drove away to the town.

The boy was not entirely alone, for there was the big black tabby-cat lying upon the floor in the kitchen, and the little yellow dog barking at the wagon as it drove away, and the big moolie-cow lowing in the pasture down by the brook. Animals are often very good company, and Bobby did not feel nearly as lonely as he would had there been no living thing about the house.

Besides he had some work to do in the garden, pulling up the weeds that grew thick in the carrot-bed, and when the last faint sounds of the wheels had died away he went into the garden and began his task.

The little dog went too, for dogs love to be with people and to watch what is going on; and he sat down near Bobby and cocked up his ears and wagged his tail and seemed to take a great interest in the weeding. Once in a while he would rush away to chase a butterfly or bark at a beetle that crawled through the garden, but he always came back to the boy and kept near his side.

By and by the cat, which found it lonely in the big, empty kitchen, now that Bobby's mother was gone, came walking into the garden also, and lay down upon a path in the sunshine and lazily watched the boy at his work. The dog and the cat were good friends, having lived together so long that they did not care to fight each other. To be sure Towser, as the little dog was called, sometimes tried to tease pussy, being himself very mischievous; but when the cat put out her sharp claws and showed her teeth, Towser, like a wise little dog, quickly ran away, and so they managed to get along in a friendly manner.

By the time the carrot-bed was well weeded, the sun was sinking behind the edge of the forest and the new moon rising in the east, and now Bobby began to feel hungry and went into the house for his dish of bread and milk.

'I think I'll take my supper down to the brook,' he said to himself, 'and sit upon the grassy bank while I eat it. And I'll take my fiddle, too, and play upon it to pass the time until father and mother come home.'

It was a good idea, for down by the brook it was cool and pleasant; so Bobby took his fiddle under his arm and carried his dish of bread and milk down to the bank that sloped to the edge of the brook. It was rather a steep bank, but Bobby sat upon the edge, and placing his fiddle beside him, leaned against a tree and began to eat his supper.

The little dog had followed at his heels, and the cat also came slowly walking after him, and as Bobby ate, they sat one on either side of him and looked earnestly into his face as if they too were hungry. So he threw some of the bread to Towser, who grabbed it eagerly and swallowed it in the twinkling of an eye. And Bobby left some of the milk in the dish for the cat, also, and she came lazily up and drank it in a dainty, sober fashion, and licked both the dish and spoon until no drop of the milk was left.

Then Bobby picked up his fiddle and tuned it and began to play some of the pretty tunes he knew. And while he played he watched the moon rise higher and higher until it was reflected in the smooth, still water of the brook. Indeed, Bobby could not tell which was the plainest to see, the moon in the sky or the moon in the water. The little dog lay quietly on one side of him, and the cat softly purred upon the other, and even the moolie-cow was attracted by the music and wandered near until she was browsing the grass at the edge of the brook.

After a time, when Bobby had played all the tunes he knew, he laid the fiddle down beside him, near to where the cat slept, and then he lay down upon the bank and began to think.

It is very hard to think long upon a dreamy summer night without falling asleep, and very soon Bobby's eyes closed and he forgot all about the dog and the cat and the cow and the fiddle, and dreamed he was Jack the Giant Killer and was just about to slay the biggest giant in the world.

And while he dreamed, the cat sat up and yawned and stretched herself; and then began wagging her long tail from side to side and watching the moon that was reflected in the water.

But the fiddle lay just behind her, and as she moved her tail, she drew it between the strings of the fiddle, where it caught fast. Then she gave her tail a jerk and pulled the fiddle against the tree, which made a loud noise. This frightened the cat greatly, and not knowing what was the matter with her tail, she started to run as fast as she could. But still the fiddle clung to her tail, and at every step it bounded along and made such a noise that she screamed with terror. And in her fright she ran straight towards the cow, which, seeing a black streak coming at her, and hearing the racket made by the fiddle, became also frightened and made such a jump to get out of the way that she jumped right across the brook, leaping over the very spot where the moon shone in the water!

Bobby had been awakened by the noise, and opened his eyes in time to see the cow jump; and at first it seemed to him that she had actually jumped over the moon in the sky, instead of the one in the brook.

The dog was delighted at the sudden excitement caused by the cat, and ran barking and dancing along the bank, so that he presently knocked against the dish, and behold! it slid down the bank, carrying the spoon with it, and fell with a splash into the water of the brook.

As soon as Bobby recovered from his surprise he ran after the cat, which had raced to the house, and soon came to where the fiddle lay upon the ground, it having at last dropped from the cat's tail. He examined it carefully, and was glad to find it was not hurt, in spite of its rough usage. And then he had to go across the brook and drive the cow back over the little bridge, and also to roll up his sleeve and reach into the water to recover the dish and the spoon.

Then he went back to the house and lighted a lamp, and sat down to compose a new tune before his father and mother returned.

The cat had recovered from her fright and lay quietly under the stove, and Towser sat upon the floor panting, with his mouth wide open, and looking so comical that Bobby thought he was actually laughing at the whole occurrence.

And these were the words to the tune that Bobby composed that night:

Hey, diddle, diddle,
The cat and the fiddle,
The cow jumped over the moon!
The little dog laughed
To see such sport,
And the dish ran off with the spoon!

COUNTRY LIFE IN CANADA
IN THE 'THIRTIES'

Canniff Haight

Country life in Western Canada in the 'Thirties' was very simple and uneventful. There were no lines of social division such as now exist. All alike had to toil to win and maintain a home; and if, as was natural, some were more successful in the rough battle of pioneer life than others, they did not feel, on that account, disposed to treat their neighbors as their inferiors. Neighbors, they well knew, were too few and too desirable to be coldly and haughtily treated. Had not all the members of each community hewn their way side by side into the fastnesses of the Canadian bush? And what could a little additional wealth do for them, when the remoteness of the centers which might supply luxuries, enforced simplicity and made superfluities almost impossible?

The furnishings of their houses were plain, and the chief articles of dress, if substantial and comfortable, were of coarse homespun—the product of their own labor. The sources of amusement were limited. The day of the harmonium or piano had not come. Music, except in its simplest vocal form, was not cultivated; only the occasional presence of some fiddler afforded rare seasons of merriment to the delight both of old and young.

The motto of 'Early to bed and early to rise' was, even in winter, the strict rule of family life. In the morning all were up, and breakfast was over usually before seven. As soon as the gray light of dawn appeared, men and boys were off to the barns, not merely to feed the cattle but to engage in the needful and tedious labor of threshing by hand. In the evenings, the family gathered together for lighter tasks and pleasant talk around a glowing fire. In firewood, at least, there was, in those days, no need for economy.

We scarcely realize how largely little things may contribute to convenience and comfort. There were no lucifer matches at that date. It was needful to cover up carefully the live coals on the hearth before going to bed, so that there might be the means of starting the fire in the morning. This precaution was rarely unsuccessful; but sometimes a member of the family had to set out for a supply of fire from a neighbor's, in order that breakfast might be prepared. I remember well having to crawl out of my warm nest and run through the keen frosty air for half a mile or more, to fetch live coals from a neighbor's. It was, however, my father's practice to keep bundles of finely split pine sticks tipped with brimstone. With the aid of these, the merest spark served to start the fire.

In the spring, tasks of various kinds crowded rapidly upon us. The hams and beef that had been salted down in casks during the preceding autumn were taken out of the brine, washed off, and hung in the smoke-house. On the earthen floor beech or maple was burned; the oily smoke, given off by the combustion of these woods in a confined space, not only acted as a preservative but also lent a special flavor to the meat. Then ploughing, fencing, sowing, and planting followed in quick succession. No hands could be spared. The children must drive the cows to and from pasture. They must also take a hand at churning. It was a weary task, I remember, well to stand, perhaps for an hour, and drive the dasher up and down through the thick cream. How often did we examine the handle for evidence that the butter was forming, and what was the relief when the monotonous task was at an end. As soon as my legs were long enough, I had to follow a team; indeed, I drove the horses, mounted on the back of one of them, when my nether limbs were scarcely sufficiently grown to give me a grip.

The instruments for the agricultural operations were few and rough. Iron ploughs with cast-iron mold-boards and shares were commonly employed. Compared with our modern ploughs, they were clumsy things, but a vast improvement on the earlier wooden ploughs which, even at that date, had not wholly gone out of use. For drags, tree-tops were frequently used.

In June came sheep-washing. The sheep were driven to the bay shore and secured in a pen. One by one they were taken out, and the fleeces carefully washed. Within a day or two, shearing followed in the barn. The wool was sorted; some was reserved to be carded by hand; the remainder was sent to the mills to be turned into rolls. Then, day after day, for weeks, the noise of the spinning-wheel was heard, accompanied by the steady beat of the girls' feet, as they walked forward and backward drawing out and twisting the thread and running it on the spindle. This was work that required some skill, for on the fineness and evenness of the thread the character of the fabric largely depended. Finally, the yarn was carried to the weavers to be converted into cloth.

The women of the family found their hands very full in the 'Thirties.' Besides the daily round of housewifely cares, every season brought its special duties. There were wild strawberries and raspberries to be picked and prepared for daily consumption, or to be preserved for winter use. Besides milking, there was the making both of butter and cheese. There was no nurse to take care of the children, no cook to prepare the dinner. To be sure, in households when the work was beyond the powers of the family, the daughter of some neighbor might come as a helper. Though hired, she was treated in all respects as one of the family, and in return was likely to take the same sort of interest in the work, as if the tie that bound her to the family was closer than wages.

In truth, such help was regarded as a favor, and not as in any way affecting the girl's social position.

The girls in those days were more at home in a kitchen than a drawing-room. They did better execution at a tub than at a spinet, and could handle a rolling-pin more satisfactorily than a sketch-book. At a pinch, they could even use a rake or fork to good purpose in field or barn. Their finishing education was received at the country school along with their brothers. Of fashion books and milliners, few of them had any experiences.

Country life in Canada was plodding in the 'Thirties' and there was no varied outlook. The girls' training for future life was mainly at the hands of their mothers; the boys followed in the footsteps of their fathers. Neither sex felt that life was cramped or burdensome on that account. They were content to live as their parents had done. And though we can see that, as compared with later conditions, there may be something wanting in such an existence, this at least we know, that, in such a school and by such masters, the foundations of Canadian character and prosperity were laid.

THE DANGER OF LYING IN BED

Mark Twain

The man in the ticket-office said:

'Have an accident insurance ticket, also?'

'No,' I said, after studying the matter over a little. 'No, I believe not; I am going to be traveling by rail all day today. However, tomorrow I don't travel. Give me one for tomorrow.'

The man looked puzzled. He said:

'But it is for accident insurance, and if you are going to travel by rail—'

'If I am going to travel by rail I sha'n't need it. Lying at home in bed is the thing *I* am afraid of.'

I had been looking into this matter. Last year I traveled twenty thousand miles, almost entirely by rail; the year before, I traveled over twenty-five thousand miles, half by sea and half by rail; and the year before that I traveled in the neighborhood of ten thousand miles, exclusively by rail. I suppose if I put in all the little odd journeys here and there, I may say I have traveled sixty thousand miles during the three years I have mentioned. *And never an accident.*

For a good while I said to myself every morning: 'Now I have escaped thus far, and so the chances are just that much increased that I shall catch it this time. I will be shrewd, and buy an accident ticket.' And to a dead moral certainty I drew a blank, and went to bed that night without a joint started or a bone splintered. I got tired of that sort of daily bother, and fell to buying accident tickets that were good for a month. I said to myself, 'A man *can't* buy thirty blanks in one bundle.'

But I was mistaken. There was never a prize in the lot. I could read of railway accidents every day—the newspaper atmosphere was foggy with them; but somehow they never came my way. I found I had spent a good deal of money in the accident business, and had nothing to show for it. My suspicions were aroused, and I began to hunt around for somebody that had won in this lottery. I found plenty of people who had invested, but not an individual that had ever had an accident or made a cent. I stopped buying accident tickets and went to ciphering. The result was astounding. *The peril lay not in traveling, but in staying at home.*

I hunted up statistics, and was amazed to find that after all the glaring newspaper headlines concerning railroad disasters, less than *three hundred* people had really lost their lives by those disasters in the preceding twelve months. The Erie road was set down as the most murderous in the list. It had killed forty-six—or twenty-six, I do not exactly remember which, but I know the number was double that of any other road. But the fact straightway suggested itself that the Erie was an immensely long road, and did more business than any other line in the country; so the double number of killed ceased to be matter for surprise.

By further figuring, it appeared that between New York and Rochester the Erie ran eight passenger-trains each way every day—16 altogether; and carried a daily average of 6,000 persons. That is about a million in six months—the population of New York City. Well, the Erie kills from 13 to 25 persons of *its* million in six months; and in the same time 13,000 of New York's million die in their beds! My flesh crept, my hair stood on end. 'This is appalling!' I said. 'The danger isn't in traveling by rail, but in trusting to those deadly beds. I will never sleep in a bed again.'

I had figured on considerably less than one-half the length of the Erie road. It was plain that the entire road must transport at least eleven or twelve thousand people every day. There are many short roads running out of Boston that do fully half as much;

a great many such roads. There are many roads scattered about the Union that do a prodigious passenger business. Therefore it was fair to presume that an average of 2,500 passengers a day for each road in the country would be almost correct. There are 846 railway lines in our country, and 846 times 2,500 are 2,115,000. So the railways of America move more than two millions of people every day; six hundred and fifty millions of people a year, without counting the Sundays. They do that, too—there is no question about it; though where they get the raw material is clear beyond the jurisdiction of my arithmetic; for I have hunted the census through and through, and I find that there are not that many people in the United States, by a matter of six hundred and ten millions at the very least. They must use some of the same people over again, likely.

San Francisco is one-eighth as populous as New York; there are 60 deaths a week in the former and 500 a week in the latter—if they have luck. That is 3,120 deaths a year in San Francisco, and eight times as many in New York—say about 25,000 or 26,000. The health of the two places is the same. So we will let it stand as a fair presumption that this will hold good all over the country, and that consequently 25,000 out of every million of people we have must die every year. That amounts to one-fortieth of our total population. One million of us, then, die annually. Out of this million ten or twelve thousand are stabbed, shot, drowned, hanged, poisoned, or meet a similarly violent death in some other popular way, such as perishing by kerosene-lamp and hoop-skirt conflagrations, getting buried in coalmines, falling off house-tops, breaking through church, or lecture-room floors, taking patent medicines, or committing suicide in other forms. The Erie railroad kills 23 to 46; the other 845 railroads kill an average of one-third of a man each; and the rest of that million, amounting in the aggregate to that appalling figure of 987,631 corpses, die naturally in their beds!

You will excuse me from taking any more chances on those beds. The railroads are good enough for me.

And my advice to all people is, Don't stay at home any more than you can help; but when you have *got* to stay at home a while, buy a package of those insurance tickets and sit up nights. You cannot be too cautious.

(One can see now why I answered that ticket-agent in the manner recorded at the top of this sketch.)

The moral of this composition is, that thoughtless people grumble more than is fair about railroad management in the United States. When we consider that every day and night of the year full fourteen thousand railway-trains of various kinds, freighted with life and armed with death, go thundering over the land, the marvel is, *not* that they kill three hundred human beings in a twelvemonth, but that they do not kill three hundred times three hundred!

THE EMPEROR'S NEW CLOTHES

Hans Christian Andersen

Many years ago, there was an emperor, who was so excessively fond of new clothes, that he spent all his money in dress. He did not trouble himself in the least about his soldiers; nor did he care to go either to the theatre or to the chase, except for the opportunities then afforded him for displaying his new clothes. He had a different suit for each hour of the day; and as of any other king or emperor, one is accustomed to say, 'he is sitting in council,' it was always said of him, 'The Emperor is sitting in his wardrobe.'

Time passed merrily in the large town which was his capital; strangers arrived every day at the court. One day, two rogues, calling themselves weavers, made their appearance. They gave out that they knew how to weave stuffs of the most beautiful colours and elaborate patterns, the clothes manufactured from which should have the wonderful property of remaining invisible to everyone who was unfit for the office he held, or who was extraordinarily simple in character.

'These must, indeed, be splendid clothes!' thought the Emperor. 'Had I such a suit, I might at once find out what men in my realms are unfit for their office, and also be able to distinguish the wise from the foolish! This stuff must be woven for me immediately.' And he caused large sums of money to be given to both the weavers in order that they might begin their work directly.

So the two pretended weavers set up two looms, and affected to work very busily, though in reality they did nothing at all.

They asked for the most delicate silk and the purest gold thread; put both into their own knapsacks; and then continued their pretended work at the empty looms until late at night.

'I should like to know how the weavers are getting on with my cloth,' said the Emperor to himself, after some little time had elapsed; he was, however, rather embarrassed, when he remembered that a simpleton, or one unfit for his office, would be unable to see the manufacture. To be sure, he thought he had nothing to risk in his own person; but yet, he would prefer sending somebody else, to bring him intelligence about the weavers, and their work, before he troubled himself in the affair. All the people throughout the city had heard of the wonderful property the cloth was to possess; and all were anxious to learn how wise, or how ignorant, their neighbours might prove to be.

'I will send my faithful old minister to the weavers,' said the Emperor at last, after some deliberation, 'he will be best able to see how the cloth looks; for he is a man of sense, and no one can be more suitable for his office than he is.'

So the faithful old minister went into the hall, where the knaves were working with all their might, at their empty looms. 'What can be the meaning of this?' thought the old man, opening his eyes very wide. 'I cannot discover the least bit of thread on the looms.' However, he did not express his thoughts aloud.

The impostors requested him very courteously to be so good as to come nearer their looms; and then asked him whether the design pleased him, and whether the colours were not very beautiful; at the same time pointing to the empty frames. The poor old minister looked and looked, he could not discover anything on the looms, for a very good reason, viz: there was nothing there. 'What!' thought he again. 'Is it possible that I am a simpleton? I have never thought so myself; and no one must know it now if I am so. Can it be, that I am unfit for my office? No, that must not be said either. I will never confess that I could not see the stuff.'

'Well, Sir Minister!' said one of the knaves, still pretending to work. 'You do not say whether the stuff pleases you.'

'Oh, it is excellent!' replied the old minister, looking at the loom through his spectacles. 'This pattern, and the colours, yes, I will tell the Emperor without delay, how very beautiful I think them.'

'We shall be much obliged to you,' said the impostors, and then they named the different colours and described the pattern of the pretended stuff. The old minister listened attentively to their words, in order that he might repeat them to the Emperor; and then the knaves asked for more silk and gold, saying that it was necessary to complete what they had begun. However, they put all that was given them into their knapsacks; and continued to work with as much apparent diligence as before at their empty looms.

The Emperor now sent another officer of his court to see how the men were getting on, and to ascertain whether the cloth would soon be ready. It was just the same with this gentleman as with the minister; he surveyed the looms on all sides, but could see nothing at all but the empty frames.

'Does not the stuff appear as beautiful to you, as it did to my lord the minister?' asked the impostors of the Emperor's second ambassador; at the same time making the same gestures as before, and talking of the design and colours which were not there.

'I am certainly not stupid!' thought the messenger. 'It must be, that I am not fit for my good, profitable office! That is very odd; however, no one shall know anything about it.' And accordingly he praised the stuff he could not see, and declared that he was delighted with both colours and patterns. 'Indeed, please Your Imperial Majesty,' said he to his sovereign when he returned, 'the cloth which the weavers are preparing is extraordinarily magnificent.'

The whole city was talking of the splendid cloth which the Emperor had ordered to be woven at his own expense.

And now the Emperor himself wished to see the costly manufacture, while it was still in the loom. Accompanied by a select number of officers of the court, among them whom were the two honest men who had already admired the cloth, he went to the crafty impostors, who, as soon as they were aware of the Emperor's approach, went on working more diligently than ever; although they still did not pass a single thread through the looms.

'Is not the work absolutely magnificent?' said the two officers of the crown, already mentioned. 'If your Majesty will only be pleased to look at it! What a splendid design! What glorious colours!' and at the same time they pointed to the empty frames; for they imagined that everyone else could see this exquisite piece of workmanship.

'How is this?' said the Emperor to himself. 'I can see nothing! This is indeed a terrible affair! Am I a simpleton, or am I unfit to be an Emperor? That would be the worst thing that could happen—Oh! the cloth is charming,' said he, aloud. 'It has my complete approbation.' And he smiled most graciously, and looked closely at the empty looms; for on no account would he say that he could not see what two of the officers of his court had praised so much. All his retinue now strained their eyes, hoping to discover something on the looms, but they could see no more than the others; nevertheless, they all exclaimed, 'Oh, how beautiful!' and advised his majesty to have some new clothes made from this splendid material, for the approaching procession. 'Magnificent! Charming! Excellent!' resounded on all sides; and everyone was uncommonly gay. The Emperor shared in the general satisfaction; and presented the impostors with the riband of an order of knighthood, to be worn in their button-holes, and the title of 'Gentlemen Weavers.'

The rogues sat up the whole of the night before the day on which the procession was to take place, and had sixteen lights burning, so that everyone might see how anxious they were to finish the Emperor's new suit. They pretended to roll the cloth off the looms; cut the air with their scissors; and sewed with needles without any thread in them. 'See!' cried they, at last. 'The Emperor's new clothes are ready!'

And now the Emperor, with all the grandees of his court, came to the weavers; and the rogues raised their arms, as if in the act of holding something up, saying, 'Here are Your Majesty's trousers! Here is the scarf! Here is the mantle! The whole suit is as light as a cobweb; one might fancy one has nothing at all on, when dressed in it; that, however, is the great virtue of this delicate cloth.'

'Yes indeed!' said all the courtiers, although not one of them could see anything of this exquisite manufacture.

'If Your Imperial Majesty will be graciously pleased to take off your clothes, we will fit on the new suit, in front of the looking glass.'

The Emperor was accordingly undressed, and the rogues pretended to array him in his new suit; the Emperor turning round, from side to side, before the looking glass.

'How splendid His Majesty looks in his new clothes, and how well they fit!' everyone cried out. 'What a design! What colours! These are indeed royal robes!'

'The canopy which is to be borne over Your Majesty, in the procession, is waiting,' announced the chief master of the ceremonies.

'I am quite ready,' answered the Emperor. 'Do my new clothes fit well?' asked he, turning himself round again before the looking glass, in order that he might appear to be examining his handsome suit.

The lords of the bedchamber, who were to carry His Majesty's train felt about on the ground, as if they were lifting up the ends of the mantle; and pretended to be carrying something; for they would by no means betray anything like simplicity, or unfitness for their office.

So now the Emperor walked under the high canopy in the midst of the procession, through the streets of his capital; and all the people standing by, and those at the windows, cried out, 'Oh! How beautiful are our Emperor's new clothes! What a magnificent train there is to the mantle; and how gracefully the scarf hangs!' in short, no one would allow that he could not see these much-admired clothes; because, in doing so, he would have declared himself either a simpleton or unfit for his office. Certainly, none of the Emperor's various suits, had ever made so great an impression, as these invisible ones.

'But the Emperor has nothing at all on!' said a little child.

'Listen to the voice of innocence!' exclaimed his father; and what the child had said was whispered from one to another.

'But he has nothing at all on!' at last cried out all the people. The Emperor was vexed, for he knew that the people were right; but he thought the procession must go on! And the lords of the bedchamber took greater pains than ever, to appear holding up a train, although, in reality, there was no train to hold.

A GERM DESTROYER

Rudyard Kipling

Pleasant it is for the Little Tin Gods
When great Jove nods;
But Little Tin Gods make their little mistakes
In missing the hour when great Jove wakes.

As a general rule, it is inexpedient to meddle with questions of State in a land where men are highly paid to work them out for you. This tale is a justifiable exception.

Once in every five years, as you know, we indent for a new Viceroy; and each Viceroy imports, with the rest of his baggage, a Private Secretary, who may or may not be the real Viceroy, just as Fate ordains. Fate looks after the Indian Empire because it is so big and so helpless.

There was a Viceroy once who brought out with him a turbulent Private Secretary—a hard man with a soft manner and a morbid passion for work. This Secretary was called Wonder—John Fennil Wonder. The Viceroy possessed no name—nothing but a string of counties and two-thirds of the alphabet after them. He said, in confidence, that he was the electro-plated figurehead of a golden administration, and he watched in a dreamy, amused way Wonder's attempts to draw matters which were entirely outside his province into his own hands. 'When we are all cherubims together,' said His Excellency once, 'my dear, good friend Wonder will head the conspiracy for plucking out Gabriel's tail feathers or stealing Peter's keys. *Then* I shall report him.'

But, though the Viceroy did nothing to check Wonder's

officiousness, other people said unpleasant things. May be the Members of Council began it; but finally all Simla agreed that there was 'too much Wonder and too little Viceroy' in that rule. Wonder was always quoting 'His Excellency.' It was 'His Excellency this,' 'His Excellency that,' 'In the opinion of His Excellency,' and so on. The Viceroy smiled; but he did not heed. He said that, so long as his old men squabbled with his 'dear, good Wonder,' they might be induced to leave the Immemorial East in peace.

'No wise man has a Policy,' said the Viceroy. 'A Policy is the blackmail levied on the Fool by the Unforeseen. I am not the former, and I do not believe in the latter.'

I do not quite see what this means, unless it refers to an Insurance Policy. Perhaps it was the Viceroy's way of saying:- 'Lie low.'

That season came up to Simla one of these crazy people with only a single idea. These are the men who make things move; but they are not nice to talk to. This man's name was Mellish, and he had lived for fifteen years on land of his own, in Lower Bengal, studying cholera. He held that cholera was a germ that propagated itself as it flew through a muggy atmosphere; and stuck in the branches of trees like a wool-flake. The germ could be rendered sterile, he said, by 'Mellish's Own Invincible Fumigatory'—a heavy violet-black powder—'the result of fifteen years' scientific investigation, Sir!'

Inventors seem very much alike as a caste. They talk loudly, especially about 'conspiracies of monopolists'; they beat upon the table with their fists; and they secrete fragments of their inventions about their persons.

Mellish said that there was a Medical 'Ring' at Simla, headed by the Surgeon-General, who was in league, apparently, with all the Hospital Assistants in the Empire.

I forget exactly how he proved it, but it had something to

do with 'skulking up to the Hills'; and what Mellish wanted was the independent evidence of the Viceroy—'Steward of our Most Gracious Majesty the Queen, Sir.' So Mellish went up to Simla, with eighty-four pounds of Fumigatory in his trunk, to speak to the Viceroy and to show him the merits of the invention.

But it is easier to see a Viceroy than to talk to him, unless you chance to be as important as Mellishe of Madras. He was a six-thousand-rupee man, so great that his daughters never 'married.' They 'contracted alliances.' He himself was not paid. He 'received emoluments,' and his journeys about the country were 'tours of observation.' His business was to stir up the people in Madras with a long pole—as you stir up stench in a pond—and the people had to come up out of their comfortable old ways and gasp—'This is Enlightenment and Progress. Isn't it fine!' Then they give Mellishe statues and jasmine garlands, in the hope of getting rid of him.

Mellishe came up to Simla 'to confer with the Viceroy.' That was one of his perquisites. The Viceroy knew nothing of Mellishe except that he was 'one of those middle-class deities who seem necessary to the spiritual comfort of this Paradise of the Middle-classes,' and that, in all probability he had 'suggested, designed, founded, and endowed all the public institutions in Madras.' Which proves that His Excellency, though dreamy, had experience of the ways of six-thousand-rupee men.

Mellishe's name was E. Mellishe, and Mellish's was E.S. Mellish, and they were both staying at the same hotel, and the Fate that looks after the Indian Empire ordained that Wonder should blunder and drop the final 'e'; that the Chaprassi should help him, and that the note which ran—

DEAR MR MELLISH,—Can you set aside your other engagements, and lunch with us at two to-morrow? His Excellency has an hour at your disposal then, should be given to Mellish with the Fumigatory. He nearly wept with pride and delight, and at the appointed hour cantered to Peterhoff, a big paper-bag full of the Fumigatory in his coat-tail pockets. He had his chance, and he meant to make the most of it. Mellishe of Madras had been so portentously solemn about his 'conference,' that Wonder had arranged for a private tiffin,—no A.-D.-C.'s, no Wonder, no one but the Viceroy, who said plaintively that he feared being left alone with unmuzzled autocrats like the great Mellishe of Madras.

But his guest did not bore the Viceroy. On the contrary, he amused him. Mellish was nervously anxious to go straight to his Fumigatory, and talked at random until tiffin was over and His Excellency asked him to smoke. The Viceroy was pleased with Mellish because he did not talk 'shop.'

As soon as the cheroots were lit, Mellish spoke like a man; beginning with his cholera-theory, reviewing his fifteen years' 'scientific labours,' the machinations of the 'Simla Ring,' and the excellence of his Fumigatory, while the Viceroy watched him between half-shut eyes and thought—'Evidently this is the wrong tiger; but it is an original animal.' Mellish's hair was standing on end with excitement, and he stammered. He began groping in his coat-tails and, before the Viceroy knew what was about to happen, he had tipped a bagful of his powder into the big silver ash-tray.

'J-j-judge for yourself, Sir,' said Mellish. 'Y' Excellency shall judge for yourself! Absolutely infallible, on my honour.'

He plunged the lighted end of his cigar into the powder, which began to smoke like a volcano, and send up fat, greasy wreaths of copper-coloured smoke. In five seconds the room was filled with a most pungent and sickening stench—a reek that took fierce hold of the trap of your wind-pipe and shut it. The powder hissed and fizzed, and sent out blue and green sparks, and the smoke rose till you could neither see, nor breathe, nor gasp. Mellish, however, was used to it.

'Nitrate of strontia,' he shouted; 'baryta, bone-meal, *etcetera*! Thousand cubic feet smoke per cubic inch. Not a germ could live—not a germ, Y' Excellency!'

But His Excellency had fled, and was coughing at the foot of the stairs, while all Peterhoff hummed like a hive. Red Lancers came in, and the head Chaprassi who speaks English came in, and mace-bearers came in, and ladies ran downstairs screaming, 'Fire'; for the smoke was drifting through the house and oozing out of the windows, and bellying along the verandahs, and wreathing and writhing across the gardens. No one could enter the room where Mellish was lecturing on his Fumigatory till that unspeakable powder had burned itself out.

Then an Aide-de-Camp, who desired the V.C., rushed through the rolling clouds and hauled Mellish into the hall. The Viceroy was prostrate with laughter, and could only waggle his hands feebly at Mellish, who was shaking a fresh bagful of powder at him.

'Glorious! Glorious!' sobbed His Excellency. 'Not a germ, as you justly observe, could exist! I can swear it. A magnificent success!'

Then he laughed till the tears came, and Wonder, who had caught the real Mellishe snorting on the Mall, entered and was deeply shocked at the scene. But the Viceroy was delighted, because he saw that Wonder would presently depart. Mellish with the Fumigatory was also pleased, for he felt that he had smashed the Simla Medical 'Ring.'

◆

Few men could tell a story like His Excellency when he took the trouble, and his account of 'my dear, good Wonder's friend with the powder' went the round of Simla, and flippant folk made Wonder unhappy by their remarks.

But His Excellency told the tale once too often—for Wonder. As he meant to do. It was at a Seepee Picnic. Wonder was sitting just behind the Viceroy.

'And I really thought for a moment,' wound up His Excellency, 'that my dear, good Wonder had hired an assassin to clear his way to the throne!'

Every one laughed; but there was a delicate sub-tinkle in the Viceroy's tone which Wonder understood. He found that his health was giving way; and the Viceroy allowed him to go, and presented him with a flaming 'character' for use at Home among big people.

'My fault entirely,' said His Excellency, in after seasons, with a twinkle in his eye. 'My inconsistency must always have been distasteful to such a masterly man.'

HIS WEDDED WIFE

Rudyard Kipling

Cry 'Murder!' in the market-place, and each
Will turn upon his neighbor anxious eyes
That ask:—'Art thou the man?' We hunted Cain
Some centuries ago, across the world,
That bred the fear our own misdeeds maintain
To-day.

—Vibart's Moralities.

Shakespeare says something about worms, or it may be giants or beetles, turning if you tread on them too severely. The safest plan is never to tread on a worm—not even on the last new subaltern from Home, with his buttons hardly out of their tissue paper, and the red of sappy English beef in his cheeks. This is the story of the worm that turned. For the sake of brevity, we will call Henry Augustus Ramsay Faizanne, 'The Worm,' although he really was an exceedingly pretty boy, without a hair on his face, and with a waist like a girl's, when he came out to the Second 'Shikarris' and was made unhappy in several ways. The 'Shikarris' are a high-caste regiment, and you must be able to do things well—play a banjo, or ride more than little, or sing, or act—to get on with them.

The Worm did nothing except fall off his pony, and knock chips out of gate posts with his trap. Even that became monotonous after a time. He objected to whist, cut the cloth at billiards, sang out of tune, kept very much to himself, and wrote to his mamma and sisters at home. Four of these five things were vices which the 'Shikarris' objected to and set themselves to eradicate. Everyone knows how subalterns are, by brother subalterns, softened and not permitted to be ferocious. It is good and wholesome, and does no one any harm, unless tempers are lost; and then there is trouble. There was a man once—but that is another story.

The 'Shikarris' shikarred The Worm very much, and he bore everything without winking. He was so good and so anxious to learn, and flushed so pink, that his education was cut short, and he was left to his own devices by everyone except the Senior Subaltern who continued to make life a burden to The Worm. The Senior Subaltern meant no harm; but his chaff was coarse, and he didn't quite understand where to stop. He had been waiting too long for his Company; and that always sours a man. Also he was in love, which made him worse.

One day, after he had borrowed The Worm's trap for a lady who never existed, had used it himself all the afternoon, had sent a note to The Worm, purporting to come from the lady, and was telling the Mess all about it, The Worm rose in his place and said, in his quiet, ladylike voice:—'That was a very pretty sell; but I'll lay you a month's pay to a month's pay when you get your step, that I work a sell on you that you'll remember for the rest of your days, and the Regiment after you when you're dead or broke.' The Worm wasn't angry in the least, and the rest of the Mess shouted. Then the Senior Subaltern looked at The Worm from the boots upward, and down again and said: 'Done, Baby.' The Worm took the rest of the Mess to witness that the bet had been taken, and retired into a book with a sweet smile.

Two months passed, and the Senior Subaltern still educated The Worm, who began to move about a little more as the hot weather came on. I have said that the Senior Subaltern was in love. The curious thing is that a girl was in love with the Senior Subaltern. Though the Colonel said awful things, and the majors snorted, and married captains looked unutterable wisdom, and the juniors scoffed, those two were engaged.

The Senior Subaltern was so pleased with getting his Company and his acceptance at the same time that he forgot to bother The Worm. The girl was a pretty girl, and had money of her own. She does not come into this story at all.

One night, at beginning of the hot weather, all the Mess, except The Worm who had gone to his own room to write home letters, were sitting on the platform outside the Mess House. The band had finished playing, but no one wanted to go in. And the captains' wives were there also. The folly of a man in love is unlimited. The Senior Subaltern had been holding forth on the merits of the girl he was engaged to, and the ladies were purring approval, while the men yawned, when there was a rustle of skirts in the dark, and a tired, faint voice lifted itself. 'Where's my husband?'

I do not wish in the least to reflect on the morality of the 'Shikarris'; but it is on record that four men jumped up as if they had been shot. Three of them were married men. Perhaps they were afraid that their wives had come from home unbeknownst. The fourth said that he had acted on the impulse of the moment. He explained this afterwards.

Then the voice cried: 'Oh Lionel!' Lionel was the Senior Subaltern's name. A woman came into the little circle of light by the candles on the peg tables, stretching out her hands to the dark where the Senior Subaltern was, and sobbing. We rose to our feet, feeling that things were going to happen and ready to believe the worst. In this bad, small world of ours, one knows so little of the life of the next man—which, after all, is entirely his own concern—that one is not surprised when a crash comes. Anything might turn up any day for anyone. Perhaps the Senior Subaltern had been trapped in his youth. Men are crippled that way occasionally. We didn't know; we wanted to hear; and the captains' wives were as anxious as we. If he *had* been trapped, he was to be excused; for the woman from nowhere, in the dusty shoes and grey travelling dress, was very lovely, with black hair and great eyes full of tears. She was tall, with a fine figure, and her voice had a running sob in it pitiful to hear. As soon as the Senior Subaltern stood up, she threw her arms round his neck, and called him 'my darling' and said she could not bear waiting alone in England, and his letters were so short and cold, and she was his to the end of the world, and would he forgive her? This did not sound quite like a lady's way of speaking. It was too demonstrative.

Things seemed black indeed, and the captains' wives peered under their eyebrows at the Senior Subaltern, and the colonel's face set like the Day of Judgment framed in grey bristles, and no one spoke for a while.

Next the Colonel said, very shortly: 'Well, sir?' and the woman sobbed afresh. The Senior Subaltern was half choked with the arms round his neck, but he gasped out: 'It's a d—d lie! I never had a wife in my life!' 'Don't swear,' said the Colonel. 'Come into the Mess. We must sift this clear somehow,' and he sighed to himself, for he believed in his 'Shikarris,' did the Colonel.

We trooped into the anteroom, under the full lights, and there we saw how beautiful the woman was. She stood up in the middle of us all, sometimes choking with crying, then hard and proud, and then holding out her arms to the Senior Subaltern. It was like the fourth act of a tragedy. She told us how the Senior Subaltern had married her when he was Home on leave eighteen months before; and she seemed to know all that we knew, and more too, of his people and his past life. He was white and ashy grey, trying now and again to break into the torrent of her words; and we, noting how lovely she was and what a criminal he looked, esteemed him a beast of the worst kind. We felt sorry for him, though.

I shall never forget the indictment of the Senior Subaltern by his wife. Nor will he. It was so sudden, rushing out of the dark, unannounced, into our dull lives. The captains' wives stood back; but their eyes were alight, and you could see that they had already convicted and sentenced the Senior Subaltern. The Colonel seemed five years older. One major was shading his eyes with his hand and watching the woman from underneath it. Another was chewing his mustache and smiling quietly as if he were witnessing a play. Full in the open space in the centre, by the whist tables, the Senior Subaltern's terrier was hunting for fleas. I remember all this as clearly as though a photograph were in my hand. I remember the look of horror on the Senior Subaltern's face. It was rather like seeing a man hanged; but much more interesting. Finally, the woman wound up by saying that the Senior Subaltern carried a double F. M. in tattoo on his left shoulder. We all knew that, and to our innocent minds it seemed to clinch the matter. But one of the bachelor majors said very politely: 'I presume that your marriage certificate would be more to the purpose?'

That roused the woman. She stood up and sneered at the Senior Subaltern for a cur, and abused the major and the Colonel and all the rest. Then she wept, and then she pulled a paper from her breast, saying imperially: 'Take that! And let my husband—my lawfully wedded husband—read it aloud—if he dare!'

There was a hush, and the men looked into each other's eyes as the Senior Subaltern came forward in a dazed and dizzy way, and took the paper. We were wondering, as we stared, whether there was anything against any one of us that might turn up later on. The Senior Subaltern's throat was dry; but, as he ran his eye over the paper, he broke out into a hoarse cackle of relief, and said to the woman: 'You young blackguard!'

But the woman had fled through a door, and on the paper was written: 'This is to certify that I, The Worm, have paid in full my debts to the Senior Subaltern, and, further, that the Senior Subaltern is my debtor, by agreement on the 23rd of February, as by the Mess attested, to the extent of one month's Captain's pay, in the lawful currency of the India Empire.'

Then a deputation set off for The Worm's quarters and found him, betwixt and between, unlacing his stays, with the hat, wig, serge dress, etc., on the bed. He came over as he was, and the 'Shikarris' shouted till the Gunners' Mess sent over to know if they might have a share of the fun. I think we were all, except the Colonel and the Senior Subaltern, a little disappointed that the scandal had come to nothing. But that is human nature. There could be no two words about The Worm's acting. It leaned as near to a nasty tragedy as anything this side of a joke can. When most of the subalterns sat upon him with sofa cushions to find out why he had not said that acting was his strong point, he answered very quietly: 'I don't think you ever asked me. I used to act at home with my sisters.' But no acting with girls could account for The Worm's display that night. Personally, I think it was in bad taste. Besides being dangerous. There is no sort of use in playing with fire, even for fun.

The 'Shikarris' made him President of the Regimental Dramatic Club; and, when the Senior Subaltern paid up his debt, which he did at once, The Worm sank the money in scenery and dresses. He was a good Worm; and the 'Shikarris' are proud of him. The only drawback is that he has been christened 'Mrs Senior Subaltern'; and, as there are now two Mrs Senior Subalterns in the station, this is sometimes confusing to strangers.

Later on, I will tell you of a case something like this, but with all the jest left out and nothing in it but real trouble.

CLIFFORD'S TOWER

Charlotte Perkins Gilman

There are few localities in New England where so much of the charm and color of old romance was given to the landscape by the work of man, as that which lay under the far reaching and dignified shadow of Clifford's Tower. The houses in the neighboring village were of no nobler character than those of any similar group of human habitations in all the country-side; neither were the lives of the citizens—if indeed we can designate with so large a title the humble dwellers in this hamlet—more dignified nor more ambitious than were those of their fellows. None the less was there a certain air of pride in the bearing of any resident when you asked him concerning the battlemented grandeur that stood so dark and tall against the evening sky.

'That,' you would have been told, with an unconscious arrogance in the tone of the speaker, 'that is Clifford's Tower.'

The Cliffords, it further appeared, were a great family in that place. They had been a great family when old Sir Mortimer Clifford received his grant of New World land from a king of whom the envious did say that he was glad to so cheaply rid himself of a too officious servant; and they were a great family now, still holding wide lands in the very heart of this fair and fertile region, and mighty industries which made them arbiters of fate to the greater part of the population.

True, some of the house of Clifford were not so great and powerful, not so prosperous and full of success, as were the main branch; yet every last bough and twig felt to the full the Clifford pride, and gloried daily in that standing record of past magnificence—Clifford's Tower. Of these poorer yet no humbler Cliffords, none were more pronounced in the characteristics of their race than Mistress Catharine Clifford and her fair daughter. Agnes Clifford knew by heart the story of her kinsman of old days—that young, proud, handsome Clifford who had traversed the four seas and levied tribute on all lands, to make fair and rich the great manor to which he was to bring home his bride. He had planted those wide acres with every tree and shrub the climate would allow—strange vines and unknown bushes, flowers from across the world—and in the midst of them he reared the walls of this gray tower, meaning to have there a manor house which should rival in this new world the ancestral glory of his family in the old.

It was no fit match for a Clifford after all; this wild slip of a country lass he had chosen for wife, a fair maiden enough, and virtuous, although her father was only a sea captain and her heart, the gossips said, was buried at sea with her first-love. But Herndon Clifford loved fair Mabel Hurd all the better that she was cold and hard to win, and the more his family showed scorn of her whom he had chosen, the more he sought to exalt her by every high observance. She should have a home such as no other lady in the land could claim, not even a Clifford; he would make for her a castle, not a house; and then as the day drew near for the completion of the building and his happiness, the sea gave up its dead—and there returned to her the lover she had mourned so long. Herndon Clifford stopped the work on the house and the work on the place at once; and all these years the gray stone tower had looked down on the unfinished walls beside it and the tangled waste of strange dark foliage below—a ruin that had never been a home; whose master wandered in far lands, an exile till he died. The Clifford pride would never sell or let the grand demesne, a broken heart might be carried with unmoved countenance, a life might pass in sorrow, but the tower stood.

And when Agnes Clifford, fair pale Agnes whose short life was passed in the very shadow of the tower—for her mother had found shelter after a stormy youth under the roof of the never finished home beside it,—when Agnes first met a lover, it was in these long whispering avenues of strange trees, and in sheltered nooks where flowers bloomed rankly, large flowers of a sort unknown to the land about.

Urgent and warm was his wooing, and he begged her to leave these sickly shadows, this dark world of green and gray and come to the cheery light of his cottage on the hillside. 'The sun shines there all day,' he said to her, 'and there are scarlet-flowered bean vines that drum merrily on the pane in the fresh sea winds. You know my sister already, and love her; she will be company for you while I am on the bay.' For Robert Hurd was a fisherman as his father and grandfather had been before him,—and he prospered in a sturdy quiet way. His sister Elsie, a blithe and wholesome lass whose bright cheeks had the fresh color of sea pinks in them, kept house for him in the new cottage he had built; and to his cheery home he sought to lead this slender, drooping maiden, whose very life seemed colored by the darkness of the tangled trees about her, and the shadow of the tower.

'Come, Agnes,' urged her lover. 'You need more air, more light. The wind never stirs under these matted boughs—it only shakes the gathered fog down on the house and on you. The sun does not get in—see—look at the green moss on the side of every tree trunk—on the roof—here even by the door-steps—and all down the tower—come! Bring your mother with you,—we will cheer her in spite of herself. She cannot live long here.'

'Agnes! Come here!' cried a weak, harsh voice from within. 'Come here, and bring that man to me!'

Agnes obeyed, and her tall lover followed, his broad shoulders and ruddy cheeks bearing a sense of youth and strength into the shadowy room where age and illness lay.

Mistress Catharine Clifford lay back upon the pillows, as she had lain for long years past, her firm thin lips and clear eyes telling of an undiminished will which had once ruled many, but whose only instrument now was this one pale girl.

'Agnes!' said she, 'What is this? What is this young man to you?' He spoke for her at once.

'Mistress Catharine Clifford,' said he firmly, 'I am come to ask your daughter's hand, and to offer her and you a home which will be more fit for human use than this. I love her well and can keep her, if not in grandeur, at least in loving comfort. You will not deny us your consent?'

The sick woman's eyes burned large and fierce as she listened, and she fixed them on him with scorn so deep that gentle Agnes was roused to quick rebellion.

'You shall not look at him so!' she cried. 'He is a good man, mother, and I love him!' Her mother turned her gaze on her daughter, with the same relentless scorn.

'You love him, do you? You love him? You, a Clifford, love this Hurd! And do you know that he is but the grandson of that Mabel Hurd for whose false faith this great house stands to-day unbuilt! He says it is unfit for human use, this house which should have been the glory of the country had that girl been true! But a Clifford was well served for loving so beneath him; and you shall fare no better if you love this man. You, a Clifford, living here on your own land, to wed a fisherman and go to live in his cheap hut—and offer *me* a home! Thank God your mother lives and can defend you yet from the weakness of your own heart! Thank God that in my very helplessness I hold you fast. You cannot leave me for a day—a night—and while I live, and while this tower shall stand, you shall not marry this man!'

A sudden darkness gathered while she spoke. In those green shades the dark came earlier always, but this fell thickly as though a curtain closed across the sky.

Not a leaf stirred; the insistent shrilling of insects filled the hot air with vibrant energy. Far off a heavy breath of sound and the soft sheeted flashes of heat lightning spoke of a gathering storm.

Robert Hurd stood pale and silent, then turned and strode away without a word. Agnes followed him to the door. He seized her hand and strained her to him once. 'Meet me once more to-night,' he begged, 'Once more, while she sleeps—at the west gate.'

It was midnight before the slow breathing of the exhausted woman told Agnes that for a few short hours she might rest beside her. Instead she stole away—softer footed than a fog wreath—and crept out to the great lodge gate where her lover waited yet her final word.

There was a fearful storm raging, but Agnes was too worn by storms within to mind the wind that wrenched the tree-tops and laid flat the dripping grass, the sheets of hammering rain, or the recurrent roar and flash that filled the heavens.

Strong arms were around her and drew her into shelter when she reached the gate. She stood panting, and looked at him in the intermittent light.

'It is the last time Robert,' said she, quietly. 'I cannot disobey my mother. She is firm and my duty is with her. Seek another wife, my strong, true friend—one who will bring you joy, not sorrow. While my mother lives and the tower stands I cannot come.'

A fearful glare poured out across the sky. Every wet leaf stood out pale green and vivid, and the driving rain was lit as it rushed down.

A crash that stunned them followed on the instant—a crash that echoed from earth to heaven and was followed by another roar, less loud but doubly awful. Before their eyes the tall tower bent and tottered, rent from turret to foundation by the stroke, and burying as it fell the ruined home and ruined life beneath it.

Strong in her pride she lived, and she died as she would have wished—by the power of the house of Clifford.

Robert bore Agnes, fainting to his sister's arms, and a newer, brighter life unfolded for the fair young girl in the bright home that now became her own.

THE KISS

Kate Chopin

It was still quite light out of doors, but inside with the curtains drawn and the smoldering fire sending out a dim, uncertain glow, the room was full of deep shadows.

Brantain sat in one of these shadows; it had overtaken him and he did not mind. The obscurity lent him courage to keep his eyes fastened as ardently as he liked upon the girl who sat in the firelight.

She was very handsome, with a certain fine, rich coloring that belongs to the healthy brune type. She was quite composed, as she idly stroked the satiny coat of the cat that lay curled in her lap, and she occasionally sent a slow glance into the shadow where her companion sat. They were talking low, of indifferent things which plainly were not the things that occupied their thoughts. She knew that he loved her—a frank, blustering fellow without guile enough to conceal his feelings, and no desire to do so. For two weeks past he had sought her society eagerly and persistently. She was confidently waiting for him to declare himself and she meant to accept him. The rather insignificant and unattractive Brantain was enormously rich; and she liked and required the entourage which wealth could give her.

During one of the pauses between their talk of the last tea and the next reception the door opened and a young man entered whom Brantain knew quite well. The girl turned her face toward him. A stride or two brought him to her side, and bending over her chair—before she could suspect his intention, for she did not realize that he had not seen her visitor—he pressed an ardent, lingering kiss upon her lips.

Brantain slowly arose; so did the girl arise, but quickly, and the newcomer stood between them, a little amusement and some defiance struggling with the confusion in his face.

'I believe,' stammered Brantain, 'I see that I have stayed too long. I—I had no idea—that is, I must wish you good-by.' He was clutching his hat with both hands, and probably did not perceive that she was extending her hand to him, her presence of mind had not completely deserted her; but she could not have trusted herself to speak.

'Hang me if I saw him sitting there, Nattie! I know it's deuced awkward for you. But I hope you'll forgive me this once—this very first break. Why, what's the matter?'

'Don't touch me; don't come near me,' she returned angrily. 'What do you mean by entering the house without ringing?'

'I came in with your brother, as I often do,' he answered coldly, in self-justification. 'We came in the side way. He went upstairs and I came in here hoping to find you. The explanation is simple enough and ought to satisfy you that the misadventure was unavoidable. But do say that you forgive me, Nathalie,' he entreated, softening.

'Forgive you! You don't know what you are talking about. Let me pass. It depends upon—a good deal whether I ever forgive you.'

At that next reception which she and Brantain had been talking about she approached the young man with a delicious frankness of manner when she saw him there.

'Will you let me speak to you a moment or two, Mr Brantain?' she asked with an engaging but perturbed smile. He seemed extremely unhappy; but when she took his arm and walked away with him, seeking a retired corner, a ray of hope mingled with the almost comical misery of his expression. She was apparently very outspoken.

'Perhaps I should not have sought this interview, Mr Brantain; but—but, oh, I have been very uncomfortable, almost miserable since that little encounter the other afternoon. When I thought how you might have misinterpreted it, and believed things'—hope was plainly gaining the ascendancy over misery in Brantain's round, guileless face—'Of course, I know it is nothing to you, but for my own sake I do want you to understand that Mr Harvy is an intimate friend of long standing. Why, we have always been like cousins—like brother and sister, I may say. He is my brother's most intimate associate and often fancies that he is entitled to the same privileges as the family. Oh, I know it is absurd, uncalled for, to tell you this; undignified even,' she was almost weeping, 'but it makes so much difference to me what you think of—of me.' Her voice had grown very low and agitated. The misery had all disappeared from Brantain's face.

'Then you do really care what I think, Miss Nathalie? May I call you Miss Nathalie?' They turned into a long, dim corridor that was lined on either side with tall, graceful plants. They walked slowly to the very end of it. When they turned to retrace their steps Brantain's face was radiant and hers was triumphant.

◆

Harvy was among the guests at the wedding; and he sought her out in a rare moment when she stood alone.

'Your husband,' he said, smiling, 'has sent me over to kiss you.'

A quick blush suffused her face and round polished throat. 'I suppose it's natural for a man to feel and act generously on an occasion of this kind. He tells me he doesn't want his marriage to interrupt wholly that pleasant intimacy which has existed between you and me. I don't know what you've been telling him,' with an insolent smile, 'but he has sent me here to kiss you.'

She felt like a chess player who, by the clever handling of his pieces, sees the game taking the course intended. Her eyes were bright and tender with a smile as they glanced up into his; and her lips looked hungry for the kiss which they invited.

'But, you know,' he went on quietly, 'I didn't tell him so, it would have seemed ungrateful, but I can tell you. I've stopped kissing women; it's dangerous.'

Well, she had Brantain and his million left. A person can't have everything in this world; and it was a little unreasonable of her to expect it.

EVELINE

James Joyce

She sat at the window watching the evening invade the avenue. Her head was leaned against the window curtains and in her nostrils was the odour of dusty cretonne. She was tired.

Few people passed. The man out of the last house passed on his way home; she heard his footsteps clacking along the concrete pavement and afterwards crunching on the cinder path before the new red houses. One time there used to be a field there in which they used to play every evening with other people's children. Then a man from Belfast bought the field and built houses in it—not like their little brown houses but bright brick houses with shining roofs. The children of the avenue used to play together in that field—the Devines, the Waters, the Dunns, little Keogh the cripple, she and her brothers and sisters. Ernest, however, never played: he was too grown up. Her father used often to hunt them in out of the field with his blackthorn stick; but usually little Keogh used to keep nix and call out when he saw her father coming. Still they seemed to have been rather happy then. Her father was not so bad then; and besides, her mother was alive. That was a long time ago; she and her brothers and sisters were all grown up; her mother was dead. Tizzie Dunn was dead, too, and the Waters had gone back to England. Everything changes. Now she was going to go away like the others, to leave her home.

Home! She looked round the room, reviewing all its familiar objects which she had dusted once a week for so many years, wondering where on earth all the dust came from. Perhaps she would never see again those familiar objects from which she had never dreamed of being divided. And yet during all those years she had never found out the name of the priest whose yellowing photograph hung on the wall above the broken harmonium beside the coloured print of the promises made to Blessed Margaret Mary Alacoque. He had been a school friend of her father. Whenever he showed the photograph to a visitor her father used to pass it with a casual word:

'He is in Melbourne now.'

She had consented to go away, to leave her home. Was that wise? She tried to weigh each side of the question. In her home anyway she had shelter and food; she had those whom she had known all her life about her. Of course she had to work hard, both in the house and at business. What would they say of her in the Stores when they found out that she had run away with a fellow? Say she was a fool, perhaps; and her place would be filled up by advertisement. Miss Gavan would be glad. She had always had an edge on her, especially whenever there were people listening.

'Miss Hill, don't you see these ladies are waiting?'

'Look lively, Miss Hill, please.'

She would not cry many tears at leaving the Stores.

But in her new home, in a distant unknown country, it would not be like that. Then she would be married—she, Eveline. People would treat her with respect then. She would not be treated as her mother had been. Even now, though she was over nineteen, she sometimes felt herself in danger of her father's violence. She knew it was that that had given her the palpitations. When they were growing up he had never gone for her, like he used to go for Harry and Ernest, because she was a girl; but latterly he had begun to threaten her and say what he would do to her only for her dead mother's sake. And now she had nobody to protect her. Ernest was dead and Harry, who was in the church decorating business, was nearly always down somewhere in the country. Besides, the invariable squabble for money on Saturday nights had begun to weary her unspeakably. She always gave her entire wages—seven shillings—and Harry always sent up what he could but the trouble was to get any money from her father. He said she used to squander the money, that she had no head, that he wasn't going to give her his hard-earned money to throw about the streets, and much more, for he was usually fairly bad on Saturday night. In the end he would give her the money and ask her had she any intention of buying Sunday's dinner. Then she had to rush out as quickly as she could and do her marketing, holding her black leather purse tightly in her hand as she elbowed her way through the crowds and returning home late under her load of provisions. She had hard work to keep the house together and to see that the two young children who had been left to her charge went to school regularly and got their meals regularly. It was hard work—a hard life—but now that she was about to leave it she did not find it a wholly undesirable life.

She was about to explore another life with Frank. Frank was very kind, manly, open-hearted. She was to go away with him by the night-boat to be his wife and to live with him in Buenos Ayres where he had a home waiting for her. How well she remembered the first time she had seen him; he was lodging in a house on the main road where she used to visit. It seemed a few weeks ago. He was standing at the gate, his peaked cap pushed back on his head and his hair tumbled forward over a face of bronze. Then they had come to know each other. He used to meet her outside the Stores every evening and see her home. He took her to see *The Bohemian Girl* and she felt elated as she sat in an unaccustomed part of the theatre with him. He was awfully fond of music and sang a little. People knew that they were courting and, when he sang about the lass that loves a sailor, she always felt pleasantly confused. He used to call her Poppens out of fun. First of all it had been an excitement for her to have a fellow and then she had begun to like him. He had tales of distant countries. He had started as a deck boy at a pound a month on a ship of the Allan Line going out to Canada. He told her the names of the ships he had been on and the names of the different services. He had sailed through the Straits of Magellan and he told her stories of the terrible Patagonians. He had fallen on his feet in Buenos Ayres, he said, and had come over to the old country just for a holiday. Of course, her father had found out the affair and had forbidden her to have anything to say to him.

'I know these sailor chaps,' he said.

One day he had quarrelled with Frank and after that she had to meet her lover secretly.

The evening deepened in the avenue. The white of two letters in her lap grew indistinct. One was to Harry; the other was to her father. Ernest had been her favourite but she liked Harry too. Her father was becoming old lately, she noticed; he would miss her. Sometimes he could be very nice. Not long before, when she had been laid up for a day, he had read her out a ghost story and made toast for her at the fire. Another day, when their mother was alive, they had all gone for a picnic to the Hill of Howth. She remembered her father putting on her mother's bonnet to make the children laugh.

Her time was running out but she continued to sit by the window, leaning her head against the window curtain, inhaling the odour of dusty cretonne. Down far in the avenue she could hear a street organ playing. She knew the air. Strange that it should come that very night to remind her of the promise to her mother, her promise to keep the home together as long as she could. She remembered the last night of her mother's illness; she was again in the close dark room at the other side of the hall and outside she heard a melancholy air of Italy. The organ-player had been ordered to go away and given sixpence. She remembered her father strutting back into the sickroom saying:

'Damned Italians! coming over here!'

As she mused the pitiful vision of her mother's life laid its spell on the very quick of her being—that life of commonplace sacrifices closing in final craziness. She trembled as she heard again her mother's voice saying constantly with foolish insistence: 'Derevaun Seraun! Derevaun Seraun!'

She stood up in a sudden impulse of terror. Escape! She must escape! Frank would save her. He would give her life, perhaps love, too. But she wanted to live. Why should she be unhappy? She had a right to happiness.

Frank would take her in his arms, fold her in his arms. He would save her.

◆

She stood among the swaying crowd in the station at the North Wall. He held her hand and she knew that he was speaking to her, saying something about the passage over and over again. The station was full of soldiers with brown baggages. Through the wide doors of the sheds she caught a glimpse of the black mass of the boat, lying in beside the quay wall, with illumined portholes. She answered nothing. She felt her cheek pale and cold and, out of a maze of distress, she prayed to God to direct her, to show her what was her duty. The boat blew a long mournful whistle into the mist. If she went, tomorrow she would be on the sea with Frank, steaming towards Buenos Ayres. Their passage had been booked. Could she still draw back after all he had done for her? Her distress awoke a nausea in her body and she kept moving her lips in silent fervent prayer.

A bell clanged upon her heart. She felt him seize her hand:
'Come!'

All the seas of the world tumbled about her heart. He was drawing her into them: he would drown her. She gripped with both hands at the iron railing.

'Come!'

No! No! No! It was impossible. Her hands clutched the iron in frenzy.

Amid the seas she sent a cry of anguish!

'Eveline! Evvy!'

He rushed beyond the barrier and called to her to follow. He was shouted at to go on but he still called to her. She set her white face to him, passive, like a helpless animal. Her eyes gave him no sign of love or farewell or recognition.

PIETY'S MONUMENT

Frank Penn-Smith

The old man gathered in his contemplation from elsewhere, and fixed his pink-edged eyes on mine. I coughed and then began: 'Didn't old Piety work the kilns above here? What sort of lime did he burn?' And I offered the old fellow my flask.

He picked up a battered jam-tin and gazed thoughtfully into it. Then he poked his finger in. Lastly, he emptied all my whisky into it, and drank it swiftly and suspiciously. 'Eh?' he said. Then something began to work in the old man; his reserve seemed to crack and come to pieces; he burst-up slowly, as it were, and crumbled into speech. 'What should you know about old Piety?' he asked, uneasily, in a sorrowful, whining tone. 'Oh, *he* could burn lime,' he went on, 'leastways, he *thought* he could. But there was as much difference between his kilns and mine as between oysters and cheese. Well! Well! You knowed him?' he whispered, stroking the bricks in the chimney behind him, thoughtfully.

'No' I replied, 'only heard of him.'

'And heard wrong,' said the old man simply. 'Now I'll tell you the facks.' Then he went off in a low, quavering whine: 'Piety owned these here kilns, an' Piety burnt lime. Leastways, he said he did, but it was me as done it. But when Piety put his finger in, the kiln was all stone. He worrited here, he worrited there, muddling and mulling every blessed kiln till he had me nigh crazed, and my fingers raw picking out stone. "Jus' give me the contrack," I'd say—"the contrack to burn lime at so much a bushel." "No you don't," says he. An' that's all I ever got out of him: "No, you don't! Not in my day." And then he went and killed the kangaroo.'

'The kangaroo?' I asked. 'What kangaroo?'

'Bill's kangaroo,' he replied, querulously. 'Bill had a pet kangaroo—Bill, the old man's grandson, as owns these here kilns now. They didn't get on, the old man and Bill, and lived in different huts. Bill was an orphan. Well, the kiln was about half-full and burning—old Piety, he was great at half-kilns—when the kangaroo hopped on to the kiln bank and ate old Piety's dinner, bread-and-butter and what not. Oho! he *was* wild when he found out. Then the beast came and rooted at him with its fore-paws, playing like. With that, he kicks it; but lor', the beast thought he was playing with it, so it just turns back upon him, a-twiddling its paws. Then he goes for it real spiteful, and give it a tremendous kick that sends it flying, right into the burning kiln.'

The old man paused here and stared into space, mumbling. Then he went on, monotonously: 'Lad! You *would* have larfed to see that kangaroo jump. But, lor'! there's no jumping out of a kiln. D'ye see the p'int?—But Bill, he didn't larf when he finds it all out. There was the last of the kangaroo smoking in the blue flame a-top of the kiln. "Oh, you old devil!" he says to Piety; "it would serve you right to go through the kiln yourself!" Then he cleared right away, and wouldn't speak to nobody. But it was the childer as did it.'

'Did what?' I asked.

'Well, it was like this,' he explained. 'My fingers was red raw with the half-burnt stone, and I was a-tying them up with rags, and abusing of old Piety. "Couldn't burn charcoal, let alone lime!" I says. And the childer they took it round to Piety hisself. Well! the kiln was emptied, and we was going to start another, when he comes toddling down. "You old weather-beaten windbag, you!" he cries. "It's you that knows what spoils the kilns!" he says; "just you clear out. I'll put the lime in myself this time." "And welcome," says I, "if you draw it yourself," says I.

'"None of your cheek!" he says, coming at me with the sieve, and so I clears away, larfing to myself at the mess he'd make of it, and waiting for his tantrum to blow over. Well, I camps here in the hut, day by day, and hears them bumbling away up the valley, putting in the kiln and lighting it. Then when it's time to draw it, I goes up to the kiln, but no Piety.

"'He's not turned up," says the quarryman.

"'And not likely," says I, "with a ki'ful o' stone. I'd be ashamed to look a man in the face," I says. So I sets to work and draws the kiln as usual. But no Piety. And what's more, he wasn't about his hut, nor nowheres. Then I begins to think and think, and I draws that kiln slow and steady. But at last I draws a sort of bit o' white stick—lime like the rest. I has a good look at it, and then says to myself, says I—'

Here the maundering old man paused, looking into space, then pulling himself together went on:

'I says to myself: "Here he comes, feet first. I thought as much!" It was the shin-bone.'

'Whose shin-bone?' I demanded.

'Why, old Piety's, of course,' he replied.

'What?—he'd fallen into the kiln?' I asked, horrified.

The old man turned viciously upon me for damaging his story.

'There you go,' he cried—'blurting the thing out! Why, of course he'd fell in the kiln—what else would he do? There were his tracks to the kiln edge, and a few bricks gone where he lost his footing. Well, I jus' leaves it there and put a bag over it. Then I goes down to Bill—a-digging in the orchard—and says to him: "About this here contrack. Will you 'gree to let me have the contrack after the old man's dead?"

"'That's looking ahead with a vengeance," he says, grinning.

"'Never mind," I says. "Good understandings makes long frien's," I says.

"'Oh, just as you like," he says, digging away. "I'm not too pertickler!"

'"That's a bargain?" I asks.

'"That's a bargain," he says, just to be rid o' me. Then I says to him: "Come up to the kiln, I want yer to help me awhile." So he comes. Then I takes the bag off the bones. "Look at that!" I says.

'"Well," says he, "and what about it?"

'"Well," I says, "that's your respected gran'father; leastwise all that's left of him."

'You could have knocked him down with a feather. When he comes to see it all he took on dreadful.

'"Good Gawd," he says, and, "'Orrible! 'Orrible!"

'Then says I: "Be a man! It might have been wuss. It might have been *me*," I says—"or yerself," I says. "It might have been *me*—and then who's to burn the lime?" But he took on all the same. He took that dreadful a view of it. Oho!' quavered the old fellow, wagging his head: 'He took a gloomby view of it, a very gloomby view of it!'

'"Now you go away!" I says to him, "and I'll draw this lime and bag it."

'"Bag that lime!" says he, "and my gran'father amongst it!"

'"My wages is in it," I says, firm, "but I'll get what I can of him out," and so I did, and put the bone or two on the shed roof, away from the childer. Put 'em there not thinking, for there came a shower of rain while I was away for the cart, and when I got back the bones had all slacked up.

'But look ye here,' went on the old man confidentially, 'I had my own little idee so as old Piety'd not be lost sight of altogether. I takes about harf the lime the bones made—real lime, mind you—and makes up a bit of mortar for this here chimbley— which I was building at the time. So you see these here bricks and that bit mortar? Well, I reckon that's old Piety's monument. But as for the rest, Bill he buried it in the orchard, and when the perlice came up there was nothing left but the buttons.'

WHARF LABOURERS

Robert Brothers

Whether wharf labourers as a class are more lurid than other casual workers I don't know, but it is my opinion that the man who lumps cargo can hold his own against any other. Language is not a gift, but he can't help himself. If you put a padlock on his lips and gave his mind a bath, he'd still think in swear-words. Not that he does think. He talks, but shifting wool and wheat doesn't give him any exercise in mentality. His brain acts sheep-like, following the lead of others, and in consequence the tongue-noise he puts in is an iteration which is only varied in frills and embroideries of obscenity. This incessant talk is not as foolish as it sounds; it is how he dodges sweating.

But to hear a wharf labourer at his best you require to sleep near a hatch on a passenger boat the night before she leaves port. I've done so on various occasions, and it has interested me so much that last night I switched on the light and made a verbatim report of what I heard. Of course, in setting it down here, I've left spaces, representing lingua incognita. You can fill them in yourself if you know how, only you must understand that the real language was worse.

First you are awakened by a terrific bumping-down of the hatch-board, and then comes the maddening clatter of the winch being tested, accompanied by the clang of iron bars being thrown about over your head. There is a terrible amount of language also, but the noise of the winch and the bars is so great that it even drowns a wharf labourer's stentorian voice. Waking from one's sleep it strikes right into one's nerves and lifts the roof from your head.

A wharf labourer is so accustomed to shouting so as to be heard above the din of winches that he keeps it up all the time. Immediately the hellish noise subsides, a raucous voice demands, 'Where's my b——'

Then it stops. It seems to remember that there are passengers aboard. There is a little sense of decency behind that voice. It has probably been well brought up—had a mother, or some good female influence. It continued: '—blessed 'ook?'

In Heaven's Book there must be recorded the noble restraint of that labourer. I am sure St Peter will remember that man and pass him in. It will be recorded that once in his lifetime he put a curb on his tongue and left unsaid the thing that he set out to say. I am glad I heard it. It is the only time I've ever heard a wharf labourer use a mild adjective.

'Anybody seen Bill's — 'ook?' roared out a man with a voice like a bull and no respect for passengers.

Then a dozen bull voices roared: 'Bill's — — 'ook's lost!'

And there came a noise of spitting.

Then one voice spoke—one which will never leave my memory—an awful voice: 'The — —'s gone an' lost his — 'ook.'

'W'y the — — doesn't 'e look after 'is — 'ook?' This voice was a commonsense sort of voice. It is the voice of the critic that you will mostly find in every crowd—the Red Page voice.

'Is it Bill's — 'ook wot's — well lost?' asked a sympathetic voice.

'— silly —,' said a weak edition of the Red Page voice.

All the time about twenty men were chasing round looking for Bill's hook, instead of working and getting the ship away up to time. It occurred to me that Bill had lost his hook on purpose. ey all talked at once on these occasions.

'Whose — 'ook is this?'

Everybody came forward to identify it, and then the bull voice rang out: 'That's not Bill's — 'ook. That — 'ook belongs to one of the —s who voted for — overtime. 'E's — well asleep behind the — wool-bales.'

'Is this Bill's — 'ook?' from another part of the hold. Another scuttle of all the wharf labourers to make another identification. And then Bill spoke: 'Yes, that's my — 'ook.'

I felt sorry to notice Bill's lapse. I am sure that Bill must have loved a good woman at one time or another of his life.

'Now we'd better get to work.' No doubt this came from a ganger.

There was no excited rush to begin sweating, as I expected.

'Yes, we'd better — well get to — work.'

Everybody began to reiterate 'getting to work', just in the sheep-like way of wharf labourers. They might have got to work in a few minutes, only for another voice. It was the First Red Page voice that said:

'Don't — well know 'ow we'll — well stow that — barley.'

'It's a — monkey's puzzle,' said the Second Red Page voice.

'It's a — — monkey's — — puzzle,' said the voice of Bill. (Oh, Bill, and the way that you must have been brought up!) You could understand Bill. No doubt, the Second Red Page voice hadn't expressed the difficulty of stowing the barley sufficiently well.

Then the Second Red Page voice said: 'We'll 'ave to — well get round the — — stack and stow the — stuff down that wing.'

Then all the voices repeated: 'We'll 'ave to — well get round the — — stack and stow the — barley down that — wing.' It took five minutes (more or less) to say it, as they didn't say it in concert.

I thought they would start work when they had finished saying it, only someone found one of them drinking a bottle of beer behind some cases, and everybody had to comment upon it, and then somebody said, 'Well, boys, let's get to — work,' and when everybody had repeated it as a necessary formula before starting work, an officer-sort of voice said: 'Who the h—I stowed this here?'

'Wasn't me, sir,' replied an awful voice, conciliatingly.

'Nor me, sir,' said the voice of Bill.

'Wasn't any of us, sir.'

''Ow the — could it be any of us, sir, when it's — wheat, and we're stowing — barley, and we're not started — work yet?'

'It was — well done by the last — shift, sir,' said the Red Page voice.

'It's got no right here, anyway,' said the officer voice, severely.

Then the Second Red Page voice must have grown sick of the sirring, or the interference of the officer voice. It said with a spit: 'Oh, shut yer — nose.'

The First Red Page voice did not seem to think that this was expressed right. It evidently knew that the meaning was, 'Oh, shut up, and don't poke your nose into things,' but it didn't take time to get it clear. It said with a louder spit:

'Oh, shut yer — nose in yer — mouth and get to — out of this — yer.'

'And now let's get to — work,' said the voice of Bill.

''As enny son of a — seen my — — 'ook?' asked the Second Red Page voice.

'Enny one seen Jim's — — 'ook?'

'Another — —'s lost 'is — 'ook.'

'W'y the —'

'Oh, 'ere's 'is — 'ook.'

'It's orright, yer —s. Jim's got 'is — 'ook.'

'And now let's get to — work.'

THE CANARY

Katherine Mansfield

...You see that big nail to the right of the front door? I can scarcely look at it even now and yet I could not bear to take it out. I should like to think it was there always even after my time. I sometimes hear the next people saying, 'There must have been a cage hanging from there.' And it comforts me; I feel he is not quite forgotten.

...You cannot imagine how wonderfully he sang. It was not like the singing of other canaries. And that isn't just my fancy. Often, from the window, I used to see people stop at the gate to listen, or they would lean over the fence by the mock-orange for quite a long time—carried away. I suppose it sounds absurd to you—it wouldn't if you had heard him—but it really seemed to me that he sang whole songs with a beginning and an end to them.

For instance, when I'd finished the house in the afternoon, and changed my blouse and brought my sewing on to the veranda here, he used to hop, hop, hop from one perch to another, tap against the bars as if to attract my attention, sip a little water just as a professional singer might, and then break into a song so exquisite that I had to put my needle down to listen to him. I can't describe it; I wish I could. But it was always the same, every afternoon, and I felt that I understood every note of it.

...I loved him. How I loved him! Perhaps it does not matter so very much what it is one loves in this world. But love something one must. Of course there was always my little house and the garden, but for some reason they were never enough.

Flowers respond wonderfully, but they don't sympathize. Then I loved the evening star. Does that sound foolish? I used to go into the backyard, after sunset, and wait for it until it shone above the dark gum tree. I used to whisper 'There you are, my darling.' And just in that first moment it seemed to be shining for me alone. It seemed to understand this…something which is like longing, and yet it is not longing. Or regret—it is more like regret. And yet regret for what? I have much to be thankful for.

…But after he came into my life I forgot the evening star; I did not need it any more. But it was strange. When the Chinaman who came to the door with birds to sell held him up in his tiny cage, and instead of fluttering, fluttering, like the poor little goldfinches, he gave a faint, small chirp, I found myself saying, just as I had said to the star over the gum tree, 'There you are, my darling.' From that moment he was mine.

…It surprises me even now to remember how he and I shared each other's lives. The moment I came down in the morning and took the cloth off his cage he greeted me with a drowsy little note. I knew it meant 'Missus! Missus!' Then I hung him on the nail outside while I got my three young men their breakfasts, and I never brought him in until we had the house to ourselves again. Then, when the washing-up was done, it was quite a little entertainment. I spread a newspaper over a corner of the table and when I put the cage on it he used to beat with his wings despairingly, as if he didn't know what was coming. 'You're a regular little actor,' I used to scold him. I scraped the tray, dusted it with fresh sand, filled his seed and water tins, tucked a piece of chickweed and half a chili between the bars. And I am perfectly certain he understood and appreciated every item of this little performance. You see by nature he was exquisitely neat. There was never a speck on his perch. And you'd only to see him enjoy his bath to realize he had a real small passion for cleanliness. His bath was put in last. And the moment it was in he positively leapt into it. First he fluttered one wing, then the other, then he ducked his head and dabbled his breast feathers. Drops of water were scattered all over the kitchen, but still he would not get out. I used to say to him, 'Now that's quite enough. You're only showing off.' And at last out he hopped and, standing on one leg, he began to peck himself dry. Finally he gave a shake, a flick, a twitter and he lifted his throat—Oh, I can hardly bear to recall it. I was always cleaning the knives at the time. And it almost seemed to me the knives sang too, as I rubbed them bright on the board.

...Company, you see—that was what he was. Perfect company. If you have lived alone you will realize how precious that is. Of course there were my three young men who came in to supper every evening, and sometimes stayed in the dining-room afterwards reading the paper. But I could not expect them to be interested in the little things that made my day. Why should they be? I was nothing to them. In fact, I overheard them one evening talking about me on the stairs as 'the Scarecrow.' No matter. It doesn't matter. Not in the least. I quite understand. They are young. Why should I mind? But I remember feeling so especially thankful that I was not quite alone that evening. I told him, after they had gone out. I said 'Do you know what they call Missus?' And he put his head on one side and looked at me with his little bright eye until I could not help laughing. It seemed to amuse him.

...Have you kept birds? If you haven't all this must sound, perhaps, exaggerated. People have the idea that birds are heartless, cold little creatures, not like dogs or cats. My washerwoman used to say on Mondays when she wondered why I didn't keep 'a nice fox terrier,' 'There's no comfort, Miss, in a canary.' Untrue. Dreadfully untrue. I remember one night. I had had a very awful dream—dreams can be dreadfully cruel—even after I had woken up I could not get over it. So I put on my dressing-gown and went down to the kitchen for a glass of water. It was a winter night and raining hard. I suppose I was still half asleep, but through the kitchen window, that hadn't a blind, it seemed to me the dark was staring in, spying. And suddenly I felt it was unbearable that I had no one to whom I could say 'I've had such a dreadful dream,' or—or 'Hide me from the dark.' I even covered my face for a minute. And then there came a little 'Sweet! Sweet!' His cage was on the table, and the cloth had slipped so that a chink of light shone through. 'Sweet! Sweet!' said the darling little fellow again, softly, as much as to say, 'I'm here, Missus! I'm here!' That was so beautifully comforting that I nearly cried.

...And now he's gone. I shall never have another bird, another pet of any kind. How could I? When I found him, lying on his back, with his eye dim and his claws wrung, when I realised that never again should I hear my darling sing, something seemed to die in me. My heart felt hollow, as if it was his cage. I shall get over it. Of course. I must. One can get over anything in time. And people always say I have a cheerful disposition. They are quite right. I thank my God I have.

...All the same, without being morbid, and giving way to— to memories and so on, I must confess that there does seem to me something sad in life. It is hard to say what it is. I don't mean the sorrow that we all know, like illness and poverty and death. No, it is something different. It is there, deep down, deep down, part of one, like one's breathing. However hard I work and tire myself I have only to stop to know it is there, waiting. I often wonder if everybody feels the same. One can never know. But isn't it extraordinary that under his sweet, joyful little singing it was just this sadness—ah, what is it?—that I heard?

THE MIRROR

Catulle Mendès

There was once a kingdom where mirrors were unknown. They had all been broken and reduced to fragments by order of the queen, and if the tiniest bit of looking-glass had been found in any house, she would not have hesitated to put all the inmates to death with the most frightful tortures.

Now for the secret of this extraordinary caprice. The queen was dreadfully ugly, and she did not wish to be exposed to the risk of meeting her own image; and, knowing herself to be hideous, it was a consolation to know that other women at least could not see that they were pretty.

You may imagine that the young girls of the country were not at all satisfied. What was the use of being beautiful if you could not admire yourself?

They might have used the brooks and lakes for mirrors; but the queen had foreseen that, and had hidden all of them under closely joined flagstones. Water was drawn from wells so deep that it was impossible to see the liquid surface, and shallow basins must be used instead of buckets, because in the latter there might be reflections.

Such a dismal state of affairs, especially for the pretty coquettes, who were no more rare in this country than in others.

The queen had no compassion, being well content that her subjects should suffer as much annoyance from the lack of a mirror as she felt at the sight of one.

However, in a suburb of the city there lived a young girl called Jacinta, who was a little better off than the rest, thanks to her sweetheart, Valentin. For if someone thinks you are beautiful, and loses no chance to tell you so, he is almost as good as a mirror.

'Tell me the truth,' she would say; 'what is the color of my eyes?'

'They are like dewy forget-me-nots.'

'And my skin is not quite black?'

'You know that your forehead is whiter than freshly fallen snow, and your cheeks are like blush roses.'

'How about my lips?'

'Cherries are pale beside them.'

'And my teeth, if you please?'

'Grains of rice are not as white.'

'But my ears, should I be ashamed of them?'

'Yes, if you would be ashamed of two little pink shells among your pretty curls.'

And so on endlessly; she delighted, he still more charmed, for his words came from the depth of his heart and she had the pleasure of hearing herself praised, he the delight of seeing her. So their love grew more deep and tender every hour, and the day that he asked her to marry him she blushed certainly, but it was not with anger. But, unluckily, the news of their happiness reached the wicked queen, whose only pleasure was to torment others, and Jacinta more than anyone else, on account of her beauty.

A little while before the marriage Jacinta was walking in the orchard one evening, when an old crone approached, asking for alms, but suddenly jumped back with a shriek as if she had stepped on a toad, crying:

'Heavens, what do I see?'

'What is the matter, my good woman? What is it you see? Tell me.'

'The ugliest creature I ever beheld.'

'Then you are not looking at me,' said Jacinta, with innocent vanity.

'Oh! Alas! yes, my poor child, it is you. I have been a long time on this earth, but never have I met anyone so hideous as you!'

'What! am I ugly?'

'A hundred times uglier than I can tell you.'

'But my eyes—'

'They are a sort of dirty gray; but that would be nothing if you had not such an outrageous squint!'

'My complexion—'

'It looks as if you had rubbed coal-dust on your forehead and cheeks.'

'My mouth—'

'It is pale and withered, like a faded flower.'

'My teeth—'

'If the beauty of teeth is to be large and yellow, I never saw any so beautiful as yours.'

'But, at least, my ears—'

'They are so big, so red, and so misshapen, under your coarse elf-locks, that they are revolting. I am not pretty myself, but I should die of shame if mine were like them.' After this last blow, the old witch, having repeated what the queen had taught her, hobbled off, with a harsh croak of laughter, leaving poor Jacinta dissolved in tears, prone on the ground beneath the apple-trees.

◆

Nothing could divert her mind from her grief. 'I am ugly—I am ugly,' she repeated constantly. It was in vain that Valentin assured and reassured her with the most solemn oaths. 'Let me alone; you are lying out of pity. I understand it all now; you never loved me; you are only sorry for me. The beggar woman had no interest in deceiving me. It is only too true—I am ugly. I do not see how you can endure the sight of me.'

To undeceive her, he brought people from far and near; every man declared that Jacinta was created to delight the eyes; even the women said as much, though they were less enthusiastic. But the poor child persisted in her conviction that she was a repulsive object, and when Valentin pressed her to name their wedding day—'I, your wife!' cried she. 'Never! I love you too dearly to burden you with a being so hideous as I am.' You can fancy the despair of the poor fellow so sincerely in love. He threw himself on his knees; he prayed; he supplicated; she answered still that she was too ugly to marry him.

What was he to do? The only way to give the lie to the old woman and prove the truth to Jacinta was to put a mirror before her. But there was no such thing in the kingdom, and so great was the terror inspired by the queen that no workman dared make one.

'Well, I shall go to court,' said the lover, in despair. 'Harsh as our mistress is, she cannot fail to be moved by the tears and the beauty of Jacinta. She will retract, for a few hours at least, this cruel edict which has caused our trouble.'

It was not without difficulty that he persuaded the young girl to let him take her to the palace. She did not like to show herself, and asked of what use would be a mirror, only to impress her more deeply with her misfortune; but when he wept, her heart was moved, and she consented, to please him.

◆

'What is all this?' said the wicked queen. 'Who are these people? and what do they want?'

'Your Majesty, you have before you the most unfortunate lover on the face of the earth.'

'Do you consider that a good reason for coming here to annoy me?'

'Have pity on me.'

'What have I to do with your love affairs?'

'If you would permit a mirror—'

The queen rose to her feet, trembling with rage. 'Who dares to speak to me of a mirror?' she said, grinding her teeth.

'Do not be angry, your Majesty, I beg of you, and deign to hear me. This young girl whom you see before you, so fresh and pretty, is the victim of a strange delusion. She imagines that she is ugly.'

'Well,' said the queen, with a malicious grin, 'she is right. I never saw a more hideous object.'

Jacinta, at these cruel words, thought she would die of mortification. Doubt was no longer possible, she must be ugly. Her eyes closed, she fell on the steps of the throne in a deadly swoon.

But Valentin was affected very differently. He cried out loudly that Her Majesty must be mad to tell such a lie. He had no time to say more. The guards seized him, and at a sign from the queen the headsman came forward. He was always beside the throne, for she might need his services at any moment.

'Do your duty,' said the queen, pointing out the man who had insulted her. The executioner raised his gleaming axe just as Jacinta came to herself and opened her eyes. Then two shrieks pierced the air. One was a cry of joy, for in the glittering steel Jacinta saw herself, so charmingly pretty—and the other a scream of anguish, as the wicked soul of the queen took flight, unable to bear the sight of her face in the impromptu mirror.

MONDAY OR TUESDAY

Virginia Woolf

Lazy and indifferent, shaking space easily from his wings, knowing his way, the heron passes over the church beneath the sky. White and distant, absorbed in itself, endlessly the sky covers and uncovers, moves and remains. A lake? Blot the shores of it out! A mountain? Oh, perfect—the sun gold on its slopes. Down that falls. Ferns then, or white feathers, for ever and ever—

Desiring truth, awaiting it, laboriously distilling a few words, for ever desiring—(a cry starts to the left, another to the right. Wheels strike divergently. Omnibuses conglomerate in conflict)—for ever desiring—(the clock asseverates with twelve distinct strokes that it is midday; light sheds gold scales; children swarm)—for ever desiring truth. Red is the dome; coins hang on the trees; smoke trails from the chimneys; bark, shout, cry 'Iron for sale'—and truth?

Radiating to a point men's feet and women's feet, black or gold-encrusted—(This foggy weather—Sugar? No, thank you—The commonwealth of the future)—the firelight darting and making the room red, save for the black figures and their bright eyes, while outside a van discharges, Miss Thingummy drinks tea at her desk, and plate-glass preserves fur coats—

Flaunted, leaf-light, drifting at corners, blown across the wheels, silver-splashed, home or not home, gathered, scattered, squandered in separate scales, swept up, down, torn, sunk, assembled—and truth?

Now to recollect by the fireside on the white square of marble. From ivory depths words rising shed their blackness, blossom and penetrate. Fallen the book; in the flame, in the smoke, in the momentary sparks—or now voyaging, the marble square pendant, minarets beneath and the Indian seas, while space rushes blue and stars glint—truth? content with closeness?

Lazy and indifferent the heron returns; the sky veils her stars; then bares them.

THE OPEN WINDOW

Saki

'My aunt will be down presently, Mr Nuttel,' said a very self-possessed young lady of fifteen; 'in the meantime you must try and put up with me.'

Framton Nuttel endeavoured to say the correct something which should duly flatter the niece of the moment without unduly discounting the aunt that was to come. Privately he doubted more than ever whether these formal visits on a succession of total strangers would do much towards helping the nerve cure which he was supposed to be undergoing.

'I know how it will be,' his sister had said when he was preparing to migrate to this rural retreat; 'you will bury yourself down there and not speak to a living soul, and your nerves will be worse than ever from moping. I shall just give you letters of introduction to all the people I know there. Some of them, as far as I can remember, were quite nice.'

Framton wondered whether Mrs Sappleton, the lady to whom he was presenting one of the letters of introduction, came into the nice division.

'Do you know many of the people round here?' asked the niece, when she judged that they had had sufficient silent communion.

'Hardly a soul,' said Framton. 'My sister was staying here, at the rectory, you know, some four years ago, and she gave me letters of introduction to some of the people here.'

He made the last statement in a tone of distinct regret.

'Then you know practically nothing about my aunt?' pursued

the self-possessed young lady.

'Only her name and address,' admitted the caller. He was wondering whether Mrs Sappleton was in the married or widowed state. An undefinable something about the room seemed to suggest masculine habitation.

'Her great tragedy happened just three years ago,' said the child; 'that would be since your sister's time.'

'Her tragedy?' asked Framton; somehow in this restful country spot tragedies seemed out of place.

'You may wonder why we keep that window wide open on an October afternoon,' said the niece, indicating a large French window that opened on to a lawn.

'It is quite warm for the time of the year,' said Framton; 'but has that window got anything to do with the tragedy?'

'Out through that window, three years ago to a day, her husband and her two young brothers went off for their day's shooting. They never came back. In crossing the moor to their favourite snipe-shooting ground they were all three engulfed in a treacherous piece of bog. It had been that dreadful wet summer, you know, and places that were safe in other years gave way suddenly without warning. Their bodies were never recovered. That was the dreadful part of it.' Here the child's voice lost its self-possessed note and became falteringly human. 'Poor aunt always thinks that they will come back some day, they and the little brown spaniel that was lost with them, and walk in at that window just as they used to do. That is why the window is kept open every evening till it is quite dusk. Poor dear aunt, she has often told me how they went out, her husband with his white waterproof coat over his arm, and Ronnie, her youngest brother, singing "Bertie, why do you bound?" as he always did to tease her, because she said it got on her nerves. Do you know, sometimes on still, quiet evenings like this, I almost get a creepy feeling that they will all walk in through that window—'

She broke off with a little shudder. It was a relief to Framton when the aunt bustled into the room with a whirl of apologies for being late in making her appearance.

'I hope Vera has been amusing you?' she said.

'She has been very interesting,' said Framton.

'I hope you don't mind the open window,' said Mrs Sappleton briskly; 'my husband and brothers will be home directly from shooting, and they always come in this way. They've been out for snipe in the marshes today, so They'll make a fine mess over my poor carpets. So like you men-folk, isn't it?'

She rattled on cheerfully about the shooting and the scarcity of birds, and the prospects for duck in the winter. To Framton it was all purely horrible. He made a desperate but only partially successful effort to turn the talk on to a less ghastly topic; he was conscious that his hostess was giving him only a fragment of her attention, and her eyes were constantly straying past him to the open window and the lawn beyond. It was certainly an unfortunate coincidence that he should have paid his visit on this tragic anniversary.

'The doctors agree in ordering me complete rest, an absence of mental excitement, and avoidance of anything in the nature of violent physical exercise,' announced Framton, who laboured under the tolerably widespread delusion that total strangers and chance acquaintances are hungry for the least detail of one's ailments and infirmities, their cause and cure. 'On the matter of diet they are not so much in agreement,' he continued.

'No?' said Mrs Sappleton, in a voice which only replaced a yawn at the last moment. Then she suddenly brightened into alert attention—but not to what Framton was saying.

'Here they are at last!' she cried. 'Just in time for tea, and don't they look as if they were muddy up to the eyes!'

Framton shivered slightly and turned towards the niece with a look intended to convey sympathetic comprehension. The child was staring out through the open window with dazed horror in her eyes. In a chill shock of nameless fear Framton swung round in his seat and looked in the same direction.

In the deepening twilight three figures were walking across the lawn towards the window; they all carried guns under their arms, and one of them was additionally burdened with a white coat hung over his shoulders. A tired brown spaniel kept close at their heels. Noiselessly they neared the house, and then a hoarse young voice chanted out of the dusk: 'I said, Bertie, why do you bound?'

Framton grabbed wildly at his stick and hat; the hall-door, the gravel-drive, and the front gate were dimly-noted stages in his headlong retreat. A cyclist coming along the road had to run into the hedge to avoid an imminent collision.

'Here we are, my dear,' said the bearer of the white mackintosh, coming in through the window; 'fairly muddy, but most of it's dry. Who was that who bolted out as we came up?'

'A most extraordinary man, a Mr Nuttel,' said Mrs Sappleton; 'could only talk about his illnesses, and dashed off without a word of good-bye or apology when you arrived. One would think he had seen a ghost.'

'I expect it was the spaniel,' said the niece calmly; 'he told me he had a horror of dogs. He was once hunted into a cemetery somewhere on the banks of the Ganges by a pack of pariah dogs, and had to spend the night in a newly dug grave with the creatures snarling and grinning and foaming just above him. Enough to make anyone lose their nerve.'

Romance at short notice was her speciality.

WHOSE DOG–?

Frances Gregg

'Hey—there's ladies here, move on—you!' The tone was authoritative and old John, the village drunkard, crouched away.

'I warn't doin' nothin',' he clutched feebly at the loose hanging rags that clothed him, 'only wanted to see same's them. Guess this pier's big enough to hold us all.'

'Halloo, John, have a drink?' A grinning boy held a can of salt water toward him.

The quick maudlin tears sprang to the old man's eyes. 'Little fellers,' he muttered, 'little fellers, they oughtn't ter act that way.'

'Give him a new necktie, he's gotta go to dinner with the Lodge.' A handful of dank sea-weed writhed around the old man's neck. 'That's a turtle, that is,' the boy went on, the need for imparting information justifying his lapse from ragging the drunkard. 'There—swimming round—it's tied to that stake. You orter've seen it at low tide when it was on the beach. It weighs ninety pounds.'

'I seen a turtle onct,' the drunkard quavered. 'It was bigger'n that. En they tied it to a stake—en it swam round—en it swam round—.' His sodden brain clutched for something more to say, some marvel with which to hold the interest of the gathered boys. It was good to talk. If only they would let him talk to them. If only they would let him sit on the store porch and smoke and gossip. He wouldn't be the town disgrace—

'Well—go on—what'd do?'

'Hey you!'—the boys were interrupted by the authoritative voice—'I told you to move on, didn't I—now if I tell you again

I'll run you in. D'yer hear? What you boys let that old bum hang around you for anyway. What's he doin' here?'

'Aw, he's fun. He warn't doin' nothin'. He was just awatchin' it swim. It's tied to that post. It don't come up no more.'

'Watchin' it swim, eh, was he? A'right. Whose dog is it?' The officer turned and sauntered away.

Sudden horror seized the old man. The liquor seemed drained out of his veins: his brain worked almost quickly. 'Whose dog— whose dog? Say!' he darted after the retreating boys. 'Say—that ain't no dog—is it—no *dog*? Tied up like that to drown—say—'

'Aw—keep off—I told you onct—it's a turtle for the Lodge dinner.' The boy shook himself free.

The old man stood a moment, shaken. His pulpy brain worked dimly toward the conception of the pain that was consuming him. 'Whose dog—' that man had asked—and he hadn't meant to help it—'whose dog!' They could do it—tie up a dog to drown in sight of people—like that—cruel. He saw the policeman coming toward him again. In a sudden frenzy he clutched his tattered garments about him and began to run, to run toward the end of the pier.

The boys raced after him. 'What yer gonter do?' they shouted. 'What yer gonter do?'

The old man turned and looked at them a moment with twitching features. 'I'm gonter die,' he said.

'Come on, you fellers—come on—the drunk's gonter dive— come on—he's cryin'!'

There was a splash. A surge of green filth and mud spread and dyed the water. A row of expectant heads leaned over the rail. 'Say—he ain't come up.' They waited.

The policeman strolled leisurely down in response to their repeated cries. '*Who* ain't come up? What, him—the drunk?' The officer leaned lethargically over the rail. 'What'm I gonter do? Why, leave 'm. He ain't got no folks gonter sit up nights waitin' fer 'm. Now you young ones go along home to your suppers,' he indulgently commanded, 'and you little fellers, if you want crabs, be 'round here early. By tomorrow this place will be fairly swarmin' with them.'

THE MASQUE OF THE RED DEATH

Edgar Allan Poe

The 'Red Death' had long devastated the country. No pestilence had ever been so fatal, or so hideous. Blood was its Avatar and its seal—the redness and the horror of blood. There were sharp pains, and sudden dizziness, and then profuse bleeding at the pores, with dissolution. The scarlet stains upon the body and especially upon the face of the victim, were the pest ban which shut him out from the aid and from the sympathy of his fellow-men. And the whole seizure, progress and termination of the disease, were the incidents of half-an-hour.

But the Prince Prospero was happy and dauntless and sagacious. When his dominions were half-depopulated, he summoned to his presence a thousand hale and light-hearted friends from among the knights and dames of his court, and with these retired to the deep seclusion of one of his castellated abbeys. This was an extensive and magnificent structure, the creation of the prince's own eccentric yet august taste. A strong and lofty wall girdled it in. This wall had gates of iron. The courtiers, having entered, brought furnaces and massy hammers and welded the bolts. They resolved to leave means neither of ingress nor egress to the sudden impulses of despair or of frenzy from within. The abbey was amply provisioned. With such precautions the courtiers might bid defiance to contagion. The external world could take care of itself. In the meantime it was folly to grieve, or to think. The prince had provided all the appliances of pleasure. There were buffoons, there were improvisatori, there were ballet-dancers, there were musicians, there was Beauty, there was wine. All these and security were within. Without was the 'Red Death'.

It was towards the close of the fifth or sixth month of his seclusion, and while the pestilence raged most furiously abroad, that the Prince Prospero entertained his thousand friends at a masked ball of the most unusual magnificence.

It was a voluptuous scene, that masquerade. But first let me tell of the rooms in which it was held. These were seven—an imperial suite. In many palaces, however, such suites form a long and straight vista, while the folding doors slide back nearly to the walls on either hand, so that the view of the whole extent is scarcely impeded. Here the case was very different, as might have been expected from the duke's love of the *bizarre*. The apartments were so irregularly disposed that the vision embraced but little more than one at a time. There was a sharp turn at every twenty or thirty yards, and at each turn a novel effect. To the right and left, in the middle of each wall, a tall and narrow Gothic window looked out upon a closed corridor which pursued the windings of the suite. These windows were of stained glass whose color varied in accordance with the prevailing hue of the decorations of the chamber into which it opened. That at the eastern extremity was hung, for example in blue—and vividly blue were its windows. The second chamber was purple in its ornaments and tapestries, and here the panes were purple. The third was green throughout, and so were the casements. The fourth was furnished and lighted with orange—the fifth with white—the sixth with violet. The seventh apartment was closely shrouded in black velvet tapestries that hung all over the ceiling and down the walls, falling in heavy folds upon a carpet of the same material and hue. But in this chamber only, the color of the windows failed to correspond with the decorations. The panes here were scarlet—a deep blood color. Now in no one of the seven apartments was there any lamp or candelabrum, amid the profusion of golden ornaments that lay scattered to and fro or depended from the roof. There was no light of any kind emanating from lamp or candle within the suite of chambers. But in the corridors that followed the suite, there stood, opposite to each window, a heavy tripod, bearing a brazier of fire, that projected its rays through the tinted glass and so glaringly illumined the room. And thus were produced a multitude of gaudy and fantastic appearances. But in the western or black chamber the effect of the fire-light that streamed upon the dark hangings through the blood-tinted panes, was ghastly in the extreme, and produced so wild a look upon the countenances of those who entered, that there were few of the company bold enough to set foot within its precincts at all.

It was in this apartment, also, that there stood against the western wall, a gigantic clock of ebony. Its pendulum swung to and fro with a dull, heavy, monotonous clang; and when the minute-hand made the circuit of the face, and the hour was to be stricken, there came from the brazen lungs of the clock a sound which was clear and loud and deep and exceedingly musical, but of so peculiar a note and emphasis that, at each lapse of an hour, the musicians of the orchestra were constrained to pause, momentarily, in their performance, to harken to the sound; and thus the waltzers perforce ceased their evolutions; and there was a brief disconcert of the whole gay company; and, while the chimes of the clock yet rang, it was observed that the giddiest grew pale, and the more aged and sedate passed their hands over their brows as if in confused revery or meditation. But when the echoes had fully ceased, a light laughter at once pervaded the assembly; the musicians looked at each other and smiled as if at their own nervousness and folly, and made whispering vows, each to the other, that the next chiming of the clock should produce in them no similar emotion; and then, after the lapse of sixty minutes, (which embrace three thousand and six hundred seconds of the Time that flies,) there came yet another chiming of the clock, and then were the same disconcert and tremulousness and meditation as before.

But, in spite of these things, it was a gay and magnificent revel. The tastes of the duke were peculiar. He had a fine eye for colors and effects. He disregarded the *decora* of mere fashion. His plans were bold and fiery, and his conceptions glowed with barbaric luster. There are some who would have thought him mad. His followers felt that he was not. It was necessary to hear and see and touch him to be *sure* that he was not.

He had directed, in great part, the movable embellishments of the seven chambers, upon occasion of this great *fête*; and it was his own guiding taste which had given character to the masqueraders. Be sure they were grotesque. There were much glare and glitter and piquancy and phantasm—much of what has been since seen in *Hernani*. There were arabesque figures with unsuited limbs and appointments. There were delirious fancies such as the madman fashions. There were much of the beautiful, much of the wanton, much of the *bizarre*, something of the terrible, and not a little of that which might have excited disgust. To and fro in the seven chambers there stalked, in fact, a multitude of dreams. And these—the dreams—writhed in and about taking hue from the rooms, and causing the wild music of the orchestra to seem as the echo of their steps. And, anon, there strikes the ebony clock which stands in the hall of the velvet. And then, for a moment, all is still, and all is silent save the voice of the clock. The dreams are stiff-frozen as they stand. But the echoes of the chime die away—they have endured but an instant—and a light, half-subdued laughter floats after them as they depart. And now again the music swells, and the dreams live, and writhe to and fro more merrily than ever, taking hue from the many tinted windows through which stream the rays from the tripods. But to the chamber which lies most westwardly of the seven, there are now none of the maskers who venture; for the night is waning away; and there flows a ruddier light through the blood-colored panes; and the blackness of the sable drapery appals; and to him whose foot falls upon the sable carpet, there comes from the near clock of ebony a muffled peal more solemnly emphatic than any which reaches *their* ears who indulged in the more remote gaieties of the other apartments.

But these other apartments were densely crowded, and in them beat feverishly the heart of life. And the revel went whirlingly on, until at length there commenced the sounding of midnight upon the clock. And then the music ceased, as I have told; and the evolutions of the waltzers were quieted; and there was an uneasy cessation of all things as before. But now there were twelve strokes to be sounded by the bell of the clock; and thus it happened, perhaps, that more of thought crept, with more of time, into the meditations of the thoughtful among those who reveled. And thus too, it happened, perhaps, that before the last echoes of the last chime had utterly sunk into silence, there were many individuals in the crowd who had found leisure to become aware of the presence of a masked figure which had arrested the attention of no single individual before. And the rumor of this new presence having spread itself whisperingly around, there arose at length from the whole company a buzz, or murmur, expressive of disapprobation and surprise—then, finally, of terror, of horror, and of disgust.

In an assembly of phantasms such as I have painted, it may well be supposed that no ordinary appearance could have excited such sensation. In truth the masquerade license of the night was nearly unlimited; but the figure in question had out-Heroded Herod, and gone beyond the bounds of even the prince's indefinite decorum. There are chords in the hearts of the most reckless which cannot be touched without emotion. Even with the utterly lost, to whom life and death are equally jests, there are matters of which no jest can be made. The whole company, indeed, seemed now deeply to feel that in the costume and bearing of the stranger neither wit nor propriety existed. The figure was tall and gaunt, and shrouded from head to foot in the habiliments of the grave. The mask which concealed the visage was made so nearly to resemble the countenance of a stiffened corpse that the closest scrutiny must have had difficulty in detecting the cheat. And yet all this might have been endured, if not approved, by the mad revelers around. But the mummer had gone so far as to assume the type of the Red Death. His vesture was dabbled in *blood*—and his broad brow, with all the features of the face, was besprinkled with the scarlet horror.

When the eyes of the Prince Prospero fell upon this spectral image (which, with a slow and solemn movement, as if more fully to sustain its role, stalked to and fro among the waltzers) he was seen to be convulsed, in the first moment with a strong shudder either of terror or distaste; but, in the next, his brow reddened with rage.

'Who dares,' he demanded hoarsely of the courtiers who stood near him—'who dares insult us with this blasphemous mockery? Seize him and unmask him that we may know whom we have to hang, at sunrise, from the battlements!'

It was in the eastern or blue chamber in which stood the Prince Prospero as he uttered these words. They rang throughout the seven rooms loudly and clearly—for the prince was a bold and robust man, and the music had become hushed at the waving of his hand.

It was in the blue room where stood the prince, with a group of pale courtiers by his side. At first, as he spoke, there was a slight rushing movement of this group in the direction of the intruder, who at the moment was also near at hand, and now, with deliberate and stately step, made closer approach to the speaker. But from a certain nameless awe with which the mad assumptions of the mummer had inspired the whole party, there were found none who put forth hand to seize him; so that, unimpeded, he passed within a yard of the prince's person; and, while the vast assembly, as if with one impulse, shrank from the centers of the rooms to the walls, he made his way uninterruptedly, but with the same solemn and measured step which had distinguished him from the first, through the blue chamber to the purple—through the purple to the green—through the green to the orange—through this again to the white—and even thence to the violet, ere a decided movement had been made to arrest him. It was then, however, that the Prince Prospero, maddening with rage and the shame of his own momentary cowardice, rushed hurriedly through the six chambers, while none followed him on account of a deadly terror that had seized upon all. He bore aloft a drawn dagger, and had approached, in rapid impetuosity, to within three or four feet of the retreating figure, when the latter, having attained the extremity of the velvet apartment, turned suddenly and confronted his pursuer. There was a sharp cry—and the dagger dropped gleaming upon the sable carpet, upon which, instantly afterwards, fell prostrate in death the Prince Prospero. Then, summoning the wild courage of despair, a throng of the revelers at once threw themselves into the black apartment, and, seizing the mummer, whose tall figure stood erect and motionless within the shadow of the ebony clock, gasped in unutterable horror at finding the grave cerements and corpse-like mask, which they handled with so violent a rudeness, untenanted by any tangible form.

And now was acknowledged the presence of the Red Death. He had come like a thief in the night. And one by one dropped the revelers in the blood-bedewed halls of their revel, and died each in the despairing posture of his fall. And the life of the ebony clock went out with that of the last of the gay. And the flames of the tripods expired. And Darkness and Decay and the Red Death held illimitable dominion over all.

WONDERWINGS

Edith Howes

Poppypink sat up in bed and yawned. 'Why is everybody getting up so early?' she asked. 'Is it a holiday?'

The older fairies were dressing themselves and brushing their long fine hair. 'Wonderwings is coming to see us,' they said. 'Jump up, little Poppypink.'

'Who is Wonderwings?' she asked.

'You will see when you are dressed. Hurry, or you will miss her.'

'Oh dear! I am so sleepy,' said Poppypink, and she yawned again. 'I don't care about Wonderwings.' She snuggled down into the bedclothes again, and went to sleep.

Presently she was awakened by the sound of the sweetest singing she had ever heard, and a flash of brilliant colour went past her window pane of crystal set in pearl.

'That must be Wonderwings,' she said. 'Oh, I must see her. I hope I am not too late.'

She sprang from bed and dressed so hurriedly that I am afraid her hair did not receive its due amount of brushing. Then she ran out into the garden.

The older fairies stood all in a group, saying loudly 'I will go,' and 'I will go.' And before them, scarcely touching the ground with the tip of her foot, stood poised a glorious fairy, taller than any other there. She was altogether beautiful; and her wings—as soon as Poppypink saw them she knew why the visitor had been called Wonderwings. For they reached high above her head and almost to the ground, and they glowed with so many colours that it seemed as if a million jewels had been hung upon them and had stuck, growing into a million flashing stars that made a million little rainbows with every sway and movement of her body.

'How lovely! Oh, how lovely!' cried Poppypink. She crept nearer to the beautiful fairy and sat among the daisies at her feet. 'See,' she cried. 'My wings are small and colourless. Tell me how I may grow wings like yours.' Just as little girls adore beautiful hair, so do little fairies adore beautiful wings.

Wonderwings smiled down at her. 'Such wings as mine are only to be won in sadder lands than these,' she said. 'If you would have them you must leave your fairyland and come where humans live, and where hunger and sorrow and death trample the city streets.'

'I will come!' cried Poppypink. 'I will come!'

'Come then,' said Wonderwings. She took the little fairy's hand, and up they all rose into the clear air, flying far and far away till they left their fairyland behind and came at last to the sadder lands where humans lived. There Wonderwings showed them where hunger and sorrow and death trampled the city streets, and the band of fairies flew lower and lower to look.

'The children tumble and fight in the dirty lanes, and cry for bread,' cried Poppypink. 'The little ones, I cannot bear to hear them sob.'

'Perhaps you can help them,' said Wonderwings.

'I am only a little fairy. What can I do?' asked Poppypink. 'I have no bread to give them.'

She flew a little lower, to gaze at them more nearly. 'What can I do?' she asked again.

No answer came. She looked around, and found herself alone. Wonderwings and the older fairies had in a moment gone from sight.

Below, a crippled child sat among rags in a dark corner of a dreary room, and tears ran down her cheeks. 'The sunshine, the pretty yellow sunshine!' she wailed. 'If only I could run and play in the pretty sunshine!'

'Here is something I can do,' thought Poppypink. She gathered armfuls of the golden sunbeams, and flying with them through the glass as only a fairy can fly, herself unseen, she heaped them over the twisted hands and pale thin face of the child, and left her playing with them and smiling happily.

Lower she flew to help the little ones who cried about the gutters. She led the starving and shelterless to comfort, the toddlers to safety; she brought a flower to the hopeless, ease to sick ones racked with pain; at night she flew with glittering dreams from room to room, so that even sad-eyed feeble babies laughed for pleasure in their sleep. Day after day, night after night she toiled, for weeks and months and years. There was so much to do! The time passed like a moment. So busy was she that she had forgotten all about her wings.

One day there came a flash of colour in the air beside her, and Wonderwings and all the older fairies stood around her. 'Dear Poppypink,' cried one, 'how your wings have grown! And how beautiful they are! They are so tall that they reach above your head and almost to the ground, and they glow with so many colours that it seems as if a million jewels had been flung upon them and had stuck, growing into a million flashing stars that make a million little rainbows with every sway and movement of your body.'

Poppypink laughed with joy. 'I am so glad, so very glad!' she said. 'I had forgotten all about my wings.'

'Yet they have grown with use,' said Wonderwings; 'and for every deed of kindness done a star has sprung, to shine in beauty there for evermore.'

ANGELA: AN INVERTED LOVE STORY

William Schwenck Gilbert

I am a poor paralysed fellow who, for many years past, has been confined to a bed or a sofa. For the last six years I have occupied a small room, giving on to one of the side canals of Venice, and having no one about me but a deaf old woman, who makes my bed and attends to my food; and there I eke out a poor income of about thirty pounds a year by making water-colour drawings of flowers and fruit (they are the cheapest models in Venice), and these I send to a friend in London, who sells them to a dealer for small sums. But, on the whole, I am happy and content.

It is necessary that I should describe the position of my room rather minutely. Its only window is about five feet above the water of the canal, and above it the house projects some six feet, and overhangs the water, the projecting portion being supported by stout piles driven into the bed of the canal. This arrangement has the disadvantage (among others) of so limiting my upward view that I am unable to see more than about ten feet of the height of the house immediately opposite to me, although, by reaching as far out of the window as my infirmity will permit, I can see for a considerable distance up and down the canal, which does not exceed fifteen feet in width. But, although I can see but little of the material house opposite, I can see its reflection upside down in the canal, and I take a good deal of inverted interest in such of its inhabitants as show themselves from time to time (always upside down) on its balconies and at its windows.

When I first occupied my room, about six years ago, my attention was directed to the reflection of a little girl of thirteen or so (as nearly as I could judge), who passed every day on a balcony just above the upward range of my limited field of view. She had a glass of flowers and a crucifix on a little table by her side; and as she sat there, in fine weather, from early morning until dark, working assiduously all the time, I concluded that she earned her living by needle-work. She was certainly an industrious little girl, and, as far as I could judge by her upside-down reflection, neat in her dress and pretty. She had an old mother, an invalid, who, on warm days, would sit on the balcony with her, and it interested me to see the little maid wrap the old lady in shawls, and bring pillows for her chair, and a stool for her feet, and every now and again lay down her work and kiss and fondle the old lady for half a minute, and then take up her work again.

Time went by, and as the little maid grew up, her reflection grew down, and at last she was quite a little woman of, I suppose, sixteen or seventeen. I can only work for a couple of hours or so in the brightest part of the day, so I had plenty of time on my hands in which to watch her movements, and sufficient imagination to weave a little romance about her, and to endow her with a beauty which, to a great extent, I had to take for granted. I saw—or fancied that I could see—that she began to take an interest in *my* reflection (which, of course, she could see as I could see hers); and one day, when it appeared to me that she was looking right at it—that is to say when her reflection appeared to be looking right at me—I tried the desperate experiment of nodding to her, and to my intense delight her reflection nodded in reply. And so our two reflections became known to one another.

It did not take me very long to fall in love with her, but a long time passed before I could make up my mind to do more than nod to her every morning, when the old woman moved me from my bed to the sofa at the window, and again in the evening, when the little maid left the balcony for that day. One day, however, when I saw her reflection looking at mine, I nodded to her, and threw a flower into the canal. She nodded several times in return, and I saw her direct her mother's attention to the incident. Then every morning I threw a flower into the water for 'good morning', and another in the evening for 'goodnight', and I soon discovered that I had not altogether thrown them in vain, for one day she threw a flower to join mine, and she laughed and clapped her hands when she saw the two flowers join forces and float away together. And then every morning and every evening she threw her flower when I threw mine, and when the two flowers met she clapped her hands, and so did I; but when they were separated, as they sometimes were, owing to one of them having met an obstruction which did not catch the other, she threw up her hands in a pretty affectation of despair, which I tried to imitate but in an English and unsuccessful fashion. And when they were rudely run down by a passing gondola (which happened not unfrequently) she pretended to cry, and I did the same. Then, in pretty pantomime, she would point downwards to the sky to tell me that it was Destiny that had caused the shipwreck of our flowers, and I, in pantomime, not nearly so pretty, would try to convey to her that Destiny would be kinder next time, and that perhaps tomorrow our flowers would be more fortunate—and so the innocent courtship went on. One day she showed me her crucifix and kissed it, and thereupon I took a little silver crucifix that always stood by me, and kissed that, and so she knew that we were one in religion.

One day the little maid did not appear on her balcony, and for several days I saw nothing of her; and although I threw my flowers as usual, no flower came to keep it company. However, after a time, she reappeared, dressed in black, and crying often, and then I knew that the poor child's mother was dead, and, as far as I knew, she was alone in the world. The flowers came no more for many days, nor did she show any sign of recognition, but kept her eyes on her work, except when she placed her handkerchief to them. And opposite to her was the old lady's chair, and I could see that, from time to time, she would lay down her work and gaze at it, and then a flood of tears would come to her relief. But at last one day she roused herself to nod to me, and then her flower came, day by day, and my flower went forth to join it, and with varying fortunes the two flowers sailed away as of yore.

But the darkest day of all to me was when a good-looking young gondolier, standing right end uppermost in his gondola (for I could see *him* in the flesh), worked his craft alongside the house, and stood talking to her as she sat on the balcony. They seemed to speak as old friends—indeed, as well as I could make out, he held her by the hand during the whole of their interview which lasted quite half an hour. Eventually he pushed off, and left my heart heavy within me. But I soon took heart of grace, for as soon as he was out of sight, the little maid threw two flowers growing on the same stem—an allegory of which I could make nothing, until it broke upon me that she meant to convey to me that he and she were brother and sister, and that I had no cause to be sad. And thereupon I nodded to her cheerily, and she nodded to me, and laughed aloud, and I laughed in return, and all went on again as before.

Then came a dark and dreary time, for it became necessary that I should undergo treatment that confined me absolutely to my bed for many days, and I worried and fretted to think that the little maid and I should see each other no longer, and worse still, that she would think that I had gone away without even hinting to her that I was going. And I lay awake at night wondering how I could let her know the truth, and fifty plans flitted through my brain, all appearing to be feasible enough at night, but absolutely wild and impracticable in the morning. One day—and it was a bright day indeed for me—the old woman who tended me told me that a gondolier had inquired whether the English signor had gone away or had died; and so I learnt that the little maid had been anxious about me, and that she had sent her brother to inquire, and the brother had no doubt taken to her the reason of my protracted absence from the window.

From that day, and ever after during my three weeks of bed-keeping, a flower was found every morning on the ledge of my window, which was within easy reach of anyone in a boat; and when at last a day came when I could be moved, I took my accustomed place on my sofa at the window, and the little maid saw me, and stood on her head (so to speak) and clapped her hands upside down with a delight that was as eloquent as my right-end-up delight could be. And so the first time the gondolier passed my window I beckoned to him, and he pushed alongside, and told me, with many bright smiles, that he was glad indeed to see me well again. Then I thanked him and his sister for their many kind thoughts about me during my retreat, and I then learnt from him that her name was Angela, and that she was the best and purest maiden in all Venice, and that anyone might think himself happy indeed who could call her sister, but that he was happier even than her brother, for he was to be married to her, and indeed they were to be married the next day.

Thereupon my heart seemed to swell to bursting, and the blood rushed through my veins so that I could hear it and nothing else for a while. I managed at last to stammer forth some words of awkward congratulation, and he left me, singing merrily, after asking permission to bring his bride to see me on the morrow as they returned from church.

'For', said he, 'my Angela has known you very long—ever since she was a child, and she has often spoken to me of the poor Englishman who was a good Catholic, and who lay all day long for years and years on a sofa at a window, and she had said over and over again how dearly she wished she could speak to him and comfort him; and one day, when you threw a flower into the canal, she asked me whether she might throw another, and

I told her yes, for he would understand that it meant sympathy for one sorely afflicted.'

And so I learned that it was pity, and not love, except indeed such love as is akin to pity, that prompted her to interest herself in my welfare, and there was an end of it all.

For the two flowers that I thought were on one stem were two flowers tied together (but I could not tell that), and they were meant to indicate that she and the gondolier were affianced lovers, and my expressed pleasure at this symbol delighted her, for she took it to mean that I rejoiced in her happiness.

And the next day the gondolier came with a train of other gondoliers, all decked in their holiday garb, and on his gondola sat Angela, happy, and blushing at her happiness. Then he and she entered the house in which I dwelt, and came into my room (and it was strange indeed, after so many years of inversion, to see her with her head above her feet!), and then she wished me happiness and a speedy restoration to good health (which could never be); and I in broken words and with tears in my eyes, gave her the little silver crucifix that had stood by my bed or my table for so many years. And Angela took it reverently, and crossed herself, and kissed it, and so departed with her delighted husband.

And as I heard the song of the gondoliers as they went their way—the song dying away in the distance as the shadows of the sundown closed around me—I felt that they were singing the requiem of the only love that had ever entered my heart.

A BABY TRAMP

Ambrose Bierce

If you had seen little Jo standing at the street corner in the rain, you would hardly have admired him. It was apparently an ordinary autumn rainstorm, but the water which fell upon Jo (who was hardly old enough to be either just or unjust, and so perhaps did not come under the law of impartial distribution) appeared to have some property peculiar to itself: one would have said it was dark and adhesive—sticky. But that could hardly be so, even in Blackburg, where things certainly did occur that were a good deal out of the common.

For example, ten or twelve years before, a shower of small frogs had fallen, as is credibly attested by a contemporaneous chronicle, the record concluding with a somewhat obscure statement to the effect that the chronicler considered it good growing-weather for Frenchmen.

Some years later Blackburg had a fall of crimson snow; it is cold in Blackburg when winter is on, and the snows are frequent and deep. There can be no doubt of it—the snow in this instance was of the colour of blood and melted into water of the same hue, if water it was, not blood. The phenomenon had attracted wide attention, and science had as many explanations as there were scientists who knew nothing about it. But the men of Blackburg—men who for many years had lived right there where the red snow fell, and might be supposed to know a good deal about the matter—shook their heads and said something would come of it.

And something did, for the next summer was made memorable

by the prevalence of a mysterious disease—epidemic, endemic, or the Lord knows what, though the physicians didn't—which carried away a full half of the population. Most of the other half carried themselves away and were slow to return, but finally came back, and were now increasing and multiplying as before, but Blackburg had not since been altogether the same.

Of quite another kind, though equally 'out of the common,' was the incident of Hetty Parlow's ghost. Hetty Parlow's maiden name had been Brownon, and in Blackburg that meant more than one would think.

The Brownons had from time immemorial—from the very earliest of the old colonial days—been the leading family of the town. It was the richest and it was the best, and Blackburg would have shed the last drop of its plebeian blood in defence of the Brownon fair fame. As few of the family's members had ever been known to live permanently away from Blackburg, although most of them were educated elsewhere and nearly all had travelled, there was quite a number of them. The men held most of the public offices, and the women were foremost in all good works. Of these latter, Hetty was most beloved by reason of the sweetness of her disposition, the purity of her character and her singular personal beauty. She married in Boston a young scapegrace named Parlow, and like a good Brownon brought him to Blackburg forthwith and made a man and a town councillor of him. They had a child which they named Joseph and dearly loved, as was then the fashion among parents in all that region. Then they died of the mysterious disorder already mentioned, and at the age of one whole year Joseph set up as an orphan.

Unfortunately for Joseph the disease which had cut off his parents did not stop at that; it went on and extirpated nearly the whole Brownon contingent and its allies by marriage; and those who fled did not return. The tradition was broken, the Brownon estates passed into alien hands, and the only Brownons remaining in that place were underground in Oak Hill Cemetery, where, indeed, was a colony of them powerful enough to resist the encroachment of surrounding tribes and hold the best part of the grounds. But about the ghost:

One night, about three years after the death of Hetty Parlow, a number of the young people of Blackburg were passing Oak Hill Cemetery in a wagon—if you have been there you will remember that the road to Greenton runs alongside it on the south. They had been attending a May Day festival at Greenton; and that serves to fix the date. Altogether there may have been a dozen, and a jolly party they were, considering the legacy of gloom left by the town's recent sombre experiences. As they passed the cemetery the man driving suddenly reined in his team with an exclamation of surprise. It was sufficiently surprising, no doubt, for just ahead, and almost at the roadside, though inside the cemetery, stood the ghost of Hetty Parlow. There could be no doubt of it, for she had been personally known to every youth and maiden in the party. That established the thing's identity; its character as ghost was signified by all the customary signs—the shroud, the long, undone hair, the 'far-away look'—everything. This disquieting apparition was stretching out its arms toward the west, as if in supplication for the evening star, which, certainly, was an alluring object, though obviously out of reach. As they all sat silent (so the story goes) every member of that party of merrymakers—they had merrymade on coffee and lemonade only—distinctly heard that ghost call the name 'Joey, Joey!' A moment later nothing was there. Of course one does not have to believe all that.

Now, at that moment, as was afterward ascertained, Joey was wandering about in the sagebrush on the opposite side of the continent, near Winnemucca, in the State of Nevada. He had been taken to that town by some good persons distantly related to his dead father, and by them adopted and tenderly cared for.

But on that evening the poor child had strayed from home and was lost in the desert.

His after history is involved in obscurity and has gaps which conjecture alone can fill. It is known that he was found by a family of Piute Indians, who kept the little wretch with them for a time and then sold him—actually sold him for money to a woman on one of the east-bound trains, at a station a long way from Winnemucca. The woman professed to have made all manner of inquiries, but all in vain: so, being childless and a widow, she adopted him herself. At this point of his career Jo seemed to be getting a long way from the condition of orphanage; the interposition of a multitude of parents between himself and that woeful state promised him a long immunity from its disadvantages.

Mrs Darnell, his newest mother, lived in Cleveland, Ohio. But her adopted son did not long remain with her. He was seen one afternoon by a policeman, new to that beat, deliberately toddling away from her house, and being questioned answered that he was 'a doin home.' He must have travelled by rail, somehow, for three days later he was in the town of Whiteville, which, as you know, is a long way from Blackburg. His clothing was in pretty fair condition, but he was sinfully dirty. Unable to give any account of himself he was arrested as a vagrant and sentenced to imprisonment in the Infants' Sheltering Home— where he was washed.

Jo ran away from the Infants' Sheltering Home at Whiteville— just took to the woods one day, and the Home knew him no more for ever.

We find him next, or rather get back to him, standing forlorn in the cold autumn rain at a suburban street corner in Blackburg; and it seems right to explain now that the raindrops falling upon him there were really not dark and gummy; they only failed to make his face and hands less so. Jo was indeed fearfully and wonderfully besmirched, as by the hand of an artist. And the forlorn little tramp had no shoes; his feet were bare, red, and swollen, and when he walked he limped with both legs. As to clothing—ah, you would hardly have had the skill to name any single garment that he wore, or say by what magic he kept it upon him. That he was cold all over and all through did not admit of a doubt; he knew it himself. Anyone would have been cold there that evening; but, for that reason, no one else was there. How Jo came to be there himself, he could not for the flickering little life of him have told, even if gifted with a vocabulary exceeding a hundred words. From the way he stared about him one could have seen that he had not the faintest notion of where (nor why) he was.

Yet he was not altogether a fool in his day and generation; being cold and hungry, and still able to walk a little by bending his knees very much indeed and putting his feet down toes first, he decided to enter one of the houses which flanked the street at long intervals and looked so bright and warm. But when he attempted to act upon that very sensible decision a burly dog came browsing out and disputed his right. Inexpressibly frightened, and believing, no doubt (with some reason, too), that brutes without meant brutality within, he hobbled away from all the houses, and with grey, wet fields to right of him and grey, wet fields to left of him—with the rain half blinding him and the night coming in mist and darkness, held his way along the road that leads to Greenton. That is to say, the road leads those to Greenton who succeed in passing the Oak Hill Cemetery. A considerable number every year do not.

Jo did not.

They found him there the next morning, very wet, very cold, but no longer hungry. He had apparently entered the cemetery gate—hoping, perhaps, that it led to a house where there was no dog—and gone blundering about in the darkness, falling over many a grave, no doubt, until he had tired of it all and given up. The little body lay upon one side, with one soiled cheek upon one soiled hand, the other hand tucked away among the rags to make it warm, the other cheek washed clean and white at last, as for a kiss from one of God's great angels. It was observed—though nothing was thought of it at the time, the body being as yet unidentified—that the little fellow was lying upon the grave of Hetty Parlow. The grave, however, had not opened to receive him. That is a circumstance which, without actual irreverence, one may wish had been ordered otherwise.

A CHILD'S DREAM OF A STAR

Charles Dickens

There was once a child, and he strolled about a good deal, and thought of a number of things. He had a sister, who was a child too, and his constant companion. These two used to wonder all day long. They wondered at the beauty of the flowers; they wondered at the height and blueness of the sky; they wondered at the depth of the bright water; they wondered at the goodness and the power of GOD, who made the lovely world.

They used to say to one another, sometimes, Supposing all the children upon earth were to die, would the flowers and the water and the sky be sorry? They believed they would be sorry. For, said they, the buds are the children of the flowers, and the little playful streams that gambol down the hillsides are the children of the water; and the smallest bright specks playing at hide-and-seek in the sky all night must surely be the children of the stars; and they would all be grieved to see their playmates, the children of men, no more.

There was one clear shining star that used to come out in the sky before the rest, near the church-spire, above the graves. It was larger and more beautiful, they thought, than all the others, and every night they watched for it, standing hand in hand at a window. Whoever saw it first cried out, 'I see the star!' And often they cried out both together, knowing so well when it would rise and where. So they grew to be such friends with it, that, before lying down in their beds, they always looked out once again, to bid it good night; and when they were turning round to sleep, they used to say, 'God bless the star!'

But while she was still very young, O, very, very young, the sister drooped, and came to be so weak that she could no longer stand in the window at night; and then the child looked sadly out by himself, and when he saw the star, turned round and said to the patient pale face on the bed, 'I see the star!' And then a smile would come upon the face, and a little weak voice used to say, 'God bless my brother and the star!'

And so the time came, all too soon! when the child looked out alone, and when there was no face on the bed; and when there was a little grave among the graves, not there before; and when the star made long rays down towards him, as he saw it through his tears.

Now, these rays were so bright, and they seemed to make such a shining way from earth to heaven, that when the child went to his solitary bed, he dreamed about the star; and dreamed that, lying where he was, he saw a train of people taken up that sparkling road by angels. And the star, opening, showed him a great world of light, where many more such angels waited to receive them.

All these angels, who were waiting, turned their beaming eyes upon the people who were carried up into the star; and some came out from the long rows in which they stood, and fell upon the people's necks, and kissed them tenderly, and went away with them down avenues of light, and were so happy in their company, that, lying in his bed, he wept for joy.

But there were many angels who did not go with them, and among them one he knew. The patient face that once had lain upon the bed was glorified and radiant, but his heart found out his sister among all the host.

His sister's angel lingered near the entrance of the star, and said to the leader among those who had brought the people thither, 'Is my brother come?'

And he said, 'No.'

She was turning hopefully away, when the child stretched out his arms, and cried, 'O sister, I am here! Take me!' And then she turned her beaming eyes upon him, and it was night; and the star was shining into the room, making long rays down towards him as he saw it through his tears.

From that hour forth, the child looked out upon the star as on the home he was to go to, when his time should come; and he thought that he did not belong to the earth alone, but to the star too, because of his sister's angel gone before.

There was a baby born to be a brother to the child; and while he was so little that he never yet had spoken word, he stretched his tiny form out on his bed, and died.

Again the child dreamed of the opened star, and of the company of angels, and the train of people, and the rows of angels with their beaming eyes all turned upon those people's faces.

Said his sister's angel to the leader, 'Is my brother come?'

And he said, 'Not that one, but another.'

As the child beheld his brother's angel in her arms, he cried, 'O sister, I am here! Take me!' And she turned and smiled upon him, and the star was shining.

He grew to be a young man, and was busy at his books when an old servant came to him and said, 'Thy mother is no more. I bring her blessing on her darling son!'

Again at night he saw the star, and all that former company. Said his sister's angel to the leader, 'Is my brother come?'

And he said, 'Thy mother!'

A mighty cry of joy went forth through all the star, because the mother was reunited to her two children. And he stretched out his arms and cried, 'O mother, sister, and brother, I am here! Take me!'

And they answered him, 'Not yet.' And the star was shining.

He grew to be a man, whose hair was turning grey; and he was sitting in his chair by the fireside, heavy with grief, and with his face bedewed with tears, when the star opened once again.

Said his sister's angel to the leader, 'Is my brother come?'

And he said, 'Nay, but his maiden daughter.'

And the man who had been the child saw his daughter, newly lost to him, a celestial creature among those three, and he said, 'My daughter's head is on my sister's bosom, and her arm is round my mother's neck, and at her feet there is the baby of old time, and I can bear the parting from her, GOD be praised!'

And the star was shining.

Thus the child came to be an old man, and his once smooth face was wrinkled, and his steps were slow and feeble, and his back was bent. And one night as he lay upon his bed, his children standing round, he cried, as he had cried so long ago, 'I see the star!'

They whispered one another, 'He is dying.'

And he said, 'I am. My age is falling from me like a garment, and I move towards the star as a child. And O my Father, now I thank thee that it has so often opened to receive those dear ones who await me!'

And the star was shining; and it shines upon his grave.

A HAUNTED HOUSE

Virginia Woolf

Whatever hour you woke there was a door shutting. From room to room they went, hand in hand, lifting here, opening there, making sure—a ghostly couple.

'Here we left it,' she said. And he added, 'Oh, but here too!' 'It's upstairs,' she murmured. 'And in the garden,' he whispered 'Quietly,' they said, 'or we shall wake them.'

But it wasn't that you woke us. Oh, no. 'They're looking for it; they're drawing the curtain,' one might say, and so read on a page or two. 'Now they've found it,' one would be certain, stopping the pencil on the margin. And then, tired of reading, one might rise and see for oneself, the house all empty, the doors standing open, only the wood pigeons bubbling with content and the hum of the threshing machine sounding from the farm. 'What did I come in here for? What did I want to find?' My hands were empty. 'Perhaps it's upstairs then?' The apples were in the loft. And so down again, the garden still as ever, only the book had slipped into the grass.

But they had found it in the drawing room. Not that one could ever see them. The window panes reflected apples, reflected roses; all the leaves were green in the glass. If they moved in the drawing room, the apple only turned its yellow side. Yet, the moment after, if the door was opened, spread about the floor, hung upon the walls, pendant from the ceiling—what? My hands were empty. The shadow of a thrush crossed the carpet; from the deepest wells of silence the wood pigeon drew its bubble of sound. 'Safe, safe, safe,' the pulse of the house beat softly. 'The treasure buried; the room...' the pulse stopped short. Oh, was that the buried treasure?

A moment later the light had faded. Out in the garden then? But the trees spun darkness for a wandering beam of sun. So fine, so rare, coolly sunk beneath the surface the beam I sought always burnt behind the glass. Death was the glass; death was between us; coming to the woman first, hundreds of years ago, leaving the house, sealing all the windows; the rooms were darkened. He left it, left her, went North, went East, saw the stars turned in the Southern sky; sought the house, found it dropped beneath the Downs. 'Safe, safe, safe,' the pulse of the house beat gladly. 'The Treasure yours.'

The wind roars up the avenue. Trees stoop and bend this way and that. Moonbeams splash and spill wildly in the rain. But the beam of the lamp falls straight from the window. The candle burns stiff and still. Wandering through the house, opening the windows, whispering not to wake us, the ghostly couple seek their joy.

'Here we slept,' she says. And he adds, 'Kisses without number.' 'Waking in the morning—' 'Silver between the trees—' 'Upstairs—' 'In the garden—' 'When summer came—' 'In winter snowtime—' The doors go shutting far in the distance, gently knocking like the pulse of a heart.

Nearer they come; cease at the doorway. The wind falls, the rain slides silver down the glass. Our eyes darken; we hear no steps beside us; we see no lady spread her ghostly cloak. His hands shield the lantern. 'Look,' he breathes. 'Sound asleep. Love upon their lips.'

Stooping, holding their silver lamp above us, long they look and deeply. Long they pause. The wind drives straightly; the flame stoops slightly. Wild beams of moonlight cross both floor and wall, and, meeting, stain the faces bent; the faces pondering; the faces that search the sleepers and seek their hidden joy.

'Safe, safe, safe,' the heart of the house beats proudly. 'Long years—' he sighs. 'Again you found me.' 'Here,' she murmurs, 'sleeping; in the garden reading; laughing, rolling apples in the loft. Here we left our treasure—' Stooping, their light lifts the lids upon my eyes. 'Safe! safe! safe!' the pulse of the house beats wildly. Waking, I cry 'Oh, is this your buried treasure? The light in the heart.'

KATSUNO'S REVENGE

Asataro Miyamori

I

A man and a woman were whispering to each other by a shaded lamp in a quiet detached room which was partly hedged by *unohana* whose snow-white flowers gleamed in the moonlight. Only the frogs croaking in the neighbouring paddy-field broke the stillness of the night.

The man was Sakuma Shichiroyemon, a councillor of Oda Nobuyuki, the lord of the castle of Iwakura, in the province, of Owari. About fifty-two years old, he was a fierce-looking man with powerful muscles and bristling grey whiskers. Haughty, quick-tempered and very jealous he tyrannized over his subordinates and was accordingly an object of hatred throughout the clan. The person with whom he was now talking was a woman close upon his own age—the supervisor of Lord Oda's maids-of-honour, by name O-Tora-no-Kata. Being a cross, cunning, and avaricious hag, she was regarded by the maids with terror and detestation. 'Birds of a feather flock together.' She had wormed her way into the good graces of Shichiroyemon in order to make her position secure; whilst the latter, on his part, had set her to spy on the actions of his lord, as well as of his colleagues and inferiors.

'What's that, Madame Tora?' asked Shichiroyemon, his face reddening with anger. 'Do you mean to tell me that our lord is going to set that green boy of a Hachiya over me as Prime Councillor?'

'I repeat what I hear;—all the maids say so....'

'Pshaw! How I do hate that Hachiya—that peasant's son born in obscurity. Who knows where he comes from? A pale, smooth-faced womanish sprig! How glibly he flatters our lord! He has never been in battle; what use is such a bookworm in these warlike days? And yet this inexperienced stripling is going to be appointed Prime Councillor! Humph, what infatuation! Ha, ha, ha!'

'It will not boil yet. The fire is not strong enough.'

'Eh! The fire?'

'Ha, ha!' said O-Tora with a disagreeable smile. 'Here I have good fuel to make you burn!'

'Don't try to annoy me like that,' said he impatiently. 'Tell me quickly.'

'It is the secret of secrets. I can't readily...w-e-l-l...sell it.' She spoke slowly, with an emphasis on the word 'sell.'

'How grasping you are! Well, then, I will buy your secret with this.' So saying, Shichiroyemon took a packet of money out of his bosom and threw it down on the mat. The crone picked it up in silence, a cunning smile playing about her lips.

'Mr Sakuma, you must not be off your guard.'

'What do you mean?'

'Well, K...; you must give her up.'

'What! Give up Katsuno?' he exclaimed, startled. 'Why? Tell me quick!'

'Don't be surprised, sir. It is our lord's pleasure to give her to Hachiya in marriage.'

Katsuno was a maid-of-honour of Oda Nobuyuki with whom she was a great favourite. A young damsel of nineteen springs, she was the incarnation of beauty, grace and sweetness of disposition, combined with refinement and dignity. In spite of his years Shichiroyemon was madly in love with the fair maiden; but though he had courted her in every way through O-Tora, she had shown no inclination to respond to his advances.

'Has Hachiya formed a liaison with Katsuno?' asked Shichiroyemon anxiously.

'Not that; you know they are both such honest blockheads; they are too stupid for that. Even if they had the inclination, it would be impossible for them to elude my vigilant eye—not even a devil could do it!'

'Is it then our lord's order?'

'That is it. To-day our lady said to me, "It is not good for Hachiya to be alone any longer; Katsuno is a beautiful and excellent-minded maid, I will give her in marriage to Hachiya before long in reward for her faithful service!" Yes, surely, our lady told me so.'

'Is that indeed so?' said Shichiroyemon, his brow darkening, and his eyes glaring with the intensity of his jealousy. 'That green peasant's son of a Hachiya! It would be infamous to put him over a man of my ability and experience, it would be an additional wrong to give Katsuno to him in marriage. What an insult! What mortification to one of my years! I cannot stand it! I shall never rest till I have taken some steps against this Hachiya—my mortal enemy! I will have my revenge! He does not provoke me with impunity!' He spoke so fiercely and the look on his face was so diabolical that the old woman was frightened.

'Your anger is quite natural, sir; but you know "Anger leads to loss." You must think more calmly about this matter.'

'Have you anything to propose?'

'Well,...of course, in the first place Hachiya must be assassinated, and then we must manage to get Katsuno out of the hands of our lord on some pretext or other;—I will undertake *that*.'

'And I will settle the other business! But, be careful, Madame Tora!'

Here a puff of cool wind swept through the room and

blowing out the light of the lamp put an end to their conference for that time.

<h1 style="text-align:center">II</h1>

It was a fine afternoon in autumn; in the gardens of the castle of Iwakura, the glowing maple leaves and vari-coloured chrysanthemums were in the height of their beauty.

To-day being the anniversary of the death of Nobuyuki's father, all the inmates of the castle had been busy since the early morning with religious services, and a visit to the deceased's grave; to-night a banquet was to be given to all the samurai.

It was now about four o'clock, and several maids-of-honour who had retired to a private chamber to enjoy an interval of rest were talking volubly.

'What chatterboxes you are, maids! You prattle like sparrows.' This from O-Tora who entering at this moment made the sneering remark that effectually put a stop to the gay talk. As she seated herself, one of the girls, a saucy young thing, ventured to say with a demure smile. 'But, Madame, women are chatterboxes by nature, aren't they? "Nightingales visit plum-blossoms" and "Sparrows and tigers visit bamboo groves"; so we chattered like sparrows hoping Madame Tora (tiger) might be induced to come to us.'

At this repartee the rest of the maids burst into peals of laughter and even the cross-grained duenna could not refrain from a sour smile.

'Your mention of sparrows reminds me of Takané (the name of a white-eye)' said she. 'It seems the bird has not uttered a note all day. Has it been fed?'

The girls started guiltily, for so busy had they been all day they had quite forgotten to attend to the bird, a great pet with their lord who had received it, together with other gifts, from the

Shogun in recognition of his military services. Nobuyuki dearly loved the bird for the sake of its song, in addition to which he prized it on account of its donor.

O-Tora, observing the consternation of the maids, revenged herself on them by saying spitefully:—

'You had better have kept your idle chattering till you had fulfilled all your duties, you good-for-nothing girls.'

'It is a shame to have forgotten all about the poor little bird!' said Katsuno, who was with her companions.

'Poor thing, how hungry it must be! I will go at once and give it some food.'

Stepping down into the garden, she went to an old plum-tree, and stretching up her arms took the beautifully ornamented cage of the bird off the branch on which it hung. As she did so the hook came off and the cage fell to the ground, with the result that the door came open and the little prisoner with a glad twitter escaped. With a cry of dismay the girl ran after it, but too late; the bird had already made its way through the trees and was now flying far away across the blue sky rejoicing in its freedom.

'What have you done, Katsuno?' cried O-Tora, from the verandah. Inwardly glad of this golden opportunity to carry out her dark scheme of getting Katsuno into disfavour, she yet cunningly concealed her delight under cover of fear and consternation. 'Alas! You have let Takané fly away. Dear, dear, what carelessness! How could you do it!'

Katsuno, gazing up at the fast disappearing bird, seemed half stupefied. At O-Tora's words she came to herself, and then overwhelmed with thought of the consequences staggered a little and fell wailing to the ground. Her young companions standing on the verandah uttered exclamations of amazement, but none of them came to her aid, or attempted to console her. 'What will you do, Katsuno?' continued the old vixen, who had by this time come down to where the unhappy girl lay, and seized her by the neck of her garment. 'You know Takané is not a common bird, but a treasured present from His Highness the Shogun. Do you realize what you have done in letting it escape? Can you atone for your fault simply by a few tears? What can you do to repair the injury you have done to me, for it is I who shall be blamed,—I shall be considered responsible for this misfortune! Come, get up, girl, what have you to say?'

'Katsuno, prepare for death!' A loud and angry voice caused them all to start. Informed of what had occurred the hot-tempered Nobuyuki had rushed to the scene, and now with a drawn sword stood over the prostrate girl in a passion of ungovernable rage.

At this critical moment another voice was heard.

My lord, my lord, wait!' It was the new Prime Councillor, Tsuda Hachiya, who thus ventured to interpose. 'Calm yourself, my lord, I beg you. Do you forget the day? Is it not the holy anniversary of the demise of your revered father? Can you sully this solemn occasion with a bloody deed committed in the heat of anger? Restrain yourself and leave this matter to my discretion.'

Nobuyuki's rage subsided as quickly as it had risen, and his better reason prevailed. At the remonstrance of his favourite he sheathed his sword and retired to the verandah.

By this time most of the retainers had arrived at the castle for the evening's banquet, and hearing of the incident hastened to the scene. Shichiroyemon was among them and under cover of the confusion whispered something to his accomplice,—then coming forward 'How about Katsuno's chastisement, my lord?' he said. 'You act wisely in not inflicting death with your own honourable hands, but as an apology to His Highness the Shogun, and as an example to the clan it is necessary—it is imperative that she should receive condign punishment.'

'W-e-l-l—' Nobuyuki hesitated; then turning to Hachiya, 'What is your opinion, Hachiya? Shall I do as Shichiroyemon says?'

'No, my lord. History tells that long, long ago, in the reign of the Emperor Takakura, one cold frosty morning, some thoughtless gardeners cut off a few branches of a beautiful maple-tree of which the young Emperor was very fond, and burned them to warm their *saké*. Fujiwara Nobunari, an official in charge of the tree, greatly shocked at this, bound the offenders hand and foot and reported the matter to the Emperor. The benevolent monarch, however, was not enraged at all, but said calmly, "A Chinese poet sings:—

In woods we gathered maple-leaves
And burned them to warm *saké*.

I wonder how these humble gardeners have learned to have such a refined taste? What a poetic idea!" Thus the Emperor acquitted the careless gardeners. This is one reason why the Emperor Takakura is revered as a great sovereign even now after the lapse of so many centuries. So I hope and pray that my lord who is as large-hearted as the Emperor, will be lenient with a young girl who through no fault of her own has been so unfortunate as to cause this accident.'

'Enough, Mr Tsuda!' broke in Shichiroyemon. 'You are doubtless a great scholar, and eloquent, but the slack measure you suggest would be a bad precedent. You are always tender and sympathetic with women, but in dealing with a matter such as this we must make no distinction of sex. As well might you pardon the offender who sets fire to the castle and reduces it to ashes, just because she is a woman and it was "by mistake"! Is that justice?'

'Your argument is absurd,' replied the younger man contemptuously. 'You speak as if severity were a good principle in government. If so, why did Kings Chow and Chieh of ancient China, and the Tairas and the Ashikagas in our own country come to such speedy ruin? Recollect that to-day is the sacred anniversary of the demise of the father of our lord, and therefore it might well have been our lord's purpose to have set the white-eye free, himself, for the peace of the revered spirit. The fault unintentionally committed by Katsuno has thus led to the humane act of setting a poor caged bird at liberty. I have somewhere read these lines:—

Though one loves the sweet songs of a caged bird,
Who knows the sadness of its inner heart?

In my opinion Katsuno has committed no fault in the true sense of the word, but on the contrary, done a good action.'

With the exception of Shichiroyemon and O-Tora, all present listened with admiration to the eloquent pleading of Hachiya on behalf of Katsuno. The black-hearted pair persisted in urging the girl's expulsion from the castle, but Nobuyuki turned a deaf ear to their arguments, and decided to let the matter rest. Katsuno, all this time on her knees in the garden, now almost worshipped her deliverer in the depth of her gratitude.

III

Tsuda Hachiya was now thirty-one. He was born the son of a farmer, but being a handsome, well educated lad, in his sixteenth year he had been appointed to the post of page in the household of Nobuyuki who soon began to treat him with great fondness. The young samurai devoted his leisure hours to a further study of literature, and to the practice of fencing; and as he speedily evinced marked administrative ability, such as was rarely found among the intellectually ill-trained samurai of those days, he rapidly rose in the service, until now, while still a young man, he was both Prime Councillor and Steward, and exercised great authority. But notwithstanding the rank and power that might well have turned the head of one so young, he behaved modestly in public and private, and served his lord with all faithfulness and diligence, gaining thereby the admiration of the whole clan for his character and virtues.

One evening Hachiya presented himself before his lord at the latter's urgent summons.

'Hachiya,' began Nobuyuki, abruptly, with a pleasant smile, 'I think it is high time for you to—, isn't it?'

'Excuse me, my lord, I do not understand you?' said Hachiya with a puzzled look.

'That important affair of yours.'

'That important affair of mine?' echoed the young man more puzzled than before.

'Ha, ha! how dull-witted you are to-day! The Katsuno affair!'

Hachiya did not speak. It was not the first time that Nobuyuki, who was enthusiastic over the question of Hachiya's marriage, had offered to act as middleman between him and Katsuno. Far from objecting to the proposed bride, Hachiya's inclination pointed that way, but his prudence, however, had hitherto prevailed, and he remembered the saying "a full moon is sure to wane." His appointment as Prime Councillor over the heads of older men was already calculated to give offence; should he marry Katsuno, the acknowledged beauty of the clan, would he not still further give cause for jealousy and ill-feeling? Moreover, he was not ignorant of Shichiroyemon's mad attachment, and had no desire to provoke his resentment; therefore, on various pretexts, he had month after month evaded his lord's importunity.

'Do you again say "until next month"?' said Nobuyuki, half threateningly, as the young man remained silent. 'Think not to deceive me in that way!'

Hachiya did not answer; his head was bent in respectful attention.

'Answer me at once! Still silent?... Tell me, do you dislike the girl?'

'Oh, no, my lord, but I fear her refusal!'

'Is that all! Set your mind at rest on that score; I have sounded her. Poor girl! Since the white-eye incident her "sickness" has become worse and she has grown quite thin!'

Observant and sympathetic, Nobuyuki had found out that Katsuno was love-sick for Hachiya.

'Do not tease me, my lord! I will tell you of my real reasons for this hesitation.'

And with this preface Hachiya gave his reasons, at each one of which the older man gave a little nod of comprehension.

'I admire your prudence and forethought,' he said when Hachiya ceased speaking. 'But remember you can never do anything if you think so much of the feelings of others. As for that doting old Shichiroyemon, do not fear him. I have set my heart on your happiness, and I never do things by halves. It is my wish, also, to give Katsuno the desire of her heart. But as it is so near the close of the year we will postpone the marriage till the New Year, and then I will listen to no more denials. Yes, yes, that is what we will do, Hachiya.'

So saying, Nobuyuki summoned a maid and in a low voice gave an order. Presently a bottle of *saké* and some cups were brought in. Then the *fusuma* between this and the next room was gently slid open and there appeared a beautiful young woman clad in a gay *uchikaké* or gown, who knelt with movements full of grace on the threshold. It was none other than Katsuno.

'What is your pleasure, my lord?' said she bowing reverently first to Nobuyuki and then to Hachiya.

'Ah, is it Katsuno? I want you to serve us with *saké*. Sit nearer to me, Hachiya; come, let us have some *saké*.'

'Excuse me, my lord. Something tells me I am needed at home; besides it is getting late. With your kind permission, I will go home at once.'

'No, no; not just yet, Hachiya. Though it is late no loved

one is waiting for your return, I imagine. Ha, ha! Come, you cannot refuse. Katsuno, pour him out a cup of *saké*!'

Katsuno hesitated bashfully, but on Nobuyuki's repeating his command, she took the bottle, and with a hand that trembled filled Hachiya's cup to the brim. Their eyes met and both blushed consciously.

'If you have drunk, let Katsuno have the cup,' said Nobuyuki.

'I should return the cup to your lordship.'

'No, I will have it after her. Give it to Katsuno.'

Hachiya had no choice but to do as he was told, and accordingly offered the cup, into which he had poured more *saké*, to the maid-of-honour, who overcome with shyness, took and sipped it with difficulty.

'Give it to me.'

Nobuyuki drank off three cupfuls and then said with a sly laugh:—

'I am mightily glad you have thus exchanged the wine-cups of betrothal! Ha, ha! You have my hearty congratulations!'

The young lovers prostrated themselves in acknowledgment of his favour, but even as they did so the loud clang, clang of the alarm-bell broke the stillness of the night and caused them all to start up to listen.

'What can it be?' exclaimed Hachiya, opening the *shōji* to look out. No need to ask that question; the lurid sky, the quickly rising flames and showers of falling sparks proclaimed all too surely a house on fire!

'A fire, my lord! And not more than five *chō* beyond the pine-trees on the bank of the moat. I must go at once!'

'No doubt as to its being a fire,' said Nobuyuki looking out also, 'Is it not in your direction?'

'Allow me to leave your presence; I fear it is as you say!'

'Then lose no time! I will give the necessary instructions to the Fire-Commissioner myself.'

With a hurried word of thanks and apology to his lord and Katsuno, Hachiya left the apartment and ran home at the top of his speed. A fierce wind had arisen and whistled through the branches of the tall old pine-trees; louder and louder clanged the iron-throated bell.

His fears were all too surely realized: he reached his home only to find it wrapped in flames! A detached room where he had been wont to study was already reduced to ashes and the fire had caught on to the main building. The trees in the garden were also burning and as the wind shook the branches they let fall a shower of sparks. A number of samurai and firemen were doing their utmost with squirts and rakes to get the fire under, but against the fierce flames fanned to fury by the strong wind their efforts were of little avail. Hachiya involuntarily heaved a deep sigh of despair, but there was no time to delay. It was imperative that he should venture into the burning building and save, if possible, important documents and ancestral treasures, as well as some highly valued gifts he had received from his lord.

As he rushed through the front gate a dark form sprang from the shade of a great pine-tree and plunged a sword into his side. Before Hachiya could draw his own weapon the assassin gave him another thrust through the heart, and the young Councillor fell lifeless to the ground.

The charred body of the hapless samurai was found in the ashes of his ruined home.

IV

On hearing of Hachiya's death, Nobuyuki clenched his teeth, and Katsuno was beside herself with grief.

A dagger—an excellent blade by Masamuné—was found near the body. Seeing it, Nobuyuki slapped his thigh in delighted recognition, for it was a well-known weapon which his elder

brother Nobunaga, Lord of Owari, had given to the elder
brother of Shichiroyemon, Gemba Morimasa, one of Nobunaga's
councillors. Except Morimasa nobody could have had it but
Shichiroyemon; therefore, Nobuyuki who knew of the terms
between his two followers, had no doubt but that his favourite
councillor had fallen a victim to the jealous malignancy of the
man he had superseded both in the favour of their master, and
in the affection of the girl on whom he had set his heart. Added
to this, a man who had been arrested on suspicion on Hachiya's
premises the night of the fire, confessed after a strict examination
that it was at the instigation of Shichiroyemon that he had set
fire to the house.

Evidence of his guilt being so strong, some sheriffs were
despatched to Shichiroyemon's residence to arrest him; but the
wily scoundrel scenting danger had fled, and it was not till after
a rigorous search that it was found that he had taken refuge
in the neighbouring province of Mino in the castle of Inaba,
belonging to Saitō Dōzō.

O-Tora-no-Kata also disappeared about this time, and rumour
had it that she was now in the mansion of Gemba Morimasa.

It was the seventh of January, and most people were enjoying
the New Year festivities. But to Nobuyuki, the season brought no
joy; he still brooded over Hachiya's tragic end. Buried in thought
as he leant on his arm-rest, he did not notice the entrance of
Katsuno, still pale and emaciated she knelt before him.

'Ah, Katsuno, I am glad to see you,' he said, 'I was thinking
of Hachiya, and of your great grief in losing your future husband
just after you had exchanged the cups of betrothal. I feel for you
with all my heart!'

'Thank you, my lord,' she replied sadly. 'You are too good
to me!'

'It is natural you should grieve,' went on Nobuyuki, after a
pause. 'But mere sorrowing does no good to any one. Far wiser

would it be to devise some way to kill the base assassin and avenge Hachiya with all speed.'

'You are right, my lord,—I think my husband in Hades would be pleased to know that your lordship is willing to do so much for his honour. May I ask what is the result of your negotiations with His Excellency, the Lord of Owari?'

Nobuyuki's brother, the Lord of Owari, being the son-in-law of Saitō Dōzō, Nobuyuki had requested his brother to arrange for the delivery of Shichiroyemon, but Dōzō had ill-naturedly refused.

'This puts difficulties in our way,' concluded the old lord disconsolately.

'I have a favour to ask of your lordship; may I venture to speak?'

'By all means.'

'Permit me to go to Inaba, my lord.'

'To Inaba! You want to go to the castle of that Saitō Dōzō?'

'Yes, my lord. I wish to enter the castle in disguise, and avenge the death of Hachiya on his murderer!'

'Not to be thought of, Katsuno!' Nobuyuki could not keep back a smile, though he saw the girl was in deadly earnest. 'A young woman, and single handed!—absurd!'

'Not so, my lord, believe me!' Katsuno's eyes gleamed, and her breath came quick and fast. 'I have thought it all out. I beseech you to let me go!'

Nobuyuki argued with her in vain. Her mind was made up, and nothing could shake her resolution. Therefore, he at length reluctantly gave her the desired permission, at the same time handing her the Masamuné dagger, to which reference has been made before, and saying:—

'This is the dagger with which our Hachiya was stabbed; thrust it up to the hilt in the throat of his murderer, and avenge his death!'

'I will, or die in the attempt! My lord, I thank you, farewell, fare....'

A burst of tears choked her utterance; she hastened from the room.

'May you have all success,' said Nobuyuki, as she disappeared, and then he returned to his thoughts.

V

In the guise of a merchant's wife, and assuming a false name, Katsuno journeyed to the castle-town of Inaba, and taking up her abode at the house of an uncle who was a farmer living in a village close to the town, watched for an opportunity to achieve her purpose.

One day, Yoshitatsu, the son of Saitō Dōzō, returning from hunting, stopped to rest at the farm-house. Katsuno waited upon him and served him with tea. Her beauty and grace of manner attracted the attention of the young nobleman. In reply to his inquiries Katsuno's uncle told him that she had recently lost her husband, a merchant, and that she was anxious to enter the service of a daimio's lady. Yoshitatsu undertook to engage her as maid-of-honour to his mother, and his offer was immediately accepted with joy. She was soon an inmate of the castle, where her faithful service pleased her mistress so much that she speedily became a great favourite.

A warm spring day, with the delicate blossoms of the cherry-trees filling all the land with their beauty, and the faint sweetness of their perfume. Since dawn a large number of workmen had been busily at work sweeping the courtyard of the castle, and spreading clean sand over it. Some important function must be on hand. Katsuno wondered what it was.

'Excuse my curiosity, my lady,' she said as she served her mistress with a cup of tea, 'but for what are those men making such great preparations? Is anything going to take place?'

'Don't you know? To-morrow there will be matches of mounted archery.'

'Mounted archery, my lady? What is that?' asked Katsuno, feigning ignorance.

'All the samurai who are skilled in archery will practise the art on horseback.'

'Are many coming, my lady?' asked Katsuno, her heart beating high with the hope that at last she might meet her enemy.

'About a hundred, I believe, to take part in the competition, and of course, all the samurai of our clan with their families will be present to look on.'

'Who are the archers?'

'Why do you ask?'

Katsuno was embarrassed for a moment, but quickly regaining her presence of mind, she replied:—

'For no special reason, my lady; but my father, though only a farmer, was very fond of archery, and so, from a child, I have been interested in the sport.'

'Ah, I see. Well, they brought me a programme of the day's events this morning; here it is; you can see the names of the archers for yourself.' The lady handed Katsuno a sheet of soft, thick paper covered with bold, black characters. With an eagerness she strove to conceal, she ran her eyes down the lines, till near the middle of the page she found the name 'Sakuma Shichiroyemon' At last! This was the time for which she had waited and planned.

'All the archers seem to be good samurai. What a splendid sight they will present! How I should like to see the sport, even from a distance.'

'There should be no difficulty about that. You have my permission.'

'My lady, I am deeply grateful.' She could say no more, but such was the state of her feelings that it was with difficulty she performed her usual duties that day, nor could she sleep at all at night.

VI

The following day the weather continued to be all that could be desired. The wide courtyard was duly prepared. The centre was enclosed for the list in the shape of an oblong square, and temporary stands had been erected all round it to accommodate the spectators; these were covered with gay carpets and soft cushions which gave colour to the scene. A dais in the very centre of the gallery on the eastern side of the lists and at a convenient distance from the target, was richly decorated with hangings of purple and white silk, which fluttered gently in the breeze. This was the place of honour for Lord Saitō and his family.

From early in the morning, samurai after samurai began to arrive at the castle, and soon every stand was crowded. The lord of the castle accompanied by his family and attended by a numerous retinue of councillors, pages, and maids-of-honour, presently appeared, and in great state seated himself in the place prepared for him. Katsuno, gaily dressed, her face powdered and painted in the usual fashion, and the Masamuné dagger concealed in the bosom of her garments, was among this company, and avoiding the attention of the others, eagerly awaited her opportunity.

'To-day, or never,' she thought to herself. 'If I let such a golden opportunity pass, I shall never get another! Dearest Hachiya, look at me from Hades! I will avenge your death before the sun sets!' Then clasping her hands she murmured a prayer, 'Oh, Hachiman, God of War, favour me with success!'

When those about to take part in the competitions were ready, the umpire, the herald, the signalman and the registrar, all betook themselves to their respective stations; a large drum being then loudly beaten to announce that the tournament was about to begin.

One after another, the archers clad in *kosodé* (silk underclothes), *hitataré* (court robes), and *mukabaki* (breeches), came forth on horseback into the lists and rode to and fro, till coming to the appointed spot from which to aim, they shot their arrows at the mark. The judge, or umpire, would then after a careful examination give his decision, the herald would loudly proclaim the name of the archer and his achievement, while the registrar would make a written record. Then it was the part of the signalman to announce the event to the spectators, who raised such shouts of applause that one might almost fancy the petals of the cherry-blossoms fell in showers from the vibration in the air.

So archer after archer exhibited his skill, until now it was the turn of 'No. 53' Sakuma Shichiroyemon. Katsuno, who had been impatiently awaiting her chance, and whose nerves were strained to the utmost, involuntarily grasped the dagger in her bosom.

Shichiroyemon rode out slowly, but as soon as he had bowed low to his lord, put spurs to his horse and dashed swiftly forward.

In her nervous excitement Katsuno pushed forward and straightening herself assumed the attitude necessary to cut at her enemy as he came up to the dais. In so doing she touched her mistress's shoulder and shrank back inadvertently, but the next moment she again pressed forward and stood ready.

Shichiroyemon galloped up with the speed of lightning, the horse's mane touched the railing of the gallery, but before the girl could act was far out of her reach.

With an exclamation of dismay she stood looking after him.

'What is the matter with you, Katsuno?' said Lady Saitō, displeased at the want of manners in her favourite maid.

Recalled to herself the girl forced a laugh but replied readily enough:—

'Forgive my rudeness, my lady! In my admiration of the heroic sport I forgot myself.'

'You are indeed fond of archery!'

'Yes, my lady, there is nothing I like so well.'

'A strange taste for a girl!' said her mistress looking curiously at her. 'But the excitement is too much for you; you are pale and your eyes are bloodshot. Have you a headache?'

'No, your ladyship, but I did not sleep last night.'

'Are you not well?'

'I am quite well; it was the thought of to-day's pleasure that kept me awake.'

'What a passionate lover of archery!' said the lady laughing, and Katsuno flushed at her mocking tone.

The performance of the various numbers on the programme required many of the archers to appear several times in the lists, Shichiroyemon among them. Every time he rode forth Katsuno eagerly watched for her chance, but to her intense mortification it nearly always happened that his horse was on the opposite side of the lists; and the few occasions on which he approached close enough to where she waited, he dashed past so swiftly she was unable to do anything. She wondered if her enemy had recognized her and was on his guard. She suffered an agony of impatience and fear, and almost gave up in despair.

The programme had been duly gone through, and there now remained only the final ceremony of *nanori* or 'declaring of names.' How would this be performed? she wondered. She feared it would not bring Shichiroyemon within her reach. Should she rush desperately into the lists and kill him there in the midst of his compeers? No, that would be too hazardous; should she fail her chance would be gone for ever. On the other hand if she let slip this opportunity was it likely she would ever get another? And she must decide quickly.

While Katsuno agonized thus, the ceremony had commenced.

Each archer in his turn rode up to the dais, bowed reverentially to his liege lord, declared his name, and slowly withdrew. Quickly making up her mind she braced herself for action.

The day had advanced and it was now the middle of the afternoon. The cherry-blossoms hung still in the bright sunshine, for the air had not movement enough to stir even their delicate petals. A langour seemed to have fallen on all and even the spectators showed signs of fatigue. Only Katsuno was keenly on the alert!

'No. 53!' At the call Shichiroyemon leapt on his horse, pausing a moment to arrange the harness. A swift glance at him as he sat in the full blaze of the sun showed Katsuno that he was splendidly arrayed in a white *kosodé*, covered with a design of nightingales perched on plum-trees. With bow and arrows in his hand, and mounted on a snow-white steed he made a gallant show, his bronze complexion and bushy whiskers adding to his grim and warlike appearance. Katsuno gnashed her teeth.

After riding three times round the lists Shichiroyemon suddenly tightened the reins and caused his horse to stop before the dais. Then slowly riding up to the foot of the gallery he bowed low, as in a clear voice he proclaimed his name. This moment, as he was about to withdraw, was Katsuno's opportunity. Slipping off her upper garment she was on the step before any one could stop her.

'Well met, Sakuma Shichiroyemon. I am the wife of Tsuda Hachiya whom you foully murdered! Taste the sharpness of my revenge!'

With these words she thrust the dagger into his side with all her strength. So sudden was the attack, and such the force lent her by desperation, that, strong man though he was, Shichiroyemon fell forward from his saddle to the ground. With the cry 'Hachiya is avenged!' she gave him another thrust which proved mortal.

A white petal wafted by the breeze fluttered softly on to the blood-stained dagger, and for a while all who witnessed the scene were speechless with horror.

VII

Saitō Dōzō, in his admiration of Katsuno's heroic deed, had it in his mind to save the girl from the consequences of her rash action; but as a samurai it did not accord with his honour to do so. This for two reasons; one being that he had refused to deliver up Shichiroyemon when asked to do so by Nobuyuki; and the other because it was a disgrace to him personally that a warrior under his protection should have been killed by a woman. Therefore, he gave orders for the close confinement of the culprit, directing that she should be strictly watched and guarded night and day.

Now that she had accomplished her long-cherished desire, and had sent word to that effect to Lord Nobuyuki, Katsuno no longer had anything to trouble her, and awaited her sentence with a tranquil mind.

One evening she was arranging some wisteria flowers which had been brought to her by one of the samurai, appointed to keep guard over her, when without any announcement Lady Saitō came into her room.

'How tastefully you have arranged those flowers, Katsuno!' she said. 'Have you recovered yourself?'

The girl smiled.

'Yes, thank you, my lady; having attained my object, I have nothing left to wish for, and am ready to meet my fate.'

'You are a pattern of womanhood! How I admire you! It is unbearable that one so virtuous should be subjected to the ignominy of imprisonment for so long. I have repeatedly implored my lord for your release, but as yet without avail.'

'You are too good; but I have no hope of release, and I am ready to die.'

'Your death would serve no end, and I do not intend to let your life be sacrificed. Listen,' she came nearer and whispered in Katsuno's ear, 'I have managed to get your guard sent away on some pretext, and to-night, Katsuno, you shall escape.'

'Indeed, no, my lady; that cannot be! I am quite prepared for death. Without Hachiya my life is nothing to me, and should his lordship discover what you had done his wrath would be terrible,—What might he not do to you!'

'Have no fears on that point. It is not likely my lord will suspect that I had any hand in your escape, but at the worst he will not kill me. Do not think of me, but fly!'

'But, my lady,...'

'Oh, how obstinate you are! Why will you throw your life away? Katsuno, as your mistress, I command you to escape this night!'

Seeing her mistress would take no refusal the girl gave in, and they proceeded to discuss plans.

'And when you are safe, Katsuno, how will you spend your life?'

'I shall become a nun and spend my life praying to Buddha for the peace of my dead husband's soul.'

'An admirable resolve, but foolish! Have you no love for your parents?—for your family and home? Ah, forgive me, your parents and brothers are dead? I did not mean to cause you pain. But do you not see that in that case it is impossible for you to give yourself up to a life of devotion? Who then could carry on the family name?'

'But, your ladyship, I became the wife of Hachiya...'

'Yes, yes, but you were only betrothed! If you had married him really, the case would be different,—an engagement is nothing. No other woman would have considered it necessary to avenge his death. Your faithfulness has been demonstrated by your heroic deed. Your devotion will be handed down to posterity as a model for all wives to admire and emulate, but now that is over; other duties remain.'

'What would you have me do, my lady?'

'You must marry.'

'A second marriage!'

'No, a first; as you told me yourself you were never married to Hachiya, so who can blame you or call you a faithless wife if you contract a marriage with another man? Even Hachiya in the spirit world would approve of it.'

Katsuno thought over these words. It was true according to the ideas in which she had been brought up that it was her duty not to let her family name die out.

'You are right,' she said at length. 'If I escape I will not refuse to marry.' But she sighed, for her heart was with Hachiya.

'I was sure you would be sensible. And now hear what I have to say; a near relative of mine, Ōsuga Katsutaka, a retainer of Lord Tokugawa of Mikawa province is looking for a wife. He is only twenty-seven, yet he is distinguished for his scholarship, bravery and above all his military achievements. He has a great future before him, and, what counts with a woman before all things, he has very good looks! Will you marry him? I have already sounded him on the subject and he is anxious you should be his wife. Do not reject such a good offer.'

Katsuno was silent, partly because of maiden modesty, and partly because it was too momentous a question to be decided without due consideration.

'Why do not you answer? What is your objection? I assure you that Ōsuga is every thing that can be desired; you would never regret marrying him—he is so brave and learned! But what is most important in your case, if you have two or three children by him you can adopt one of them to succeed to your father's house and carry on the family name.'

'I am deeply grateful to you for all your kindness, my lady.

I will do as you advise; you are wiser than I, and you know what is best.'

'Then you agree? That is right, you are a good girl, Katsuno, and deserve to be happy, as I know you will be with Ōsuga. But it is getting very late and it is time you went. A palanquin is ready with ten strong footmen to convey you to the home of Ōsuga. I am sorry to part from you but it has to be, Farewell.'

As she spoke, Lady Saitō handed Katsuno a letter addressed to Ōsuga Katsutaka, and a packet of money for her travelling expenses. The girl accepted them with many thanks, and bidding farewell to her mistress made her way to the postern gate from whence she safely effected her escape from the castle arriving at her destination without adventure.

VIII

Ōsuga Katsutaka married Katsuno with the hearty approval of his lord, Tokugawa Iyeyasu, who greatly struck with admiration of the girl's heroic deed, readily promised to accord her his special protection.

On hearing of this, Shichiroyemon's brother Gemba Morimasa, a well-known warrior, who had won for himself the nickname of Gemba the Tiger, clenched his teeth in wrath and mortification, and going to his lord, Nobunaga, gave him a minute account of all that had happened, requesting him to take immediately some steps to wrest Katsuno from Iyeyasu's hand.

'If this be left undone,' he continued fiercely, 'my brother's spirit will never be at peace, nor will my outraged feelings allow me to rest. You must see this, my lord.'

'Calm yourself, Morimasa. You speak wildly.'

'Who could help it, my lord! Just think of the case! Not only was my brother murdered by a mere woman, but she, my mortal enemy, has been taken under the protection of a powerful noble, so that I am powerless to touch her! If I allow the matter to stand my reputation as a warrior will be compromised. If you decline to interfere, I will go myself and negotiate with Lord Tokugawa. At least you will allow me to do that!'

'If you are so set upon it, I will see what I can do,' said Nobunaga, reluctantly; and he accordingly sent a warrior to Iyeyasu to request the delivery of Katsuno.

Iyeyasu readily granted the messenger an interview, but after listening to what he had to say, replied bluntly:—

'I am sorry, but I cannot consent. Katsuno is a heroine, and such a woman as is rarely found in Japan. To speak frankly, Shichiroyemon did not behave well. I understand that because Katsuno would have nothing to say to him, and because Hachiya, to whom she was affianced, was a favourite with his lord, Shichiroyemon, out of a mean jealousy, unworthy of a samurai, caused his house to be set on fire and himself to be assassinated. In my opinion,—in the opinion of all right-minded men, he richly deserved his fate, and it was fitting he should die as he did. What can his brother urge in extenuation of his crime? His demand is preposterous! Think of Katsuno! For the sake of a man to whom she was merely betrothed, she boldly avenged his death, stabbing a strong warrior in the midst of a large concourse. What courage! It might well put a man to shame! And this heroic woman comes to me for protection, honouring me by her confidence! Do you imagine I will give her up? Never! Tell your lord that Iyeyasu is not one to betray his trust, and that he emphatically refuses to deliver up this brave woman to her enemies.'

There was nothing more to be said. The messenger returned to his lord and gave the answer he had received. Nobunaga admitted its reasonableness, and not even the hot-tempered Morimasa could deny its truth. But being of a stubborn and revengeful nature, he brooded over his grievance, and secretly schemed for the attainment of his purpose.

One fine autumn day Katsuno, attended by a maid, was strolling in the grounds at the back of her residence. Sweet and beautiful she looked, with the calm happiness of a contented young wife. To the west of the garden were to be seen the quarters of her husband's retainers, and the twang of bowstrings accompanied by the whistling arrows showed that the samurai were strenuously practising their archery. A grove of maple-trees bounded the east, and their red leaves effectively contrasted with the dark green of their background. In front, to the south, the view led across paddy-fields to the tall black pines enclosing the precincts of the village shrine. A few little birds flitting here and there, and softly twittering, gave life to the scene.

Standing by a pond in the garden Katsuno was idly throwing some food to the carp which came at her call, when the little gate that gave entrance to the grounds suddenly opened, and an elderly woman came in.

'I am glad to see you, Miss Katsuno, nay, I should say Mrs Ōsuga,' said the newcomer bowing politely.

'Madame O-Tora!' exclaimed Katsuno, in surprise, quite taken aback by this unexpected visitation. 'Is it indeed you? I am very glad to see you, it is long since I had that pleasure. How did you find your way here?'

'By a mere chance,' replied the elder woman, smiling as though overjoyed at the meeting, and speaking in propitiatory tones. 'As I was passing along this lane I happened to glance through the hedge and to my great astonishment and joy recognised you in the garden. What a happy home you have! I could envy you your good fortune!'

Katsuno made no reply to her honeyed speech, but asked curtly:—

'How do you *happen* to be in these parts? Have you come to live here?'

'That is a long story,' said O-Tora in an agitated manner. 'I can't tell it in a few words. I cannot stop to tell you to-day, but I will come again soon when I have more time to spare and tell you all about it. Now I must say Good-bye.'

'Where are you staying?'

'Not far from here...but I'll come again soon... Good-bye!'

And she hurried away. Katsuno stood gazing after her retreating figure with an expression of mingled wonder and doubt, when suddenly from the grove of maples an arrow whizzed past and grazing her sash pierced the *shōji* of the samurai's rooms. Instantly an uproar arose, but before anything could be done another arrow whistled through the still air. Quick to think and act, Katsuno flung herself on to the ground but her maid, too much alarmed to move, stood upright where she was.

By this time the young samurai had rushed forth with loud shouts.

'The villain is hiding behind the maples,' cried Katsuno. 'Do not let him escape, quick, quick!'

With drawn swords the party dashed into the grove, scattering the red leaves as they pushed through.

IX

While this was occurring, Katsuno's husband was away from home having gone up to the castle on duty. Two ruffians were caught, but unfortunately the samurai, being unacquainted with O-Tora's personality and evil intentions, did not think of trying to seize her also, though it would have been quite easy as she ran wildly hither and thither in her bewilderment and alarm.

Closely questioned, the men confessed that they were spies, and had been hired by Gemba Morimasa to assassinate Katsuno, O-Tora being decoy.

Iyeyasu, in righteous anger, caused them to be decapitated,

and their heads were exposed in front of one of the castle gates with a notice which ran as follows:—

'These villains, on a strict examination, confessed that at the instigation of Sakuma Gemba Morimasa, a high retainer of Oda Nobunaga, they had come disguised to our castle-town with intent to murder. However, it may be that they were common thieves and only made up the above story to conceal their mean purposes. Therefore, we have judged them as thieves, and expose their heads accordingly.'

At the failure of his plans, Morimasa flew into a terrible passion; nor could Nobunaga allow the matter to pass without notice. He despatched a messenger to Iyeyasu with a protest, to which he received the following reply:—

'If an honourable samurai of Gemba Morimasa's rank and position really intended to take his revenge on an enemy he would have come openly and in person. He would not intrust so important a task to low nameless assassins! He could not so debase his honour! This was an act worthy of a peasant, a mere tradesman, or a *ronin*. So I concluded that those men were common thieves and in that supposition caused that notice to be written. Can Lord Oda say anything against it?'

What could Nobunaga or Morimasa urge against this temperate reply? They could not confess that the would-be murderers were indeed what they had said, and not the thieves that Iyeyasu affected to believe them. Thus were they again baffled. But Nobunaga was exceedingly enraged and determined to go to war with Iyeyasu in order to wipe out his disgrace. He diligently set about his preparations.

It was not difficult to foretell the issue of a struggle between the rival lords; Iyeyasu, with his small following, had no chance against his more powerful enemy. Katsuno was in despair. It was all through her that this danger threatened Lord Tokugawa, it was because he had refused to give her up that all this trouble had come. She had forfeited her life by her act of vengeance at the castle of Inaba, and but for the mercy of Lady Saitō she would have died long before. Though her husband loved her devotedly and she was not unhappy, still she had no desire to live, and if she were to die, there would no longer be any object in commencing a disastrous war. Therefore she would die.

In the silent watches of a winter's night when the silver moon flooded all the land with quiet beauty, Katsuno rose from her bed and with a dagger put an end to her life,—in the flower of her womanhood, at the age of twenty-two!

Katsuno left behind her four long letters addressed espectively to Iyeyasu, her husband, Katsutaka, Lady Saitō, and her former lord, Oda Nobuyuki, giving the reason for her rash act, and repeatedly thanking them for all their kindness.

THE LOYALTY OF A BOY SAMURAI

Asataro Miyamori

Matsudaira Nobutsuna was one of the ministers of the Shogun Iyemitsu, next to Iyeyasu, the ablest of all the Tokugawa Shoguns. A man of great sagacity, he contributed not a little to Iyemitsu's wise administration.

When Iyemitsu was a young boy named Takechiyo, Nobutsuna who was called at that time Chōshirō served him as one of his attendants and playmates.

One morning when the young nobleman was passing along a corridor accompanied by Chōshirō and two other boys, on the way to the private apartments of his father, the Shogun Hidetada, his attention was caught by some fledgling sparrows that were hopping about and chirping gaily on the tiles of the roof. Takechiyo, then but ten years of age, was seized with a fancy to have them; and turning to Chōshirō, three years older than himself, he commanded:—

'Catch those little sparrows for me, Chōshirō.'

'With pleasure, your lordship; but should I be found catching sparrows I should be reprimanded by his Highness and the officials. Fortunately I shall be on duty to-night; so to-night I will climb out on to the roof when there is no one to see me, and give you the little birds in the morning. Will you please to wait till then, my master?'

'I suppose I must.' And the small company passed on.

That night when all was quiet, Chōshirō managed somehow or other to get out on to the roof, and crawling carefully on all fours to the spot where the parent birds had built their nest, reached out one hand and seized one of the little sparrows. Poor little things! Surprised in their sleep they were not able to escape. Transferring his captive to the left hand Chōshirō again stretched out his right and caught another. Whether the attainment of his purpose caused him to relax his care or for some other reason, certain it is that at this moment his foot slipped and with a heavy thud he fell down into the court-yard below. As he fell he involuntarily clutched the birds more firmly so that they were instantly squeezed to death. With the dead birds in his hands, he fainted. But the roof was comparatively low, and he also had the good fortune to fall on to some bushes so that he was not killed as might have been the case.

The sound of the fall awoke the Shogun. He started up and followed by his consort and some attendants went out on to the verandah and opening a sliding shutter looked down. By the light of a lantern held by one of the servants he perceived the boy lying on the ground just beneath. Chōshirō had now recovered consciousness and was trying to rise though the pain he felt all over his body rendered the operation one of considerable difficulty. His consternation was great when the light of the lantern revealed his person to those on the verandah.

'Chōshirō, is that you?' called his lord, recognizing the boy at once. 'It is strange that you should be on my roof at this time of night! Come up instantly and explain your conduct. This must be inquired into.'

The boy, still holding the dead sparrows, obeyed. Prostrating himself before the Shogun he waited for him to speak.

'What have you in your hands, Chōshirō?'

'Sparrows, my lord.'

'Sparrows? Do you then climb roofs at midnight to catch sparrows? A strange fancy!'

'Yes, my lord. I will tell you the truth. When Takechiyo Sama and I were passing along the corridor this morning his attention was attracted by some little sparrows on the roof and we stopped to watch them. Takechiyo Sama said "What dear little things they are!" and the desire then arose in my mind to get them for him that he might play with them. So to-night when everyone was asleep I climbed out on to the roof of your apartments in disregard to the respect I should have shown to your august person, and caught two of the young sparrows. But how quickly the punishment of Heaven followed my crime! I fell down as you see and my wickedness was discovered. I am ready for any chastisement your lordship sees fit to inflict.'

'My lord,' here broke in Lady Eyo, the Shogun's consort. 'Excuse my interference, but I think Takechiyo must have ordered Chōshirō to catch these sparrows. There is no doubt about it.'

It should be explained that Lady Eyo had two sons—Takechiyo and Kunimatsu. Takechiyo, the elder, was sharp-witted and active though rather rough in his manners; his brother, on the contrary, was quiet and effeminate. For this and probably some other unknown reason the younger son was his mother's favourite, and it was her desire that he should be appointed heir to the Shogunate in place of his elder brother. She therefore lost no opportunity to disparage Takechiyo in the estimation of his father, hoping thereby to attain her object in due time.

'What a thoughtless boy Takechiyo is!' agreed the Shogun. 'This was undoubtedly done at his instigation. How cruel to command Chōshirō to endanger his life by catching birds on a roof at night! Though he is but a child there is no excuse for him. The proverb says "A snake bites even when it is only an inch long." One who is so inconsiderate to his attendants when young cannot be expected to govern wisely and well when more power is invested in his hands. Now, Chōshirō,' turning to the boy who still knelt at his feet, 'Takechiyo ordered you to get the sparrows; is it not so?'

Chōshirō had heard with surprise the unkind words of the

Shogun and his lady about his adored master. What did they mean by the words 'A snake bites even when it is only an inch long?' If their feelings towards the boy were already so antagonistic what would they think and do should the real facts of the case be disclosed? Chōshirō firmly resolved to take all the blame even at the risk of his life.

'Oh, no, my lord,' said he earnestly. 'Takechiyo Sama never gave me such a command, never! I caught these sparrows quite of my own accord. I meant one for Takechiyo Sama, and one for myself.'

'Nonsense! Whatever you say I know Takechiyo is at the bottom of it. You are a bold fellow to dare to tell me an untruth!... Let me see, what shall I do to you?... Here, bring me one of those bags.'

The Shogun pointed to some large, strong leather bags, resembling a money-pouch in shape, in which in the event of a fire or of an earthquake his valuables would be incased before putting them into the *dozō* or fire-proof godown.

When the bag was brought the Shogun said:—

'Now, Chōshirō, if you don't confess the truth, I will have you put into this bag and never allow you to go home again, nor give you any food. Do you still persist in your falsehood?'

'It is no falsehood, my lord. It is the truth that I caught the sparrows of my own wish. No one but myself is responsible for my misdeed. My fall from the roof was the punishment of Heaven. It is right that you should chastise me also. I beg you to do so.'

With these words, Chōshirō, betraying no signs of fear, put himself into the bag.

'What a stubborn boy!' exclaimed the Shogun in anger.

Then with the help of his consort he tightly fastened up the bag with the boy in it, and had it hung from a peg on the wall of the corridor. Leaving the poor child in this state all retired once more to their broken rest.

Late the next morning, having had breakfast and finished her toilet, Lady Eyo, attended by two maids of honour, came out to the corridor where the bag still hung and ordered it to be taken down. On opening it the boy was found still holding the dead sparrows.

'Good morning, your ladyship,' said Chōshirō, rubbing his eyes with his closed fists.

'You were ordered by Takechiyo to take the sparrows, is it not so?' said Lady Eyo kindly, hoping to make the boy confess the truth.

'No, my lady. It was my own idea. Takechiyo Sama had nothing whatever to do with the matter.'

'Come, boy, if you are so obstinate you will have to remain a prisoner always, and never have anything to eat. But if you confess what I am convinced is the truth, you shall be released and have food at once. Now tell the truth.'

'My lady, as you command me to do so I will tell the truth; but I am so hungry that I find it difficult to speak at all. May I ask for some food first? If you will allow me to have even some *musubi*, I will say all you wish.'

'Good boy, you shall have some *musubi* at once.'

The lady gave the order and soon the boy was eagerly devouring the rice-cakes. Three or four large ones made a good meal.

'Thank you, my lady; I am now able to speak.'

'Then confess the truth, good boy, confess quickly; I am tired of waiting.'

'Forgive me, my lady; I caught the sparrows of my own accord. I received no order direct or indirect from Takechiyo Sama. That is the truth.'

The lady for once forgot herself and flew into a passion. Stamping her foot on the floor, she rushed into the Shogun's room and gave him an exaggerated account of what had happened. He was very angry.

'The young rascal,' cried he, rising, and taking his Yoshimitsu sword in his hand, 'I will kill him myself. Tango Hasegawa, bring Chōshirō here.'

Tango found the culprit sitting in the bag his hands on his lap.

'Chōshirō,' he said, 'His lordship is terribly angry with you—your stubbornness and insolence are past endurance. He intends to kill you with his own hands. Prepare yourself for instant death!'

'I am quite prepared, sir.'

'Your father is my old friend,' went on the man pitifully. 'If you have any farewell message for him I will undertake to deliver it.'

'Thank you, sir; but I have no words to send to my father. It is the duty of a samurai to sacrifice his life for the sake of loyalty. After my death my motive for refusing to confess what my lord the Shogun desires will become clear. Tell my father only that I met my doom fearlessly by my lord's own sword. My one sorrow is that my mother is now ill and this news may lead to her death also. That is my only regret.'

'What a truly heroic resolve!' cried Tango, unable to restrain his tears. 'Your father may well be proud of you, boy, when I tell him how you met death.'

Taking Chōshirō by the hand Tango conducted him into the presence of the Shogun and his lady. The stern noble stood up on their entrance and laying his hand on the hilt of his sword motioned to them to approach nearer. The brave boy kneeling down pushed the stray locks from his neck, and with clasped hands and closed eyes calmly awaited decapitation. The Shogun's manly compassion was not proof against this pathetic sight. Throwing his sword away, 'Chōshirō, you are forgiven!' he cried. 'I recognize your supreme fidelity to your young master—faithful unto death! Tango, I foretell that when Takechiyo succeeds me as Shogun, no one will be able to assist him in the task of ruling this people so well as this courageous young samurai. Chōshirō, you are pardoned!'

LOVE, FAITH AND HOPE

Leonid Andreyev

He loved.

According to his passport, he was called Max Z. But as it was stated in the same passport that he had no special peculiarities about his features, I prefer to call him Mr N+1. He represented a long line of young men who possess wavy, dishevelled locks, straight, bold, and open looks, well-formed and strong bodies, and very large and powerful hearts.

All these youths have loved and perpetuated their love. Some of them have succeeded in engraving it on the tablets of history, like Henry IV; others, like Petrarch, have made literary preserves of it; some have availed themselves for that purpose of the newspapers, wherein the happenings of the day are recorded, and where they figured among those who had strangled themselves, shot themselves, or who had been shot by others; still others, the happiest and most modest of all, perpetuated their love by entering it in the birth records—by creating posterity.

The love of N+1 was as strong as death, as a certain writer put it; as strong as life, he thought.

Max was firmly convinced that he was the first to have discovered the method of loving so intensely, so unrestrainedly, so passionately, and he regarded with contempt all who had loved before him. Still more, he was convinced that even after him no one would love as he did, and he felt sorry that with his death the secret of true love would be lost to mankind. But, being a modest young man, he attributed part of his achievement to her—to his beloved. Not that she was perfection itself, but she came very close to it, as close as an ideal can come to reality.

There were prettier women than she, there were wiser women, but was there ever a better woman? Did there ever exist a woman on whose face was so clearly and distinctly written that she alone was worthy of love—of infinite, pure, and devoted love? Max knew that there never were, and that there never would be such women. In this respect, he had no special peculiarities, just as Adam did not have them, just as you, my reader, do not have them. Beginning with Grandmother Eve and ending with the woman upon whom your eyes were directed—before you read these lines—the same inscription is to be clearly and distinctly read on the face of every woman at a certain time. The difference is only in the quality of the ink.

A very nasty day set in—it was Monday or Tuesday—when Max noticed with a feeling of great terror that the inscription upon the dear face was fading. Max rubbed his eyes, looked first from a distance, then from all sides; but the fact was undeniable— the inscription was fading. Soon the last letter also disappeared— the face was white like the recently whitewashed wall of a new house. But he was convinced that the inscription had disappeared not of itself, but that some one had wiped it off. Who?

Max went to his friend, John N. He knew and he felt sure that such a true, disinterested, and honest friend there never was and never would be. And in this respect, too, as you see, Max had no special peculiarities. He went to his friend for the purpose of taking his advice concerning the mysterious disappearance of the inscription, and found John N. exactly at the moment when he was wiping away that inscription by his kisses. It was then that the records of the local occurrences were enriched by another unfortunate incident, entitled 'An Attempt at Suicide.'

◆

It is said that death always comes in due time. Evidently, that time had not yet arrived for Max, for he remained alive—that is, he ate, drank, walked, borrowed money and did not return it, and altogether he showed by a series of psycho-physiological acts that he was a living being, possessing a stomach, a will, and a mind—but his soul was dead, or, to be more exact, it was absorbed in lethargic sleep. The sound of human speech reached his ears, his eyes saw tears and laughter, but all that did not stir a single echo, a single emotion in his soul. I do not know what space of time had elapsed. It may have been one year, and it may have been ten years, for the length of such intermissions in life depends on how quickly the actor succeeds in changing his costume.

One beautiful day—it was Wednesday or Thursday—Max awakened completely. A careful and guarded liquidation of his spiritual property made it clear that a fair piece of Max's soul, the part which contained his love for woman and for his friends, was dead, like a paralysis-stricken hand or foot. But what remained was, nevertheless, enough for life. That was love for and faith in mankind. Then Max, having renounced personal happiness, started to work for the happiness of others.

That was a new phase—he believed.

All the evil that is tormenting the world seemed to him to be concentrated in a 'red flower,' in one red flower. It was but necessary to tear it down, and the incessant, heart-rending cries and moans which rise to the indifferent sky from all points of the earth, like its natural breathing, would be silenced. The evil of the world, he believed, lay in the evil will and in the madness of the people. They themselves were to blame for being unhappy, and they could be happy if they wished. This seemed so clear and simple that Max was dumfounded in his amazement at human stupidity. Humanity reminded him of a crowd huddled together in a spacious temple and panic-stricken at the cry of 'Fire!'

Instead of passing calmly through the wide doors and saving

themselves, the maddened people, with the cruelty of frenzied beasts, cry and roar, crush one another and perish—not from the fire (for it is only imaginary), but from their own madness. It is enough sometimes when one sensible, firm word is uttered to this crowd—the crowd calms down and imminent death is thus averted. Let, then, a hundred calm, rational voices be raised to mankind, showing them where to escape and where the danger lies—and heaven will be established on earth, if not immediately, then at least within a very brief time.

Max began to utter his word of wisdom. How he uttered it you will learn later. The name of Max was mentioned in the newspapers, shouted in the market places, blessed and cursed; whole books were written on what Max N+1 had done, what he was doing, and what he intended to do. He appeared here and there and everywhere. He was seen standing at the head of the crowd, commanding it; he was seen in chains and under the knife of the guillotine. In this respect Max did not have any special peculiarities, either. A preacher of humility and peace, a stern bearer of fire and sword, he was the same Max—Max the believer. But while he was doing all this, time kept passing on. His nerves were shattered; his wavy locks became thin and his head began to look like that of Elijah the Prophet; here and there he felt a piercing pain...

The earth continued to turn light-mindedly around the sun, now coming nearer to it, now retreating coquettishly, and giving the impression that it fixed all its attention upon its household friend, the moon; the days were replaced by other days, and the dark nights by other dark nights, with such pedantic German punctuality and correctness that all the artistic natures were compelled to move over to the far north by degrees, where the devil himself would break his head endeavouring to distinguish between day and night—when suddenly something happened to Max.

Somehow it happened that Max became misunderstood. He had calmed the crowd by his words of wisdom many a time before and had saved them from mutual destruction but now he was not understood. They thought that it was he who had shouted 'Fire!' With all the eloquence of which he was capable he assured them that he was exerting all his efforts for their sake alone; that he himself needed absolutely nothing, for he was alone, childless; that he was ready to forget the sad misunderstanding and serve them again with faith and truth—but all in vain. They would not trust him. And in this respect Max did not have any special peculiarities, either. The sad incident ended for Max in a new intermission.

◆

Max was alive, as was positively established by medical experts, who had made a series of simple tests. Thus, when they pricked a needle into his foot, he shook his foot and tried to remove the needle. When they put food before him, he ate it, but he did not walk and did not ask for any loans, which clearly testified to the complete decline of his energy. His soul was dead—as much as the soul can be dead while the body is alive. To Max all that he had loved and believed in was dead. Impenetrable gloom wrapped his soul. There were neither feelings in it, nor desires, nor thoughts. And there was not a more unhappy man in the world than Max, if he was a man at all.

But he was a man.

According to the calendar, it was Friday or Saturday, when Max awakened as from a prolonged sleep. With the pleasant sensation of an owner to whom his property has been restored which had wrongly been taken from him, Max realized that he was once more in possession of all his five senses.

His sight reported to him that he was all alone, in a place which might in justice be called either a room or a chimney.

Each wall of the room was about a metre and a half wide and about ten metres high. The walls were straight, white, smooth, with no openings, except one through which food was brought to Max. An electric lamp was burning brightly on the ceiling. It was burning all the time, so that Max did not know now what darkness was. There was no furniture in the room, and Max had to lie on the stone floor. He lay curled together, as the narrowness of the room did not permit him to stretch himself.

His sense of hearing reported to him that until the day of his death he would not leave this room... Having reported this, his hearing sank into inactivity, for not the slightest sound came from without, except the sounds which Max himself produced, tossing about, or shouting until he was hoarse, until he lost his voice.

Max looked into himself. In contrast to the outward light which never went out he saw within himself impenetrable, heavy, and motionless darkness. In that darkness his love and faith were buried.

Max did not know whether time was moving or whether it stood motionless. The same even, white light poured down on him—the same silence and quiet. Only by the beating of his heart Max could judge that Chronos had not left his chariot. His body was aching ever more from the unnatural position in which it lay, and the constant light and silence were growing ever more tormenting. How happy are they for whom night exists, near whom people are shouting, making noise, beating drums; who may sit on a chair, with their feet hanging down, or lie with their feet outstretched, placing the head in a corner and covering it with the hands in order to create the illusion of darkness.

Max made an effort to recall and to picture to himself what there is in life; human faces, voices, the stars... He knew that his eyes would never in life see that again. He knew it, and yet he lived. He could have destroyed himself, for there is no position in which a man can not do that, but instead Max worried about his health, trying to eat, although he had no appetite, solving mathematical problems to occupy his mind so as not to lose his reason. He struggled against death as if it were not his deliverer, but his enemy; and as if life were to him not the worst of infernal tortures—but love, faith, and happiness. Gloom in the Past, the grave in the Future, and infernal tortures in the Present—and yet he lived. Tell me, John N., where did he get the strength for that?

He hoped.

HER LOVER

Maxim Gorky

An acquaintance of mine once told me the following story.

When I was a student at Moscow I happened to live alongside one of those ladies whose repute is questionable. She was a Pole, and they called her Teresa. She was a tallish, powerfully-built brunette, with black, bushy eyebrows and a large coarse face as if carved out by a hatchet—the bestial gleam of her dark eyes, her thick bass voice, her cabman-like gait and her immense muscular vigour, worthy of a fishwife, inspired me with horror. I lived on the top flight and her garret was opposite to mine. I never left my door open when I knew her to be at home. But this, after all, was a very rare occurrence. Sometimes I chanced to meet her on the staircase or in the yard, and she would smile upon me with a smile which seemed to me to be sly and cynical. Occasionally, I saw her drunk, with bleary eyes, tousled hair, and a particularly hideous grin. On such occasions she would speak to me.

'How d'ye do, Mr Student!' and her stupid laugh would still further intensify my loathing of her. I should have liked to have changed my quarters in order to have avoided such encounters and greetings; but my little chamber was a nice one, and there was such a wide view from the window, and it was always so quiet in the street below—so I endured.

And one morning I was sprawling on my couch, trying to find some sort of excuse for not attending my class, when the door opened, and the bass voice of Teresa the loathsome resounded from my threshold:

'Good health to you, Mr Student!'

'What do you want?' I said. I saw that her face was confused and supplicatory... It was a very unusual sort of face for her.

'Sir! I want to beg a favour of you. Will you grant it me?'

I lay there silent, and thought to myself:

'Gracious!... Courage, my boy!'

'I want to send a letter home, that's what it is,' she said; her voice was beseeching, soft, timid.

'Deuce take you!' I thought; but up I jumped, sat down at my table, took a sheet of paper, and said:

'Come here, sit down, and dictate!'

She came, sat down very gingerly on a chair, and looked at me with a guilty look.

'Well, to whom do you want to write?'

'To Boleslav Kashput, at the town of Svieptziana, on the Warsaw Road...'

'Well, fire away!'

'My dear Boles...my darling...my faithful lover. May the Mother of God protect thee! Thou heart of gold, why hast thou not written for such a long time to thy sorrowing little dove, Teresa?'

I very nearly burst out laughing. 'A sorrowing little dove!' more than five feet high, with fists a stone and more in weight, and as black a face as if the little dove had lived all its life in a chimney, and had never once washed itself! Restraining myself somehow, I asked:

'Who is this Bolest?'

'Boles, Mr Student,' she said, as if offended with me for blundering over the name, 'he is Boles—my young man.'

'Young man!'

'Why are you so surprised, sir? Cannot I, a girl, have a young man?' She? A girl? Well!

'Oh, why not?' I said. 'All things are possible. And has he been your young man long?'

'Six years.'

'Oh, ho!' I thought. 'Well, let us write your letter...'

And I tell you plainly that I would willingly have changed places with this Boles if his fair correspondent had been not Teresa but something less than she.

'I thank you most heartily, sir, for your kind services,' said Teresa to me, with a curtsey. 'Perhaps *I* can show *you* some service, eh?'

'No, I most humbly thank you all the same.'

'Perhaps, sir, your shirts or your trousers may want a little mending?'

I felt that this mastodon in petticoats had made me grow quite red with shame, and I told her pretty sharply that I had no need whatever of her services.

She departed.

A week or two passed away. It was evening. I was sitting at my window whistling and thinking of some expedient for enabling me to get away from myself. I was bored; the weather was dirty. I didn't want to go out, and out of sheer ennui I began a course of self-analysis and reflection. This also was dull enough work, but I didn't care about doing anything else. Then the door opened. Heaven be praised! Some one came in.

'Oh, Mr Student, you have no pressing business, I hope?' It was Teresa. Humph!

'No. What is it?'

'I was going to ask you, sir, to write me another letter.'

'Very well! To Boles, eh?'

'No, this time it is from him.'

'Wha-at?'

'Stupid that I am! It is not for me, Mr Student, I beg your pardon. It is for a friend of mine, that is to say, not a friend but an acquaintance—a man acquaintance. He has a sweetheart just like me here, Teresa. That's how it is. Will you, sir, write a letter to this Teresa?'

I looked at her—her face was troubled, her fingers were trembling. I was a bit fogged at first—and then I guessed how it was.

'Look here, my lady,' I said, 'there are no Boleses or Teresas at all, and you've been telling me a pack of lies. Don't you come sneaking about me any longer. I have no wish whatever to cultivate your acquaintance. Do you understand?'

And suddenly she grew strangely terrified and distraught; she began to shift from foot to foot without moving from the place, and spluttered comically, as if she wanted to say something and couldn't. I waited to see what would come of all this, and I saw and felt that, apparently, I had made a great mistake in suspecting her of wishing to draw me from the path of righteousness. It was evidently something very different.

'Mr Student!' she began, and suddenly, waving her hand, she turned abruptly towards the door and went out. I remained with a very unpleasant feeling in my mind. I listened. Her door was flung violently to—plainly the poor wench was very angry... I thought it over, and resolved to go to her, and, inviting her to come in here, write everything she wanted.

I entered her apartment. I looked round. She was sitting at the table, leaning on her elbows, with her head in her hands.

'Listen to me,' I said.

Now, whenever I come to this point in my story, I always feel horribly awkward and idiotic. Well, well!

'Listen to me,' I said.

She leaped from her seat, came towards me with flashing eyes, and laying her hands on my shoulders, began to whisper, or rather to hum in her peculiar bass voice:

'Look you, now! It's like this. There's no Boles at all, and there's no Teresa either. But what's that to you? Is it a hard thing for you to draw your pen over paper? Eh? Ah, and *you*, too!

Still such a little fair-haired boy! There's nobody at all, neither Boles, nor Teresa, only me. There you have it, and much good may it do you!'

'Pardon me!' said I, altogether flabbergasted by such a reception, 'what is it all about? There's no Boles, you say?'

'No. So it is.'

'And no Teresa either?'

'And no Teresa. I'm Teresa.'

I didn't understand it at all. I fixed my eyes upon her, and tried to make out which of us was taking leave of his or her senses. But she went again to the table, searched about for something, came back to me, and said in an offended tone:

'If it was so hard for you to write to Boles, look, there's your letter, take it! Others will write for me.'

I looked. In her hand was my letter to Boles. Phew!

'Listen, Teresa! What is the meaning of all this? Why must you get others to write for you when I have already written it, and you haven't sent it?'

'Sent it where?'

'Why, to this—Boles.'

'There's no such person.'

I absolutely did not understand it. There was nothing for me but to spit and go. Then she explained.

'What is it?' she said, still offended. 'There's no such person, I tell you,' and she extended her arms as if she herself did not understand why there should be no such person. 'But I wanted him to be... Am I then not a human creature like the rest of them? Yes, yes, I know, I know, of course... Yet no harm was done to any one by my writing to him that I can see...'

'Pardon me—to whom?'

'To Boles, of course.'

'But he doesn't exist.'

'Alas! alas! But what if he doesn't? He doesn't exist, but he *might!* I write to him, and it looks as if he did exist. And Teresa— that's me, and he replies to me, and then I write to him again…'

I understood at last. And I felt so sick, so miserable, so ashamed, somehow. Alongside of me, not three yards away, lived a human creature who had nobody in the world to treat her kindly, affectionately, and this human being had invented a friend for herself!

'Look, now! you wrote me a letter to Boles, and I gave it to some one else to read it to me; and when they read it to me I listened and fancied that Boles was there. And I asked you to write me a letter from Boles to Teresa—that is to me. When they write such a letter for me, and read it to me, I feel quite sure that Boles is there. And life grows easier for me in consequence.'

'Deuce take you for a blockhead!' said I to myself when I heard this.

And from thenceforth, regularly, twice a week, I wrote a letter to Boles, and an answer from Boles to Teresa. I wrote those answers well… She, of course, listened to them, and wept like anything, roared, I should say, with her bass voice. And in return for my thus moving her to tears by real letters from the imaginary Boles, she began to mend the holes I had in my socks, shirts, and other articles of clothing. Subsequently, about three months after this history began, they put her in prison for something or other. No doubt by this time she is dead.

My acquaintance shook the ash from his cigarette, looked pensively up at the sky, and thus concluded:

Well, well, the more a human creature has tasted of bitter things the more it hungers after the sweet things of life. And we, wrapped round in the rags of our virtues, and regarding others through the mist of our self-sufficiency, and persuaded of our universal impeccability, do not understand this.

And the whole thing turns out pretty stupidly—and very cruelly. The fallen classes, we say. And who are the fallen classes,

I should like to know? They are, first of all, people with the same bones, flesh, and blood and nerves as ourselves. We have been told this day after day for ages. And we actually listen—and the devil only knows how hideous the whole thing is. Or are we completely depraved by the loud sermonizing of humanism?

In reality, we also are fallen folks, and, so far as I can see, very deeply fallen into the abyss of self-sufficiency and the conviction of our own superiority. But enough of this. It is all as old as the hills—so old that it is a shame to speak of it. Very old indeed—yes, that's what it is!

IVAN MATVEYITCH

Anton Chekhov

Between five and six in the evening. A fairly well-known man of learning—we will call him simply the man of learning—is sitting in his study nervously biting his nails.

'It's positively revolting,' he says, continually looking at his watch. 'It shows the utmost disrespect for another man's time and work. In England such a person would not earn a farthing, he would die of hunger. You wait a minute, when you do come...'

And feeling a craving to vent his wrath and impatience upon someone, the man of learning goes to the door leading to his wife's room and knocks.

'Listen, Katya,' he says in an indignant voice. 'If you see Pyotr Danilitch, tell him that decent people don't do such things. It's abominable! He recommends a secretary, and does not know the sort of man he is recommending! The wretched boy is two or three hours late with unfailing regularity every day. Do you call that a secretary? Those two or three hours are more precious to me than two or three years to other people. When he does come I will swear at him like a dog, and won't pay him and will kick him out. It's no use standing on ceremony with people like that!'

'You say that every day, and yet he goes on coming and coming.'

'But to-day I have made up my mind. I have lost enough through him. You must excuse me, but I shall swear at him like a cabman.'

At last a ring is heard. The man of learning makes a grave face; drawing himself up, and, throwing back his head, he goes into the entry. There his amanuensis Ivan Matveyitch, a young man of eighteen, with a face oval as an egg and no moustache, wearing a shabby, mangy overcoat and no goloshes, is already standing by the hatstand. He is in breathless haste, and scrupulously wipes his huge clumsy boots on the doormat, trying as he does so to conceal from the maidservant a hole in his boot through which a white sock is peeping. Seeing the man of learning he smiles with that broad, prolonged, somewhat foolish smile which is seen only on the faces of children or very good-natured people.

'Ah, good evening!' he says, holding out a big wet hand. 'Has your sore throat gone?'

'Ivan Matveyitch,' says the man of learning in a shaking voice, stepping back and clasping his hands together. 'Ivan Matveyitch.'

Then he dashes up to the amanuensis, clutches him by the shoulders, and begins feebly shaking him.

'What a way to treat me!' he says with despair in his voice. 'You dreadful, horrid fellow, what a way to treat me! Are you laughing at me, are you jeering at me? Eh?'

Judging from the smile which still lingered on his face Ivan Matveyitch had expected a very different reception, and so, seeing the man of learning's countenance eloquent of indignation, his oval face grows longer than ever, and he opens his mouth in amazement.

'What is... what is it?' he asks.

'And you ask that?' the man of learning clasps his hands. 'You know how precious time is to me, and you are so late. You are two hours late!... Have you no fear of God?'

'I haven't come straight from home,' mutters Ivan Matveyitch, untying his scarf irresolutely. 'I have been at my aunt's name-day party, and my aunt lives five miles away... If I had come straight from home, then it would have been a different thing.'

'Come, reflect, Ivan Matveyitch, is there any logic in your conduct? Here you have work to do, work at a fixed time, and you go flying off after name-day parties and aunts! But do make haste and undo your wretched scarf! It's beyond endurance, really!'

The man of learning dashes up to the amanuensis again and helps him to disentangle his scarf.

'You are done up like a peasant woman,... Come along,... Please make haste!'

Blowing his nose in a dirty, crumpled-up handkerchief and pulling down his grey reefer jacket, Ivan Matveyitch goes through the hall and the drawing-room to the study. There a place and paper and even cigarettes had been put ready for him long ago.

'Sit down, sit down,' the man of learning urges him on, rubbing his hands impatiently. 'You are an unsufferable person... You know the work has to be finished by a certain time, and then you are so late. One is forced to scold you. Come, write,... Where did we stop?'

Ivan Matveyitch smooths his bristling cropped hair and takes up his pen. The man of learning walks up and down the room, concentrates himself, and begins to dictate:

'The fact is...comma...that so to speak fundamental forms... have you written it?...forms are conditioned entirely by the essential nature of those principles...comma...which find in them their expression and can only be embodied in them... New line,... There's a stop there, of course... More independence is found...is found...by the forms which have not so much a political...comma...as a social character...'

'The high-school boys have a different uniform now...a grey one,' said Ivan Matveyitch, 'when I was at school it was better: they used to wear regular uniforms.'

'Oh dear, write please!' says the man of learning wrathfully. 'Character...have you written it? Speaking of the forms relating to the organization...of administrative functions, and not to the regulation of the life of the people...comma...it cannot be said that they are marked by the nationalism of their forms...the last three words in inverted commas…Aie, aie…tut, tut…so what did you want to say about the high school?'

'That they used to wear a different uniform in my time.'

'Aha!…indeed,… Is it long since you left the high school?'

'But I told you that yesterday. It is three years since I left school… I left in the fourth class.'

'And why did you give up high school?' asks the man of learning, looking at Ivan Matveyitch's writing.

'Oh, through family circumstances.'

'Must I speak to you again, Ivan Matveyitch? When will you get over your habit of dragging out the lines? There ought not to be less than forty letters in a line.'

'What, do you suppose I do it on purpose?' says Ivan Matveyitch, offended. 'There are more than forty letters in some of the other lines… You count them. And if you think I don't put enough in the line, you can take something off my pay.'

'Oh dear, that's not the point. You have no delicacy, really… At the least thing you drag in money. The great thing is to be exact, Ivan Matveyitch, to be exact is the great thing. You ought to train yourself to be exact.'

The maidservant brings in a tray with two glasses of tea on it, and a basket of rusks… Ivan Matveyitch takes his glass awkwardly with both hands, and at once begins drinking it. The tea is too hot. To avoid burning his mouth Ivan Matveyitch tries to take a tiny sip. He eats one rusk, then a second, then a third, and, looking sideways, with embarrassment, at the man of learning, timidly stretches after a fourth… The noise he makes in swallowing, the relish with which he smacks his lips, and the expression of hungry greed in his raised eyebrows irritate the man of learning.

'Make haste and finish, time is precious.'

'You dictate, I can drink and write at the same time… I must confess I was hungry.'

'I should think so after your walk!'

'Yes, and what wretched weather! In our parts there is a scent of spring by now... There are puddles everywhere; the snow is melting.'

'You are a southerner, I suppose?'

'From the Don region... It's quite spring with us by March. Here it is frosty, everyone's in a fur coat,...but there you can see the grass...it's dry everywhere, and one can even catch tarantulas.'

'And what do you catch tarantulas for?'

'Oh!...to pass the time...' says Ivan Matveyitch, and he sighs. 'It's fun catching them. You fix a bit of pitch on a thread, let it down into their hole and begin hitting the tarantula on the back with the pitch, and the brute gets cross, catches hold of the pitch with his claws, and gets stuck... And what we used to do with them! We used to put a basinful of them together and drop a bihorka in with them.'

'What is a bihorka?'

'That's another spider, very much the same as a tarantula. In a fight one of them can kill a hundred tarantulas.'

'H'm!... But we must write,... Where did we stop?'

The man of learning dictates another twenty lines, then sits plunged in meditation.

Ivan Matveyitch, waiting while the other cogitates, sits and, craning his neck, puts the collar of his shirt to rights. His tie will not set properly, the stud has come out, and the collar keeps coming apart.

'H'm!...' says the man of learning. 'Well, haven't you found a job yet, Ivan Matveyitch?'

'No. And how is one to find one? I am thinking, you know, of volunteering for the army. But my father advises my going into a chemist's.'

'H'm!... But it would be better for you to go into the university. The examination is difficult, but with patience and hard work you could get through. Study, read more... Do you read much?'

'Not much, I must own...' says Ivan Matveyitch, lighting a cigarette.

'Have you read Turgenev?'

'N-no...'

'And Gogol?'

'Gogol. H'm!... Gogol... No, I haven't read him!'

'Ivan Matveyitch! Aren't you ashamed? Aie! aie! You are such a nice fellow, so much that is original in you...you haven't even read Gogol! You must read him! I will give you his works! It's essential to read him! We shall quarrel if you don't!'

Again a silence follows. The man of learning meditates, half reclining on a soft lounge, and Ivan Matveyitch, leaving his collar in peace, concentrates his whole attention on his boots. He has not till then noticed that two big puddles have been made by the snow melting off his boots on the floor. He is ashamed.

'I can't get on to-day...' mutters the man of learning. 'I suppose you are fond of catching birds, too, Ivan Matveyitch?'

'That's in autumn,... I don't catch them here, but there at home I always did.'

'To be sure... very good. But we must write, though.'

The man of learning gets up resolutely and begins dictating, but after ten lines sits down on the lounge again.

'No... Perhaps we had better put it off till to-morrow morning,' he says. 'Come to-morrow morning, only come early, at nine o'clock. God preserve you from being late!'

Ivan Matveyitch lays down his pen, gets up from the table and sits in another chair. Five minutes pass in silence, and he begins to feel it is time for him to go, that he is in the way; but in the man of learning's study it is so snug and light and warm, and the impression of the nice rusks and sweet tea is still so fresh that there is a pang at his heart at the mere thought of home.

At home there is poverty, hunger, cold, his grumbling father, scoldings, and here it is so quiet and unruffled, and interest even is taken in his tarantulas and birds.

The man of learning looks at his watch and takes up a book.

'So you will give me Gogol?' says Ivan Matveyitch, getting up.

'Yes, yes! But why are you in such a hurry, my dear boy? Sit down and tell me something...'

Ivan Matveyitch sits down and smiles broadly. Almost every evening he sits in this study and always feels something extraordinarily soft, attracting him, as it were akin, in the voice and the glance of the man of learning. There are moments when he even fancies that the man of learning is becoming attached to him, used to him, and that if he scolds him for being late, it's simply because he misses his chatter about tarantulas and how they catch goldfinches on the Don.

OPEN IT!

Saadat Hasan Manto

The special train left Amritsar at two in the afternoon, taking eight hours to reach Mughalpura. Quite a few passengers were killed along the way, several received injuries, and some just wandered off to God knows where.

At ten in the morning, when Sirajuddin opened his eyes on the ice-cold ground of the refugee camp, he saw a surging tide of men, women and children all around him and even his small remaining ability to think and comprehend deserted him. He stared at the murky sky for the longest time. Amidst the incredible din, his ears seemed to be firmly plugged against any sound. Seeing him in this state anyone would have thought he was deeply engrossed in thought. That, of course, was not the case. He was totally numb. His entire being seemed to be suspended in space.

Gazing blankly at the murky sky his eyes collided with the sun and a shaft of intense light penetrated every fiber of his being. Suddenly he snapped back into consciousness. A series of images flitted across his mind—images of plunder, fire, stampede, the train station, gunshots, night, and Sakina.

Sirajuddin jumped up with a start and made his way through the interminable tide of humanity around him like a man possessed.

For three full hours he scoured the camp calling out 'Sakina! Sakina!' but found no trace of his only daughter, a teenager. The whole area was rife with ear-splitting noise. Someone was looking for his child, another for his mother, still another for his wife or daughter. Finally Sirajuddin gave up and plopped down off to one side from sheer exhaustion, straining his memory to retrieve the moment when Sakina had become separated from him. However, each effort to recall ended with his mind jammed at the sight of his wife's mutilated body, her guts spilling out, and he couldn't go any further.

Sakina's mother was dead. She had died right in front of Sirajuddin's eyes. But where was Sakina? As she lay dying, Sakina's mother had urged him, 'Don't worry about me. Just take Sakina and run!'

Sakina was with him. Both of them were running barefooted. Her dupatta slipped off and when he stopped to pick it up, Sakina shouted, 'Abba Ji, leave it!' He retrieved it anyway. Thinking about it now, his eyes spontaneously drifted toward the bulge in the pocket of his coat. He plunged his hand into the pocket and took out the piece of cloth. It was the same dupatta. There could be no doubt about it. But where was Sakina herself?

Sirajuddin strained his memory but his tired mind was muddled. Had he been able to bring her to the station? Was she with him aboard the train? Had he passed out when the rioters forced the train to stop and stormed in? Was it then they carried her off?

His mind was bursting with questions, but there were no answers. He needed sympathy, but everyone around him needed it too. He wanted to cry, but couldn't. His tears had dried up.

Six days later, when Sirajuddin was able to pick himself up a bit, he met some people who were willing to help him. Eight young men equipped with a lorry and rifles. He blessed them and described Sakina for them. 'She is fair and exceedingly pretty. She takes after her mother, not me. She is about seventeen, with big eyes and dark hair. She has a beautiful big mole on her right cheek. She's my only daughter. Please find her. May God bless you!'

The young volunteers assured old Sirajuddin with tremendous fervor that if his daughter was alive he would be reunited with her in a few days. The volunteers didn't spare any effort. Putting their lives in harm's way, they went to Amritsar. They rescued several women, men, and children and brought them to safety. Ten days passed but they found no trace of Sakina.

One day they were heading off to Amritsar on their rescue mission aboard the same lorry when they spotted a girl trudging along the road near Chuhrat. The sound of the lorry startled the girl and she took off in a panic. The boys stopped the lorry and ran after her. Eventually they caught up with her in a field. She was stunningly beautiful and had a big black mole on her right cheek. 'Don't be afraid,' one of the boys tried to reassure her. 'Are you Sakina?'

The girl turned deathly pale. She didn't reply. When the boys, all of them, reassured her gently, her fear subsided and she admitted that she was indeed Sakina, Sirajuddin's daughter.

The young men tried every which way to please her. They fed her, gave her milk to drink, and then helped her to get into the lorry. One of them even took off his jacket and gave it to her because she was feeling quite awkward without her dupatta, making repeated but futile attempts to cover her chest with her arms.

Several days went by without Sirajuddin receiving any news of Sakina. He spent his days making the rounds of different camps and offices but had no success in tracing his missing daughter. At night he prayed for the success of the volunteers who had assured him that if she was alive they would find her in a matter of days.

One day he saw those volunteers at the camp. They were sitting inside the lorry. Just as the lorry was about to take off Sirajuddin rushed over to them and asked, 'Son, did you find my Sakina?'

'Oh, we will, we will,' they said in unison and the lorry took off. Once again Sirajuddin prayed for the success of these young men, which took some of the weight off his heart.

That evening he noticed some hullabaloo close to where he was sitting. Four men were carrying a stretcher. Upon inquiring he was told a girl was found lying unconscious by the train tracks. He followed them. They handed the girl over to the hospital staff and left.

For a while he stood leaning against the wooden post outside the facility and then he walked slowly inside. There was no one in the room. All he could see was the same stretcher with a corpse lying on it. Sirajuddin advanced toward it taking small, hesitant steps. All of a sudden the room lit up. 'Sakina!' he screamed spotting the big black mole gleaming on the blanched face of the dead girl.

'What is it?' the doctor who had turned on the light asked him.

'I... sir, I... I'm her father!' the words came out of his raspy throat.

The doctor glanced at the body lying on the stretcher. He felt the pulse and, pointing at the window, told Sirajuddin, 'Open it!'

Sakina's body stirred ever so faintly on the stretcher. With lifeless hands she slowly undid the knot of her waistband and lowered her shalwar.

'She's alive! My daughter is alive!' Old Sirajuddin screamed with unbounded joy.

The doctor broke into a cold sweat.

THE CHINESE LILY

Sui Sin Far

Mermei lived in an upstairs room of a Chinatown dwelling-house. There were other little Chinese women living on the same floor, but Mermei never went amongst them. She was not as they were. She was a cripple. A fall had twisted her legs so that she moved around with difficulty and scarred her face so terribly that none save Lin John cared to look upon it. Lin John, her brother, was a laundryman, working for another of his countrymen. Lin John and Mermei had come to San Francisco with their parents when they were small children. Their mother had died the day she entered the foreign city, and the father the week following, both having contracted a fever on the steamer. Mermei and Lin John were then taken in charge by their father's brother, and although he was a poor man he did his best for them until called away by death.

Long before her Uncle died Mermei had met with the accident that had made her not as other girls; but that had only strengthened her brother's affection, and old Lin Wan died happy in the knowledge that Lin John would ever put Mermei before himself.

So Mermei lived in her little upstairs room, cared for by Lin John, and scarcely an evening passed that he did not call to see her. One evening, however, Lin John failed to appear, and Mermei began to feel very sad and lonely. Mermei could embroider all day in contented silence if she knew that in the evening someone would come to whom she could communicate all the thoughts that filled a small black head that knew nothing of life save what it saw from an upstairs window. Mermei's window looked down upon the street, and she would sit for hours, pressed close against it, watching those who passed below and all that took place. That day she had seen many things which she had put into her mental portfolio for Lin John's edification when evening should come. Two yellow-robed priests had passed below on their way to the joss house in the next street; a little bird with a white breast had fluttered against the window pane; a man carrying an image of a Gambling Cash Tiger had entered the house across the street; and six young girls of about her own age, dressed gaily as if to attend a wedding, had also passed over the same threshold.

But when nine o'clock came and no Lin John, the girl began to cry softly. She did not often shed tears, but for some reason unknown to Mermei herself, the sight of those joyous girls caused sad reflections. In the midst of her weeping a timid knock was heard. It was not Lin John. He always gave a loud rap, then entered without waiting to be bidden. Mermei hobbled to the door, pulled it open, and there, in the dim light of the hall without, beheld a young girl—the most beautiful young girl that Mermei had ever seen—and she stood there extending to Mermei a blossom from a Chinese lily plant. Mermei understood the meaning of the offered flower, and accepting it, beckoned for her visitor to follow her into her room.

What a delightful hour that was to Mermei! She forgot that she was scarred and crippled, and she and the young girl chattered out their little hearts to one another. 'Lin John is dear, but one can't talk to a man, even if he is a brother, as one can to one the same as oneself,' said Mermei to Sin Far—her new friend, and Sin Far, the meaning of whose name was Pure Flower, or Chinese Lily, answered:

'Yes, indeed. The woman must be the friend of the woman, and the man the friend of the man. Is it not so in the country that Heaven loves?'

'What beneficent spirit moved you to come to my door?' asked Mermei.

'I know not,' replied Sin Far, 'save that I was lonely. We have but lately moved here, my sister, my sister's husband, and myself. My sister is a bride, and there is much to say between her and her husband. Therefore, in the evening, when the day's duties are done, I am alone. Several times, hearing that you were sick, I ventured to your door; but failed to knock, because always when I drew near, I heard the voice of him whom they call your brother. Tonight, as I returned from an errand for my sister, I heard only the sound of weeping—so I hastened to my room and plucked the lily for you.'

The next evening when Lin John explained how he had been obliged to work the evening before Mermei answered brightly that that was all right. She loved him just as much as ever and was just as glad to see him as ever; but if work prevented him from calling he was not to worry. She had found a friend who would cheer her loneliness.

Lin John was surprised, but glad to hear such news, and it came to pass that when he beheld Sin Far, her sweet and gentle face, her pretty drooped eyelids and arched eyebrows, he began to think of apple and peach and plum trees showering their dainty blossoms in the country that Heaven loves.

It was about four o'clock in the afternoon. Lin John, working in his laundry, paid little attention to the street uproar and the clang of the engines rushing by. He had no thought of what it meant to him and would have continued at his work undisturbed had not a boy put his head into the door and shouted:

'Lin John, the house in which your sister lives is on fire!'

The tall building was in flames when Lin John reached it. The uprising tongues licked his face as he sprung up the ladder no other man dared ascend.

'I will not go. It is best for me to die,' and Mermei resisted her friend with all her puny strength.

'The ladder will not bear the weight of both of us. You are his sister,' calmly replied Sin Far.

'But he loves you best. You and he can be happy together. I am not fit to live.'

'May Lin John decide, Mermei?'

'Yes, Lin John may decide.'

Lin John reached the casement. For one awful second he wavered. Then his eyes sought the eyes of his sister's friend.

'Come, Mermei,' he called.

'Where is Sin Far?' asked Mermei when she became conscious.

'Sin Far is in the land of happy spirits.'

'And I am still in this sad, dark world.'

'Speak not so, little one. Your brother loves you and will protect you from the darkness.'

'But you loved Sin Far better—and she loved you.'

Lin John bowed his head.

'Alas!' wept Mermei. 'That I should live to make others sad!'

'Nay,' said Lin John, 'Sin Far is happy. And I—I did my duty with her approval, aye, at her bidding. How then, little sister, can I be sad?'

THE THREE SOULS OF AH SO NAN

Sui Sin Far

I

The sun was conquering the morning fog, dappling with gold the gray waters of San Francisco's bay, and throwing an emerald radiance over the islands around.

Close to the long line of wharves lay motionless brigs and schooners, while farther off in the harbor were ships of many nations riding at anchor.

A fishing fleet was steering in from the open sea, scudding before the wind like a flock of seabirds. All night long had the fishers toiled in the deep. Now they were returning with the results of their labor.

A young Chinese girl, watching the fleet from the beach of Fisherman's Cove, shivered in the morning air. Over her blue cotton blouse she wore no wrap; on her head, no covering. All her interest was centred in one lone boat which lagged behind the rest, being heavier freighted. The fisherman was of her own race. When his boat was beached he sprang to her side.

'O'Yam, what brings you here?' he questioned low, for the curious eyes of his fellow fishermen were on her.

'Your mother is dying,' she answered.

The young man spake a few words in English to a Greek whose boat lay alongside his. The Greek answered in the same tongue. Then Fou Wang threw down his nets and, with the girl following, walked quickly along the waterfront, past the wharves, the warehouses, and the grogshops, up a zigzag hill and into the heart of Chinatown. Neither spoke until they reached their destination, a dingy three-storied building.

The young man began to ascend the stairs, the girl to follow. Fou Wang looked back and shook his head. The girl paused on the lowest step.

'May I not come?' she pleaded.

'Today is for sorrow,' returned Fou Wang. 'I would, for a time, forget all that belongs to the joy of life.'

The girl threw her sleeve over her head and backed out of the open door.

'What is the matter?' inquired a kind voice, and a woman laid her hand upon her shoulder.

O'Yam's bosom heaved.

'Oh, Liuchi,' she cried, 'the mother of Fou Wang is dying, and you know what that means to me.'

The woman eyed her compassionately.

'Your father, I know,' said she, as she unlocked a door and led her companion into a room opening on to the street, 'has long wished for an excuse to set at naught your betrothal to Fou Wang; but I am sure the lad to whom you are both sun and moon will never give him one.'

She offered O'Yam some tea, but the girl pushed it aside. 'You know not Fou Wang,' she replied, sadly yet proudly. 'He will follow his conscience, though he lose the sun, the moon, and the whole world.'

A young woman thrust her head through the door.

'The mother of Fou Wang is dead,' cried she.

'She was a good woman—a kind and loving mother,' said Liuchi, as she gazed down upon the still features of her friend.

The young daughter of Ah So Nan burst into fresh weeping. Her pretty face was much swollen. Ah So Nan had been well loved by her children, and the falling tears were not merely waters of ceremony.

At the foot of the couch upon which the dead was laid, stood Fou Wang, his face stern and immovable, his eye solemn, yet luminous with a steadfast fire. Over his head was thrown a white cloth. From morn till eve had he stood thus, contemplating the serene countenance of his mother and vowing that nothing should be left undone which could be done to prove his filial affection and desire to comfort her spirit in the land to which it had flown. 'Three years, O mother, will I give to thee and grief. Three years will I minister to thy three souls,' he vowed within himself, remembering how sacred to the dead woman were the customs and observances of her own country. They were also sacred to him. Living in America, in the midst of Americans and Americanized Chinese, the family of Fou Wang, with the exception of one, had clung tenaciously to the beliefs of their forefathers.

'All the living must die, and dying, return to the ground. The limbs and the flesh moulder away below, and hidden away, become the earth of the fields; but the spirit issues forth and is displayed on high in a condition of glorious brightness,' quoted a yellow-robed priest, swinging an incense burner before a small candle-lighted altar.

It was midnight when the mourning friends of the family of Fou Wang left the chief mourner alone with his dead mother.

His sister, Fin Fan, and the girl who was his betrothed wife brushed his garments as they passed him by. The latter timidly touched his hand—an involuntary act of sympathy—but if he were conscious of that sympathy, he paid no heed to it, and his gaze never wavered from the face of the dead.

II

'My girl, Moy Ding Fong is ready if Fou Wang is not, and you must marry this year. I have sworn you shall.'

Kien Lung walked out of the room with a determined step. He was an Americanized Chinese and had little regard for what he derided as 'the antiquated customs of China,' save when it was to his interest to follow them. He was also a widower desirous of marrying again, but undesirous of having two women of like years, one his wife, the other his daughter, under the same roof-tree.

Left alone, O'Yam's thoughts became sorrowful, almost despairing. Six moons had gone by since Ah So Nan had passed away, yet the son of Ah So Nan had not once, during that time, spoken one word to his betrothed wife. Occasionally she had passed him on the street; but always he had gone by with uplifted countenance, and in his eyes the beauty of piety and peace. At least, so it seemed to the girl, and the thought of marriage with him had seemed almost sacrilegious. But now it had come to this. If Fou Wang adhered to his resolve to mourn three years for his mother, what would become of her? She thought of old Moy Ding Fong and shuddered. It was bitter, bitter.

There was a rapping at the door. A young girl lifted the latch and stepped in. It was Fin Fan, the sister of her betrothed.

'I have brought my embroidery work,' said she, 'I thought we could have a little talk before sundown when I must away to prepare the evening meal.'

O'Yam, who was glad to see her visitor, brewed some fresh tea and settled down for an exchange of confidences.

'I am not going to abide by it,' said Fin Fan at last. 'Hom Hing is obliged to return to China two weeks hence, and with or without Fou Wang's consent I go with the man to whom my mother betrothed me.'

'Without Fou Wang's consent!' echoed O'Yam.

'Yes,' returned Fin Fan, snapping off a thread. 'Without my honorable brother's consent.'

'And your mother gone but six moons!'

O'Yam's face wore a shocked expression.

'Does the fallen leaf grieve because the green one remains on the tree?' queried Fin Fan.

'You must love Hom Hing well,' murmured O'Yam—'more than Fou Wang loves me.'

'Nay,' returned her companion, 'Fou Wang's love for you is as big as mine for Hom Hing. It is my brother's conscience alone that stands between him and you. You know that.'

'He loves not me,' sighed O'Yam.

'If he does not love you,' returned Fin Fan, 'why, when we heard that you were unwell, did he sleeplessly pace his room night after night until the news came that you were restored to health? Why does he treasure a broken fan you have cast aside?'

'Ah, well!' smiled O'Yam.

Fin Fan laughed softly.

'Fou Wang is not as other men,' said she. 'His conscience is an inheritance from his great-great-grandfather.' Her face became pensive as she added: 'It is sad to go across the sea without an elder brother's blessing.'

She repeated this to Liuchi and Mai Gwi Far, the widow, whom she met on her way home.

'Why should you,' inquired the latter, 'when there is a way by which to obtain it?'

'How?'

'Did Ah So Nan leave no garments behind her—such garments as would well fit her three souls—and is it not always easy to delude the serious and the wise?'

'Ah!'

III

O'Yam climbed the stairs to the joss house. The desire for solitude brought her there; but when she had closed the door upon herself, she found that she was not alone. Fou Wang was there. Before the images of the Three Wise Ones he stood, silent, motionless.

'He is communing with his mother's spirit,' thought O'Yam. She beheld him through a mist of tears. Love filled her whole being. She dared not move, because she was afraid he would turn and see her, and then, of course, he would go away. She would stay near him for a few moments and then retire.

The dim light of the place, the quietness in the midst of noise, the fragrance of some burning incense, soothed and calmed her. It was as if all the sorrow and despair that had overwhelmed her when her father had told her to prepare for her wedding with Moy Ding Fong had passed away.

After a few moments she stepped back softly towards the door. But she was too late. Fou Wang turned and beheld her.

She fluttered like a bird until she saw that, surprised by her presence, he had forgotten death and thought only of life—of life and love. A glad, eager light shone in his eyes. He made a swift step towards her. Then—he covered his face with his hands.

'Fou Wang!' cried O'Yam, love at last overcoming superstition, 'must I become the wife of Moy Ding Fong?'

'No, ah no!' he moaned.

'Then,' said the girl in desperation, 'take me to yourself.'

Fou Wang's hands fell to his side. For a moment he looked into that pleading face—and wavered.

A little bird flew in through an open window, and perching itself upon an altar, began twittering.

Fou Wang started back, the expression on his face changing.

'A warning from the dead,' he muttered, 'a warning from the dead!'

An iron hand gripped O'Yam's heart. Life itself seemed to have closed upon her.

IV

It was afternoon before evening, and the fog was rolling in from the sea. Quietness reigned in the plot of ground sacred to San Francisco's Chinese dead when Fou Wang deposited a bundle at the foot of his mother's grave and prepared for the ceremony of ministering to her three souls.

The fragrance from a wall of fir trees near by stole to his nostrils as he cleared the weeds and withered leaves from his parent's resting place. As he placed the bowls of rice and chicken and the vase of incense where he was accustomed to place it, he became dimly conscious of a presence or presences behind the fir wall.

He sighed deeply. No doubt the shade of his parent was restless, because—

'Fou Wang,' spake a voice, low but distinct.

The young man fell upon his knees.

'Honored Mother!' he cried.

'Fou Wang,' repeated the voice, 'though my name is on thy lips, O'Yam's is in thy heart.'

Conscience-stricken, Fou Wang yet retained spirit enough to gasp:

'Have I not been a dutiful son? Have I not sacrificed all for thee, O Mother! Why, then, dost thou reproach me?'

'I do not reproach thee,' chanted three voices, and Fou Wang, lifting his head, saw three figures emerge from behind the fir wall. 'I do not reproach thee. Thou hast been a most dutiful son, and thy offerings at my grave and in the temple have been fully appreciated. Far from reproaching thee, I am here to say to thee that the dead have regard for the living who faithfully mourn and minister to them, and to bid thee sacrifice no more until thou hast satisfied thine own heart by taking to wife the daughter of Kien Lung and given to thy sister and thy sister's husband an elder brother's blessing. Thy departed mother requires not the sacrifice of a broken heart. The fallen leaf grieves not because the green leaf still clings to the bough.'

Saying this, the three figures flapped the loose sleeves of the well-known garments of Ah So Nan and faded from his vision.

For a moment Fou Wang gazed after them as if spellbound. Then he arose and rushed towards the fir wall, behind which they seemed to have vanished.

'Mother, honored parent! Come back and tell me of the new birth!' he cried.

But there was no response.

Fou Wang returned to the grave and lighted the incense. But he did not wait to see its smoke ascend. Instead he hastened to the house of Kien Lung and said to the girl who met him at the door:

'No more shall my longing for thee take the fragrance from the flowers and the light from the sun and moon.'

THE HEAVENLY CHRISTMAS TREE

Fyodor Dostoevsky

I am a novelist, and I suppose I have made up this story. I write 'I suppose,' though I know for a fact that I have made it up, but yet I keep fancying that it must have happened somewhere at some time, that it must have happened on Christmas Eve in some great town in a time of terrible frost.

I have a vision of a boy, a little boy, six years old or even younger. This boy woke up that morning in a cold damp cellar. He was dressed in a sort of little dressing-gown and was shivering with cold. There was a cloud of white steam from his breath, and sitting on a box in the corner, he blew the steam out of his mouth and amused himself in his dullness watching it float away. But he was terribly hungry. Several times that morning he went up to the plank bed where his sick mother was lying on a mattress as thin as a pancake, with some sort of bundle under her head for a pillow. How had she come here? She must have come with her boy from some other town and suddenly fallen ill. The landlady who let the 'corners' had been taken two days before to the police station, the lodgers were out and about as the holiday was so near, and the only one left had been lying for the last twenty-four hours dead drunk, not having waited for Christmas. In another corner of the room a wretched old woman of eighty, who had once been a children's nurse but was now left to die friendless, was moaning and groaning with rheumatism, scolding and grumbling at the boy so that he was afraid to go near her corner. He had got a drink of water in the outer room, but could not find a crust anywhere, and had been on the point of waking his mother a dozen times. He felt frightened at last in the darkness: it had long been dusk, but no light was kindled. Touching his mother's face, he was surprised that she did not move at all, and that she was as cold as the wall. 'It is very cold here,' he thought. He stood a little, unconsciously letting his hands rest on the dead woman's shoulders, then he breathed on his fingers to warm them, and then quietly fumbling for his cap on the bed, he went out of the cellar. He would have gone earlier, but was afraid of the big dog which had been howling all day at the neighbour's door at the top of the stairs. But the dog was not there now, and he went out into the street.

Mercy on us, what a town! He had never seen anything like it before. In the town from which he had come, it was always such black darkness at night. There was one lamp for the whole street, the little, low-pitched, wooden houses were closed up with shutters, there was no one to be seen in the street after dusk, all the people shut themselves up in their houses, and there was nothing but the howling of packs of dogs, hundreds and thousands of them barking and howling all night. But there it was so warm and he was given food, while here—oh, dear, if he only had something to eat! And what a noise and rattle here, what light and what people, horses and carriages, and what a frost! The frozen steam hung in clouds over the horses, over their warmly breathing mouths; their hoofs clanged against the stones through the powdery snow, and every one pushed so, and—oh, dear, how he longed for some morsel to eat, and how wretched he suddenly felt. A policeman walked by and turned away to avoid seeing the boy.

Here was another street—oh, what a wide one, here he would be run over for certain; how everyone was shouting, racing and driving along, and the light, the light! And what was this? A huge glass window, and through the window a tree reaching up to the ceiling; it was a fir tree, and on it were ever so many lights, gold papers and apples and little dolls and horses; and there were children clean and dressed in their best running about the room, laughing and playing and eating and drinking something. And then a little girl began dancing with one of the boys, what a pretty little girl! And he could hear the music through the window. The boy looked and wondered and laughed, though his toes were aching with the cold and his fingers were red and stiff so that it hurt him to move them. And all at once the boy remembered how his toes and fingers hurt him, and began crying, and ran on; and again through another window-pane he saw another Christmas tree, and on a table cakes of all sorts—almond cakes, red cakes and yellow cakes, and three grand young ladies were sitting there, and they gave the cakes to any one who went up to them, and the door kept opening, lots of gentlemen and ladies went in from the street. The boy crept up, suddenly opened the door and went in. Oh, how they shouted at him and waved him back! One lady went up to him hurriedly and slipped a kopeck into his hand, and with her own hands opened the door into the street for him! How frightened he was. And the kopeck rolled away and clinked upon the steps; he could not bend his red fingers to hold it tight. The boy ran away and went on, where he did not know. He was ready to cry again but he was afraid, and ran on and on and blew his fingers. And he was miserable because he felt suddenly so lonely and terrified, and all at once, mercy on us! What was this again? People were standing in a crowd admiring. Behind a glass window there were three little dolls, dressed in red and green dresses, and exactly, exactly as though they were alive. One was a little old man sitting and playing a big violin, the two others were standing close by and playing little violins and nodding in time, and looking at one another, and their lips moved, they were speaking, actually speaking, only one couldn't hear through the glass. And at first the boy thought they were alive, and when he grasped that they were dolls he laughed. He had never seen such dolls before, and had no idea there were such dolls! And he wanted to cry, but he felt amused, amused by the dolls. All at once he fancied that some one caught at his smock behind: a wicked big boy was standing beside him and suddenly hit him on the head, snatched off his cap and tripped him up. The boy fell down on the ground, at once there was a shout, he was numb with fright, he jumped up and ran away. He ran, and not knowing where he was going, ran in at the gate of some one's courtyard, and sat down behind a stack of wood: 'They won't find me here, besides it's dark!'

He sat huddled up and was breathless from fright, and all at once, quite suddenly, he felt so happy: his hands and feet suddenly left off aching and grew so warm, as warm as though he were on a stove; then he shivered all over, then he gave a start, why, he must have been asleep. How nice to have a sleep here! 'I'll sit here a little and go and look at the dolls again,' said the boy, and smiled thinking of them. 'Just as though they were alive!...' And suddenly he heard his mother singing over him. 'Mammy, I am asleep; how nice it is to sleep here!'

'Come to my Christmas tree, little one,' a soft voice suddenly whispered over his head.

He thought that this was still his mother, but no, it was not she. Who it was calling him, he could not see, but some one bent over and embraced him in the darkness; and he stretched out his hands to him, and...and all at once—oh, what a bright light! Oh, what a Christmas tree! And yet it was not a fir tree, he had never seen a tree like that! Where was he now? Everything was bright and shining, and all round him were dolls; but no, they were not dolls, they were little boys and girls, only so bright and shining. They all came flying round him, they all kissed him, took him and carried him along with them, and he was flying himself, and he saw that his mother was looking at him and laughing joyfully. 'Mammy, Mammy; oh, how nice it is here, Mammy!' And again he kissed the children and wanted to tell them at once of those dolls in the shop window. 'Who are you, boys? Who are you, girls?' he asked, laughing and admiring them.

'This is Christ's Christmas tree,' they answered. 'Christ always has a Christmas tree on this day, for the little children who have no tree of their own...' And he found out that all these little boys and girls were children just like himself; that some had been frozen in the baskets in which they had as babies been laid on the doorsteps of well-to-do Petersburg people, others had been boarded out with Finnish women by the Foundling and had been suffocated, others had died at their starved mother's breasts (in the Samara famine), others had died in the third-class railway carriages from the foul air; and yet they were all here, they were all like angels about Christ, and He was in the midst of them and held out His hands to them and blessed them and their sinful mothers... And the mothers of these children stood on one side weeping; each one knew her boy or girl, and the children flew up to them and kissed them and wiped away their tears with their little hands, and begged them not to weep because they were so happy.

And down below in the morning the porter found the little dead body of the frozen child on the woodstack; they sought out his mother too... She had died before him. They met before the Lord God in heaven.

Why have I made up such a story, so out of keeping with an ordinary diary, and a writer's above all? And I promised two stories dealing with real events! But that is just it, I keep fancying that all this may have happened really—that is, what took place in the cellar and on the woodstack; but as for Christ's Christmas tree, I cannot tell you whether that could have happened or not.

THE HOME-COMING

Rabindranath Tagore

Phatik Chakravorti was ringleader among the boys of the village. A new mischief got into his head. There was a heavy log lying on the mud-flat of the river waiting to be shaped into a mast for a boat. He decided that they should all work together to shift the log by main force from its place and roll it away. The owner of the log would be angry and surprised, and they would all enjoy the fun. Every one seconded the proposal, and it was carried unanimously.

But just as the fun was about to begin, Mākhan, Phatik's younger brother, sauntered up and sat down on the log in front of them all without a word. The boys were puzzled for a moment. He was pushed, rather timidly, by one of the boys and told to get up; but he remained quite unconcerned. He appeared like a young philosopher meditating on the futility of games. Phatik was furious. 'Mākhan,' he cried, 'if you don't get down this minute I'll thrash you!'

Mākhan only moved to a more comfortable position.

Now, if Phatik was to keep his regal dignity before the public, it was clear he ought to carry out his threat. But his courage failed him at the crisis. His fertile brain, however, rapidly seized upon a new manœuvre which would discomfit his brother and afford his followers an added amusement. He gave the word of command to roll the log and Mākhan over together. Mākhan heard the order and made it a point of honour to stick on. But he overlooked the fact, like those who attempt earthly fame in other matters, that there was peril in it.

The boys began to heave at the log with all their might,

calling out, 'One, two, three, go!' At the word 'go' the log went; and with it went Mākhan's philosophy, glory and all.

The other boys shouted themselves hoarse with delight. But Phatik was a little frightened. He knew what was coming. And, sure enough, Mākhan rose from Mother Earth blind as Fate and screaming like the Furies. He rushed at Phatik and scratched his face and beat him and kicked him, and then went crying home. The first act of the drama was over.

Phatik wiped his face, and sat down on the edge of a sunken barge by the river bank, and began to chew a piece of grass. A boat came up to the landing and a middle-aged man, with grey hair and dark moustache, stepped on shore. He saw the boy sitting there doing nothing and asked him where the Chakravortis lived. Phatik went on chewing the grass and said: 'Over there,' but it was quite impossible to tell where he pointed. The stranger asked him again. He swung his legs to and fro on the side of the barge and said: 'Go and find out,' and continued to chew the grass as before.

But now a servant came down from the house and told Phatik his mother wanted him. Phatik refused to move. But the servant was the master on this occasion. He took Phatik up roughly and carried him, kicking and struggling in impotent rage.

When Phatik came into the house, his mother saw him. She called out angrily: 'So you have been hitting Mākhan again?'

Phatik answered indignantly: 'No, I haven't! Who told you that?'

His mother shouted: 'Don't tell lies! You have.'

Phatik said sullenly: 'I tell you, I haven't. You ask Mākhan!' But Mākhan thought it best to stick to his previous statement. He said: 'Yes, mother. Phatik did hit me.'

Phatik's patience was already exhausted. He could not bear this injustice. He rushed at Mākhan and hammered him with blows: 'Take that,' he cried, 'and that, and that, for telling lies.'

His mother took Mākhan's side in a moment, and pulled

Phatik away, beating him with her hands. When Phatik pushed her aside, she shouted out: 'What! you little villain! Would you hit your own mother?'

It was just at this critical juncture that the grey-haired stranger arrived. He asked what was the matter. Phatik looked sheepish and ashamed.

But when his mother stepped back and looked at the stranger, her anger was changed to surprise. For she recognized her brother and cried: 'Why, Dada! Where have you come from?'

As she said these words, she bowed to the ground and touched his feet. Her brother had gone away soon after she had married; and he had started business in Bombay. His sister had lost her husband while he was there. Bishamber had now come back to Calcutta and had at once made enquiries about his sister. He had then hastened to see her as soon as he found out where she was.

The next few days were full of rejoicing. The brother asked after the education of the two boys. He was told by his sister that Phatik was a perpetual nuisance. He was lazy, disobedient, and wild. But Mākhan was as good as gold, as quiet as a lamb, and very fond of reading. Bishamber kindly offered to take Phatik off his sister's hands and educate him with his own children in Calcutta. The widowed mother readily agreed. When his uncle asked Phatik if he would like to go to Calcutta with him, his joy knew no bounds and he said: 'Oh, yes, uncle!' in a way that made it quite clear that he meant it.

It was an immense relief to the mother to get rid of Phatik. She had a prejudice against the boy, and no love was lost between the two brothers. She was in daily fear that he would either drown Mākhan some day in the river, or break his head in a fight, or run him into some danger. At the same time she was a little distressed to see Phatik's extreme eagerness to get away.

Phatik, as soon as all was settled, kept asking his uncle every minute when they were to start. He was on pins and needles all day long with excitement and lay awake most of the night. He bequeathed to Mākhan, in perpetuity, his fishing-rod, his big kite, and his marbles. Indeed, at this time of departure, his generosity towards Mākhan was unbounded.

When they reached Calcutta, Phatik made the acquaintance of his aunt for the first time. She was by no means pleased with this unnecessary addition to her family. She found her own three boys quite enough to manage without taking any one else. And to bring a village lad of fourteen into their midst was terribly upsetting. Bishamber should really have thought twice before committing such an indiscretion.

In this world of human affairs there is no worse nuisance than a boy at the age of fourteen. He is neither ornamental nor useful. It is impossible to shower affection on him as on a little boy; and he is always getting in the way. If he talks with a childish lisp he is called a baby, and if he answers in a grown-up way he is called impertinent. In fact any talk at all from him is resented. Then he is at the unattractive, growing age. He grows out of his clothes with indecent haste; his voice grows hoarse and breaks and quavers; his face grows suddenly angular and unsightly. It is easy to excuse the shortcomings of early childhood, but it is hard to tolerate even unavoidable lapses in a boy of fourteen. The lad himself becomes painfully self-conscious. When he talks with elderly people he is either unduly forward, or else so unduly shy that he appears ashamed of his very existence.

Yet it is at this very age when, in his heart of hearts, a young lad most craves for recognition and love; and he becomes the devoted slave of any one who shows him consideration. But none dare openly love him, for that would be regarded as undue indulgence and therefore bad for the boy. So, what with scolding and chiding, he becomes very much like a stray dog that has lost his master.

For a boy of fourteen his own home is the only Paradise. To live in a strange house with strange people is little short of torture, while the height of bliss is to receive the kind looks of women and never to be slighted by them.

It was anguish to Phatik to be the unwelcome guest in his aunt's house, despised by this elderly woman and slighted on every occasion. If ever she asked him to do anything for her, he would be so overjoyed that he would overdo it; and then she would tell him not to be so stupid, but to get on with his lessons.

The cramped atmosphere of neglect oppressed Phatik so much that he felt that he could hardly breathe. He wanted to go out into the open country and fill his lungs with fresh air. But there was no open country to go to. Surrounded on all sides by Calcutta houses and walls, he would dream night after night of his village home and long to be back there. He remembered the glorious meadow where he used to fly his kite all day long; the broad river-banks where he would wander about the live-long day singing and shouting for joy; the narrow brook where he could go and dive and swim at any time he liked. He thought of his band of boy companions over whom he was despot; and, above all, the memory of that tyrant mother of his, who had such a prejudice against him, occupied him day and night. A kind of physical love like that of animals, a longing to be in the presence of the one who is loved, an inexpressible wistfulness during absence, a silent cry of the inmost heart for the mother, like the lowing of a calf in the twilight,—this love, which was almost an animal instinct, agitated the shy, nervous, lean, uncouth and ugly boy. No one could understand it, but it preyed upon his mind continually.

There was no more backward boy in the whole school than Phatik. He gaped and remained silent when the teacher asked him a question, and like an overladen ass patiently suffered all the blows that came down on his back. When other boys were out at play, he stood wistfully by the window and gazed at the roofs of the distant houses. And if by chance he espied children playing on the open terrace of any roof, his heart would ache with longing.

One day he summoned up all his courage and asked his uncle: 'Uncle, when can I go home?'

His uncle answered: 'Wait till the holidays come.'

But the holidays would not come till October and there was a long time still to wait.

One day Phatik lost his lesson book. Even with the help of books he had found it very difficult indeed to prepare his lesson. Now it was impossible. Day after day the teacher would cane him unmercifully. His condition became so abjectly miserable that even his cousins were ashamed to own him. They began to jeer and insult him more than the other boys. He went to his aunt at last and told her that he had lost his book.

His aunt pursed her lips in contempt and said: 'You great clumsy, country lout! How can I afford, with all my family, to buy you new books five times a month?'

That night, on his way back from school, Phatik had a bad headache with a fit of shivering. He felt he was going to have an attack of malarial fever. His one great fear was that he would be a nuisance to his aunt.

The next morning Phatik was nowhere to be seen. All searches in the neighbourhood proved futile. The rain had been pouring in torrents all night, and those who went out in search of the boy got drenched through to the skin. At last Bishamber asked help from the police.

At the end of the day a police van stopped at the door before the house. It was still raining and the streets were all flooded. Two constables brought out Phatik in their arms and placed him before Bishamber. He was wet through from head to foot, muddy all over, his face and eyes flushed red with fever and his limbs trembling. Bishamber carried him in his arms and took him into the inner apartments. When his wife saw him she exclaimed: 'What a heap of trouble this boy has given us! Hadn't you better send him home?'

Phatik heard her words and sobbed out loud: 'Uncle, I was just going home; but they dragged me back again.'

The fever rose very high, and all that night the boy was delirious. Bishamber brought in a doctor. Phatik opened his eyes, flushed with fever, and looked up to the ceiling and said vacantly: 'Uncle, have the holidays come yet?'

Bishamber wiped the tears from his own eyes and took Phatik's lean and burning hands in his own and sat by him through the night. The boy began again to mutter. At last his voice became excited: 'Mother!' he cried, 'don't beat me like that... Mother! I *am* telling the truth!'

The next day Phatik became conscious for a short time. He turned his eyes about the room, as if expecting some one to come. At last, with an air of disappointment, his head sank back on the pillow. He turned his face to the wall with a deep sigh.

Bishamber knew his thoughts and bending down his head whispered: 'Phatik, I have sent for your mother.'

The day went by. The doctor said in a troubled voice that the boy's condition was very critical.

Phatik began to cry out: 'By the mark—three fathoms. By the mark—four fathoms. By the mark—.' He had heard the sailor on the river-steamer calling out the mark on the plumb-line. Now he was himself plumbing an unfathomable sea.

Later in the day Phatik's mother burst into the room, like a whirlwind, and began to toss from side to side and moan and cry in a loud voice.

Bishamber tried to calm her agitation, but she flung herself on the bed, and cried: 'Phatik, my darling, my darling.'

Phatik stopped his restless movements for a moment. His hands ceased beating up and down. He said: 'Eh?'

The mother cried again: 'Phatik, my darling, my darling.'

Phatik very slowly turned his head and without seeing anybody said: 'Mother, the holidays have come.'

THE POSTMASTER

Rabindranath Tagore

The postmaster first took up his duties in the village of Ulapur. Though the village was a small one, there was an indigo factory near by, and the proprietor, an Englishman, had managed to get a post office established.

Our postmaster belonged to Calcutta. He felt like a fish out of water in this remote village. His office and living-room were in a dark thatched shed, not far from a green, slimy pond, surrounded on all sides by a dense growth.

The men employed in the indigo factory had no leisure; moreover, they were hardly desirable companions for decent folk. Nor is a Calcutta boy an adept in the art of associating with others. Among strangers he appears either proud or ill at ease. At any rate, the postmaster had but little company; nor had he much to do.

At times he tried his hand at writing a verse or two. That the movement of the leaves and the clouds of the sky were enough to fill life with joy—such were the sentiments to which he sought to give expression. But God knows that the poor fellow would have felt it as the gift of a new life, if some genie of the *Arabian Nights* had in one night swept away the trees, leaves and all, and replaced them with a macadamized road, hiding the clouds from view with rows of tall houses.

The postmaster's salary was small. He had to cook his own meals, which he used to share with Ratan, an orphan girl of the village, who did odd jobs for him.

When in the evening the smoke began to curl up from the

village cowsheds, and the cicalas chirped in every bush; when the mendicants of the Baül sect sang their shrill songs in their daily meeting-place, when any poet, who had attempted to watch the movement of the leaves in the dense bamboo thickets, would have felt a ghostly shiver run down his back, the postmaster would light his little lamp, and call out 'Ratan.'

Ratan would sit outside waiting for this call, and, instead of coming in at once, would reply, 'Did you call me, sir?'

'What are you doing?' the postmaster would ask.

'I must be going to light the kitchen fire,' would be the answer.

And the postmaster would say: 'Oh, let the kitchen fire be for awhile; light me my pipe first.'

At last Ratan would enter, with puffed-out cheeks, vigorously blowing into a flame a live coal to light the tobacco. This would give the postmaster an opportunity of conversing. 'Well, Ratan,' perhaps he would begin, 'do you remember anything of your mother?' That was a fertile subject. Ratan partly remembered, and partly didn't. Her father had been fonder of her than her mother; him she recollected more vividly. He used to come home in the evening after his work, and one or two evenings stood out more clearly than others, like pictures in her memory. Ratan would sit on the floor near the postmaster's feet, as memories crowded in upon her. She called to mind a little brother that she had—and how on some bygone cloudy day she had played at fishing with him on the edge of the pond, with a twig for a make-believe fishing-rod. Such little incidents would drive out greater events from her mind. Thus, as they talked, it would often get very late, and the postmaster would feel too lazy to do any cooking at all. Ratan would then hastily light the fire, and toast some unleavened bread, which, with the cold remnants of the morning meal, was enough for their supper.

On some evenings, seated at his desk in the corner of the big empty shed, the postmaster too would call up memories of his own home, of his mother and his sister, of those for whom in his exile his heart was sad,—memories which were always haunting him, but which he could not talk about with the men of the factory, though he found himself naturally recalling them aloud in the presence of the simple little girl. And so it came about that the girl would allude to his people as mother, brother, and sister, as if she had known them all her life. In fact, she had a complete picture of each one of them painted in her little heart.

One noon, during a break in the rains, there was a cool soft breeze blowing; the smell of the damp grass and leaves in the hot sun felt like the warm breathing of the tired earth on one's body. A persistent bird went on all the afternoon repeating the burden of its one complaint in Nature's audience chamber.

The postmaster had nothing to do. The shimmer of the freshly washed leaves, and the banked-up remnants of the retreating rain-clouds were sights to see; and the postmaster was watching them and thinking to himself: 'Oh, if only some kindred soul were near—just one loving human being whom I could hold near my heart!' This was exactly, he went on to think, what that bird was trying to say, and it was the same feeling which the murmuring leaves were striving to express. But no one knows, or would believe, that such an idea might also take possession of an ill-paid village postmaster in the deep, silent mid-day interval of his work.

The postmaster sighed, and called out 'Ratan.' Ratan was then sprawling beneath the guava-tree, busily engaged in eating unripe guavas. At the voice of her master, she ran up breathlessly, saying: 'Were you calling me, Dada?' 'I was thinking,' said the postmaster, 'of teaching you to read.' And then for the rest of the afternoon he taught her the alphabet.

Thus, in a very short time, Ratan had got as far as the double consonants.

It seemed as though the showers of the season would never

end. Canals, ditches, and hollows were all overflowing with water. Day and night the patter of rain was heard, and the croaking of frogs. The village roads became impassable, and marketing had to be done in punts.

One heavily clouded morning, the postmaster's little pupil had been long waiting outside the door for her call, but, not hearing it as usual, she took up her dog-eared book, and slowly entered the room. She found her master stretched out on his bed, and, thinking that he was resting, she was about to retire on tip-toe, when she suddenly heard her name—'Ratan!' She turned at once and asked: 'Were you sleeping, Dada?' The postmaster in a plaintive voice said: 'I am not well. Feel my head; is it very hot?'

In the loneliness of his exile, and in the gloom of the rains, his ailing body needed a little tender nursing. He longed to remember the touch on the forehead of soft hands with tinkling bracelets, to imagine the presence of loving womanhood, the nearness of mother and sister. And the exile was not disappointed. Ratan ceased to be a little girl. She at once stepped into the post of mother, called in the village doctor, gave the patient his pills at the proper intervals, sat up all night by his pillow, cooked his gruel for him, and every now and then asked: 'Are you feeling a little better, Dada?'

It was some time before the postmaster, with weakened body, was able to leave his sick-bed. 'No more of this,' said he with decision. 'I must get a transfer.' He at once wrote off to Calcutta an application for a transfer, on the ground of the unhealthiness of the place.

Relieved from her duties as nurse, Ratan again took up her old place outside the door. But she no longer heard the same old call. She would sometimes peep inside furtively to find the postmaster sitting on his chair, or stretched on his bed, and staring absent-mindedly into the air. While Ratan was awaiting her call, the postmaster was awaiting a reply to his application.

The girl read her old lessons over and over again,—her great fear was lest, when the call came, she might be found wanting in the double consonants. At last, after a week, the call did come one evening. With an overflowing heart Ratan rushed into the room with her—'Were you calling me, Dada?'

The postmaster said: 'I am going away to-morrow, Ratan.'

'Where are you going, Dada?'

'I am going home.'

'When will you come back?'

'I am not coming back.'

Ratan asked no other question. The postmaster, of his own accord, went on to tell her that his application for a transfer had been rejected, so he had resigned his post and was going home.

For a long time neither of them spoke another word. The lamp went on dimly burning, and from a leak in one corner of the thatch water dripped steadily into an earthen vessel on the floor beneath it.

After a while Ratan rose, and went off to the kitchen to prepare the meal; but she was not so quick about it as on other days. Many new things to think of had entered her little brain. When the postmaster had finished his supper, the girl suddenly asked him: 'Dada, will you take me to your home?'

The postmaster laughed. 'What an idea!' said he; but he did not think it necessary to explain to the girl wherein lay the absurdity.

That whole night, in her waking and in her dreams, the postmaster's laughing reply haunted her—'What an idea!'

On getting up in the morning, the postmaster found his bath ready. He had stuck to his Calcutta habit of bathing in water drawn and kept in pitchers, instead of taking a plunge in the river as was the custom of the village. For some reason or other, the girl could not ask him about the time of his departure, so she had fetched the water from the river long before sunrise, that it should be ready as early as he might want it. After the bath came a call for Ratan. She entered noiselessly, and looked silently into her master's face for orders. The master said: 'You need not be anxious about my going away, Ratan; I shall tell my successor to look after you.' These words were kindly meant, no doubt: but inscrutable are the ways of a woman's heart!

Ratan had borne many a scolding from her master without complaint, but these kind words she could not bear. She burst out weeping, and said: 'No, no, you need not tell anybody anything at all about me; I don't want to stay on here.'

The postmaster was dumbfounded. He had never seen Ratan like this before.

The new incumbent duly arrived, and the postmaster, having given over charge, prepared to depart. Just before starting he called Ratan and said: 'Here is something for you; I hope it will keep you for some little time.' He brought out from his pocket the whole of his month's salary, retaining only a trifle for his travelling expenses. Then Ratan fell at his feet and cried: 'Oh, Dada, I pray you, don't give me anything, don't in any way trouble about me,' and then she ran away out of sight.

The postmaster heaved a sigh, took up his carpet bag, put his umbrella over his shoulder, and, accompanied by a man carrying his many-coloured tin trunk, he slowly made for the boat.

When he got in and the boat was under way, and the rain-swollen river, like a stream of tears welling up from the earth, swirled and sobbed at her bows, then he felt a pain at heart; the grief-stricken face of a village girl seemed to represent for him the great unspoken pervading grief of Mother Earth herself. At one time he had an impulse to go back, and bring away along with him that lonesome waif, forsaken of the world. But the wind had just filled the sails, the boat had got well into the middle of the turbulent current, and already the village was left behind, and its outlying burning-ground came in sight.

So the traveller, borne on the breast of the swift-flowing river, consoled himself with philosophical reflections on the numberless meetings and partings going on in the world—on death, the great parting, from which none returns.

But Ratan had no philosophy. She was wandering about the post office in a flood of tears. It may be that she had still a lurking hope in some corner of her heart that her Dada would return, and that is why she could not tear herself away. Alas for our foolish human nature! Its fond mistakes are persistent. The dictates of reason take a long time to assert their own sway. The surest proofs meanwhile are disbelieved. False hope is clung to with all one's might and main, till a day comes when it has sucked the heart dry and it forcibly breaks through its bonds and departs. After that comes the misery of awakening, and then once again the longing to get back into the maze of the same mistakes.

THE CABULIWALLAH

Rabindranath Tagore

My five years' old daughter Mini cannot live without chattering. I really believe that in all her life she has not wasted a minute in silence. Her mother is often vexed at this, and would stop her prattle, but I would not. To see Mini quiet is unnatural, and I cannot bear it long. And so my own talk with her is always lively.

One morning, for instance, when I was in the midst of the seventeenth chapter of my new novel, my little Mini stole into the room, and putting her hand into mine, said: 'Father! Ramdayal the door-keeper calls a crow a krow! He doesn't know anything, does he?'

Before I could explain to her the differences of language in this world, she was embarked on the full tide of another subject. 'What do you think, Father? Bhola says there is an elephant in the clouds, blowing water out of his trunk, and that is why it rains!'

And then, darting off anew, while I sat still making ready some reply to this last saying: 'Father! what relation is Mother to you?'

With a grave face I contrived to say: 'Go and play with Bhola, Mini! I am busy!'

The window of my room overlooks the road. The child had seated herself at my feet near my table, and was playing softly, drumming on her knees. I was hard at work on my seventeenth chapter, where Pratap Singh, the hero, had just caught Kanchanlata, the heroine, in his arms, and was about to escape with her by the third-story window of the castle, when all of a sudden Mini left her play, and ran to the window, crying:

'A Cabuliwallah! a Cabuliwallah!' Sure enough in the street below was a Cabuliwallah, passing slowly along. He wore the loose, soiled clothing of his people, with a tall turban; there was a bag on his back, and he carried boxes of grapes in his hand.

I cannot tell what were my daughter's feelings at the sight of this man, but she began to call him loudly. 'Ah!' I thought, 'he will come in, and my seventeenth chapter will never be finished!' At which exact moment the Cabuliwallah turned, and looked up at the child. When she saw this, overcome by terror, she fled to her mother's protection and disappeared. She had a blind belief that inside the bag, which the big man carried, there were perhaps two or three other children like herself. The pedlar meanwhile entered my doorway and greeted me with a smiling face.

So precarious was the position of my hero and my heroine, that my first impulse was to stop and buy something, since the man had been called. I made some small purchases, and a conversation began about Abdurrahman, the Russians, the English, and the Frontier Policy.

As he was about to leave, he asked: 'And where is the little girl, sir?'

And I, thinking that Mini must get rid of her false fear, had her brought out.

She stood by my chair, and looked at the Cabuliwallah and his bag. He offered her nuts and raisins, but she would not be tempted, and only clung the closer to me, with all her doubts increased.

This was their first meeting.

One morning, however, not many days later, as I was leaving the house, I was startled to find Mini, seated on a bench near the door, laughing and talking, with the great Cabuliwallah at her feet. In all her life, it appeared, my small daughter had never found so patient a listener, save her father. And already the corner of her little *sari* was stuffed with almonds and raisins, the gift of her visitor. 'Why did you give her those?' I said, and taking out an eight-anna bit, I handed it to him. The man accepted the money without demur, and slipped it into his pocket.

Alas, on my return an hour later, I found the unfortunate coin had made twice its own worth of trouble! For the Cabuliwallah had given it to Mini; and her mother, catching sight of the bright round object, had pounced on the child with: 'Where did you get that eight-anna bit?'

'The Cabuliwallah gave it me,' said Mini cheerfully.

'The Cabuliwallah gave it you!' cried her mother much shocked. 'O Mini! how could you take it from him?'

I, entering at the moment, saved her from impending disaster, and proceeded to make my own inquiries.

It was not the first or second time, I found, that the two had met. The Cabuliwallah had overcome the child's first terror by a judicious bribery of nuts and almonds, and the two were now great friends.

They had many quaint jokes, which afforded them much amusement. Seated in front of him, looking down on his gigantic frame in all her tiny dignity, Mini would ripple her face with laughter and begin: 'O Cabuliwallah! Cabuliwallah! what have you got in your bag?'

And he would reply, in the nasal accents of the mountaineer: 'An elephant!' Not much cause for merriment, perhaps; but how they both enjoyed the fun! And for me, this child's talk with a grown-up man had always in it something strangely fascinating.

Then the Cabuliwallah, not to be behindhand, would take his turn: 'Well, little one, and when are you going to the father-in-law's house?'

Now most small Bengali maidens have heard long ago about the father-in-law's house; but we, being a little new-fangled, had kept these things from our child, and Mini at this question must have been a trifle bewildered. But she would not show it, and with ready tact replied: 'Are *you* going there?'

Amongst men of the Cabuliwallah's class, however, it is well known that the words *father-in-law's house* have a double meaning. It is a euphemism for *jail*, the place where we are well cared for, at no expense to ourselves. In this sense would the sturdy pedlar take my daughter's question. 'Ah,' he would say, shaking his fist at an invisible policeman, 'I will thrash my father-in-law!' Hearing this, and picturing the poor discomfited relative, Mini would go off into peals of laughter, in which her formidable friend would join.

These were autumn mornings, the very time of year when kings of old went forth to conquest; and I, never stirring from my little corner in Calcutta, would let my mind wander over the whole world. At the very name of another country, my heart would go out to it, and at the sight of a foreigner in the streets, I would fall to weaving a network of dreams,—the mountains, the glens, and the forests of his distant home, with his cottage in its setting, and the free and independent life of far-away wilds. Perhaps the scenes of travel conjure themselves up before me and pass and repass in my imagination all the more vividly, because I lead such a vegetable existence that a call to travel would fall upon me like a thunder-bolt. In the presence of this Cabuliwallah I was immediately transported to the foot of arid mountain peaks, with narrow little defiles twisting in and out amongst their towering heights. I could see the string of camels bearing the merchandise, and the company of turbanned merchants carrying some their queer old firearms, and some their spears, journeying downward towards the plains. I could see—. But at some such point Mini's mother would intervene, imploring me to 'beware of that man.'

Mini's mother is unfortunately a very timid lady. Whenever she hears a noise in the street, or sees people coming towards the house, she always jumps to the conclusion that they are either thieves, or drunkards, or snakes, or tigers, or malaria, or cockroaches, or caterpillars. Even after all these years of experience, she is not able to overcome her terror. So she was full of doubts about the Cabuliwallah, and used to beg me to keep a watchful eye on him.

I tried to laugh her fear gently away, but then she would turn round on me seriously, and ask me solemn questions:—

Were children never kidnapped?

Was it, then, not true that there was slavery in Cabul?

Was it so very absurd that this big man should be able to carry off a tiny child?

I urged that, though not impossible, it was highly improbable. But this was not enough, and her dread persisted. As it was indefinite, however, it did not seem right to forbid the man the house, and the intimacy went on unchecked.

Once a year in the middle of January Rahmun, the Cabuliwallah, was in the habit of returning to his country, and as the time approached he would be very busy, going from house to house collecting his debts. This year, however, he could always find time to come and see Mini. It would have seemed to an outsider that there was some conspiracy between the two, for when he could not come in the morning, he would appear in the evening.

Even to me it was a little startling now and then, in the corner of a dark room, suddenly to surprise this tall, loose-garmented, much bebagged man; but when Mini would run in smiling, with her 'O Cabuliwallah! Cabuliwallah!' and the two friends, so far apart in age, would subside into their old laughter and their old jokes, I felt reassured.

One morning, a few days before he had made up his mind to go, I was correcting my proof sheets in my study. It was chilly weather. Through the window the rays of the sun touched my feet, and the slight warmth was very welcome. It was almost eight o'clock, and the early pedestrians were returning home with their heads covered. All at once I heard an uproar in the street, and, looking out, saw Rahmun being led away bound between two policemen, and behind them a crowd of curious boys. There were blood-stains on the clothes of the Cabuliwallah, and one of the policemen carried a knife. Hurrying out, I stopped them, and inquired what it all meant. Partly from one, partly from another, I gathered that a certain neighbour had owed the pedlar something for a Rampuri shawl, but had falsely denied having bought it, and that in the course of the quarrel Rahmun had struck him. Now, in the heat of his excitement, the prisoner began calling his enemy all sorts of names, when suddenly in a verandah of my house appeared my little Mini, with her usual exclamation: 'O Cabuliwallah! Cabuliwallah!' Rahmun's face lighted up as he turned to her. He had no bag under his arm to-day, so she could not discuss the elephant with him. She at once therefore proceeded to the next question: 'Are you going to the father-in-law's house?' Rahmun laughed and said: 'Just where I am going, little one!' Then, seeing that the reply did not amuse the child, he held up his fettered hands. 'Ah!' he said, 'I would have thrashed that old father-in-law, but my hands are bound!'

On a charge of murderous assault, Rahmun was sentenced to some years' imprisonment.

Time passed away and he was not remembered. The accustomed work in the accustomed place was ours, and the thought of the once free mountaineer spending his years in prison seldom or never occurred to us. Even my light-hearted Mini, I am ashamed to say, forgot her old friend. New companions filled her life. As she grew older, she spent more of her time with girls. So much time indeed did she spend with them that she came no more, as she used to do, to her father's room. I was scarcely on speaking terms with her.

Years had passed away. It was once more autumn and we

had made arrangements for our Mini's marriage. It was to take place during the Puja Holidays. With Durga returning to Kailas, the light of our home also was to depart to her husband's house, and leave her father's in the shadow.

The morning was bright. After the rains, there was a sense of ablution in the air, and the sun-rays looked like pure gold. So bright were they, that they gave a beautiful radiance even to the sordid brick walls of our Calcutta lanes. Since early dawn that day the wedding-pipes had been sounding, and at each beat my own heart throbbed. The wail of the tune, Bhairavi, seemed to intensify my pain at the approaching separation. My Mini was to be married that night.

From early morning noise and bustle had pervaded the house. In the courtyard the canopy had to be slung on its bamboo poles; the chandeliers with their tinkling sound must be hung in each room and verandah. There was no end of hurry and excitement. I was sitting in my study, looking through the accounts, when some one entered, saluting respectfully, and stood before me. It was Rahmun the Cabuliwallah. At first I did not recognise him. He had no bag, nor the long hair, nor the same vigour that he used to have. But he smiled, and I knew him again.

'When did you come, Rahmun?' I asked him.

'Last evening,' he said, 'I was released from jail.'

The words struck harsh upon my ears. I had never before talked with one who had wounded his fellow, and my heart shrank within itself when I realised this; for I felt that the day would have been better-omened had he not turned up.

'There are ceremonies going on,' I said, 'and I am busy. Could you perhaps come another day?'

At once he turned to go; but as he reached the door he hesitated, and said: 'May I not see the little one, sir, for a moment?' It was his belief that Mini was still the same. He had pictured her running to him as she used, calling 'O Cabuliwallah!

Cabuliwallah!' He had imagined too that they would laugh and talk together, just as of old. In fact, in memory of former days he had brought, carefully wrapped up in paper, a few almonds and raisins and grapes, obtained somehow from a countryman; for his own little fund was dispersed.

I said again: 'There is a ceremony in the house, and you will not be able to see any one to-day.'

The man's face fell. He looked wistfully at me for a moment, then said 'Good morning,' and went out.

I felt a little sorry, and would have called him back, but I found he was returning of his own accord. He came close up to me holding out his offerings with the words: 'I brought these few things, sir, for the little one. Will you give them to her?'

I took them and was going to pay him, but he caught my hand and said: 'You are very kind, sir! Keep me in your recollection. Do not offer me money!—You have a little girl: I too have one like her in my own home. I think of her, and bring fruits to your child—not to make a profit for myself.'

Saying this, he put his hand inside his big loose robe, and brought out a small and dirty piece of paper. With great care he unfolded this, and smoothed it out with both hands on my table. It bore the impression of a little hand. Not a photograph. Not a drawing. The impression of an ink-smeared hand laid flat on the paper. This touch of his own little daughter had been always on his heart, as he had come year after year to Calcutta to sell his wares in the streets.

Tears came to my eyes. I forgot that he was a poor Cabuli fruit-seller, while I was——. But no, what was I more than he? He also was a father.

That impression of the hand of his little *Pārbati* in her distant mountain home reminded me of my own little Mini.

I sent for Mini immediately from the inner apartment. Many difficulties were raised, but I would not listen. Clad in the red silk of her wedding-day, with the sandal paste on her forehead, and adorned as a young bride, Mini came, and stood bashfully before me.

The Cabuliwallah looked a little staggered at the apparition. He could not revive their old friendship. At last he smiled and said: 'Little one, are you going to your father-in-law's house?'

But Mini now understood the meaning of the word 'father-in-law,' and she could not reply to him as of old. She flushed up at the question, and stood before him with her bride-like face turned down.

I remembered the day when the Cabuliwallah and my Mini had first met, and I felt sad. When she had gone, Rahmun heaved a deep sigh, and sat down on the floor. The idea had suddenly come to him that his daughter too must have grown in this long time, and that he would have to make friends with her anew. Assuredly he would not find her as he used to know her. And besides, what might not have happened to her in these eight years?

The marriage-pipes sounded, and the mild autumn sun streamed round us. But Rahmun sat in the little Calcutta lane, and saw before him the barren mountains of Afghanistan.

I took out a bank-note and gave it to him, saying: 'Go back to your own daughter, Rahmun, in your own country, and may the happiness of your meeting bring good fortune to my child!'

Having made this present, I had to curtail some of the festivities. I could not have the electric lights I had intended, nor the military band, and the ladies of the house were despondent at it. But to me the wedding-feast was all the brighter for the thought that in a distant land a long-lost father met again with his only child.

OF A MIRROR AND A BELL

Lafcadio Hearn

Eight centuries ago, the priests of Mugenyama, in the province of Tōtōmi, wanted a big bell for their temple; and they asked the women of their parish to help them by contributing old bronze mirrors for bell-metal.

[Even to-day, in the courts of certain Japanese temples, you may see heaps of old bronze mirrors contributed for such a purpose. The largest collection of this kind that I ever saw was in the court of a temple of the Jōdo sect, at Hakata, in Kyūshū: the mirrors had been given for the making of a bronze statue of Amida, thirty-three feet high.]

There was at that time a young woman, a farmer's wife, living at Mugenyama, who presented her mirror to the temple, to be used for bell-metal. But afterwards she much regretted her mirror. She remembered things that her mother had told her about it; and she remembered that it had belonged, not only to her mother but to her mother's mother and grandmother; and she remembered some happy smiles which it had reflected. Of course, if she could have offered the priests a certain sum of money in place of the mirror, she could have asked them to give back her heirloom. But she had not the money necessary. Whenever she went to the temple, she saw her mirror lying in the court-yard, behind a railing, among hundreds of other mirrors heaped there together. She knew it by the *Shō-Chiku-Bai* in relief on the back of it,— those three fortunate emblems of Pine, Bamboo, and Plumflower, which delighted her baby-eyes when her mother first showed her the mirror. She longed for some chance to steal the mirror, and hide it,—that she might thereafter treasure it always. But the chance did not come; and she became very unhappy,—felt as if she had foolishly given away a part of her life. She thought about the old saying that a mirror is the Soul of a Woman—(a saying mystically expressed, by the Chinese character for Soul, upon the backs of many bronze mirrors),—and she feared that it was true in weirder ways than she had before imagined. But she could not dare to speak of her pain to anybody.

Now, when all the mirrors contributed for the Mugenyama bell had been sent to the foundry, the bell-founders discovered that there was one mirror among them which would not melt. Again and again they tried to melt it; but it resisted all their efforts. Evidently the woman who had given that mirror to the temple must have regretted the giving. She had not presented her offering with all her heart; and therefore her selfish soul, remaining attached to the mirror, kept it hard and cold in the midst of the furnace.

Of course everybody heard of the matter, and everybody soon knew whose mirror it was that would not melt. And because of this public exposure of her secret fault, the poor woman became very much ashamed and very angry. And as she could not bear the shame, she drowned herself, after having written a farewell letter containing these words:—

> 'When I am dead, it will not be difficult to melt the mirror
> and to cast the bell. But, to the person who breaks that bell
> by ringing it, great wealth will be given by the ghost of me.'

—You must know that the last wish or promise of anybody who dies in anger, or performs suicide in anger, is generally supposed to possess a supernatural force. After the dead woman's mirror had been melted, and the bell had been successfully cast, people remembered the words of that letter. They felt sure that the spirit of the writer would give wealth to the breaker of the bell; and, as soon as the bell had been suspended in the court of the temple, they went in multitude to ring it. With all their might and main they swung the ringing-beam; but the bell proved to be a good bell, and it bravely withstood their assaults. Nevertheless, the people were not easily discouraged. Day after day, at all hours, they continued to ring the bell furiously,—caring nothing whatever for the protests of the priests. So the ringing became an affliction; and the priests could not endure it; and they got rid of the bell by rolling it down the hill into a swamp. The swamp was deep, and swallowed it up,—and that was the end of the bell. Only its legend remains; and in that legend it is called the *Mugen-Kané*, or Bell of Mugen.

◆

Now there are queer old Japanese beliefs in the magical efficacy of a certain mental operation implied, though not described, by the verb *nazoraëru*. The word itself cannot be adequately rendered by any English word; for it is used in relation to many kinds of mimetic magic, as well as in relation to the performance of many religious acts of faith. Common meanings of *nazoraëru*, according to dictionaries, are 'to imitate,' 'to compare,' 'to liken;' but the esoteric meaning is *to substitute, in imagination, one object or action for another, so as to bring about some magical or miraculous result.*

For example:—you cannot afford to build a Buddhist temple; but you can easily lay a pebble before the image of the Buddha, with the same pious feeling that would prompt you to build a temple if you were rich enough to build one. The merit of so offering the pebble becomes equal, or almost equal, to the merit of erecting a temple... You cannot read the six thousand seven hundred and seventy-one volumes of the Buddhist texts; but you can make a revolving library, containing them, turn round, by pushing it like a windlass. And if you push with an earnest wish that you could read the six thousand seven hundred and seventy-one volumes, you will acquire the same merit as the reading of them would enable you to gain... So much will perhaps suffice to explain the religious meanings of *nazoraëru*.

The magical meanings could not all be explained without a great variety of examples; but, for present purposes, the following will serve. If you should make a little man of straw, for the same reason that Sister Helen made a little man of wax,—and nail it, with nails not less than five inches long, to some tree in a temple-grove at the Hour of the Ox,—and if the person, imaginatively represented by that little straw man, should die thereafter in atrocious agony,—that would illustrate one signification of *nazoraëru*... Or, let us suppose that a robber has entered your house during the night, and carried away your valuables. If you can discover the footprints of that robber in your garden, and then promptly burn a very large moxa on each of them, the soles of the feet of the robber will become inflamed, and will allow him no rest until he returns, of his own accord, to put himself at your mercy. That is another kind of mimetic magic expressed by the term *nazoraëru*. And a third kind is illustrated by various legends of the Mugen-Kané.

After the bell had been rolled into the swamp, there was, of course, no more chance of ringing it in such wise as to break it. But persons who regretted this loss of opportunity would strike and break objects imaginatively substituted for the bell,—thus hoping to please the spirit of the owner of the mirror that had made so much trouble. One of these persons was a woman called Umégaë,—famed in Japanese legend because of her relation to Kajiwara Kagesue, a warrior of the Heiké clan. While the pair were travelling together, Kajiwara one day found himself in great straits for want of money; and Umégaë, remembering the tradition of the Bell of Mugen, took a basin of bronze, and, mentally representing it to be the bell, beat upon it until she broke it,—crying out, at the same time, for three hundred pieces of gold. A guest of the inn where the pair were stopping made inquiry as to the cause of the banging and the crying, and, on learning the story of the trouble, actually presented Umégaë with three hundred *ryō* in gold. Afterwards a song was made about Umégaë's basin of bronze; and that song is sung by dancing girls even to this day:—

Umégaë no chōzubachi tataïté
O-kané ga déru naraba
Mina San mi-uké wo
Sōré tanomimasu

['*If, by striking upon the wash-basin of Umégaë, I could make honourable money come to me, then would I negotiate for the freedom of all my girl-comrades.*']

After this happening, the fame of the Mugen-Kané became great; and many people followed the example of Umégaë,—thereby hoping to emulate her luck. Among these folk was a dissolute farmer who lived near Mugenyama, on the bank of the Ōïgawa. Having wasted his substance in riotous living, this farmer made for himself, out of the mud in his garden, a clay-model of the Mugen-Kané; and he beat the clay-bell, and broke it,—crying out the while for great wealth.

Then, out of the ground before him, rose up the figure of a white-robed woman, with long loose-flowing hair, holding a covered jar. And the woman said: 'I have come to answer your fervent prayer as it deserves to be answered. Take, therefore, this jar.' So saying, she put the jar into his hands, and disappeared.

Into his house the happy man rushed, to tell his wife the good news. He set down in front of her the covered jar,—which was heavy,—and they opened it together. And they found that it was filled, up to the very brim, with...

But no!—I really cannot tell you with what it was filled.

BLACKOUT

Roger Mais

The city was in partial blackout; the street lights had not been turned on, because of the wartime policy of conserving electricity; and the houses behind their discreet *aurelia* hedges were wrapped in an atmosphere of exclusive respectability.

The young woman waiting at the bus stop was not in the least nervous, in spite of the wave of panic that had been sweeping the city about bands of hooligans roaming the streets after dark and assaulting unprotected women. She was a sensible young woman to begin with, who realized that one good scream would be sufficient to bring a score of respectable suburban householders running to her assistance. On the other hand she was an American, and fully conscious of the tradition of American young women that they don't scare easily.

Even that slinking black shadow that seemed to be materializing out of the darkness at the other side of the street did not disconcert her. She was only slightly curious now that she observed that the shadow was approaching her, slowly.

It was a young man dressed in conventional shirt and pants, and wearing a pair of canvas shoes. That was what lent the suggestion of slinking to his movements, because he went along noiselessly—that, and the mere suggestion of a stoop. He was very tall. There was a curious look of hunger and unrest about his eyes. But the thing that struck her immediately was the fact that he was black; the other particulars scarcely made any impression at all in comparison. In her country not every night a white woman could be nonchalantly approached by a black man. There was enough novelty in all this to intrigue her. She seemed to remember that any sort of adventure might be experienced in one of these tropical islands of the West Indies.

'Could you give me a light, lady?' the man said.

It is true she was smoking, but she had only just lit this one from the stub of the cigarette she had thrown away. The fact was she had no matches. Would he believe her, she wondered? 'I am sorry. I haven't got a match.'

The young man looked into her face, seemed to hesitate an instant and said, his brow slightly wrinkled in perplexity: 'But you are smoking.'

There was no argument against that. Still, she was not particular about giving him a light from the cigarette she was smoking. It may be stupid, but there was a suggestion of intimacy about such an act, simple as it was, that, call it what you may, she could not accept just like that.

There was a moment's hesitation on her part now, during which time the man's steady gaze never left her face. There was pride and challenge in his look, curiously mingled with quiet amusement. She held out her cigarette toward him between two fingers.

'Here,' she said, 'you can light from that.'

In the act of bending his head to accept the proffered light, he came quite close to her. He did not seem to understand that she meant him to take the lighted cigarette from her hand. He just bent over her hand to light his.

Presently he straightened up, inhaled a deep lungful of soothing smoke and exhaled again with satisfaction. She saw then that he was smoking the half of a cigarette, which had been clinched and saved for future consumption.

'Thank you,' said the man, politely; and was in the act of moving off when he noticed that instead of returning her cigarette to her lips she had casually, unthinkingly flicked it away. He observed this in the split part of a second that it took him to say those two words. It was almost a whole cigarette she had thrown away. She had been smoking it with evident enjoyment a moment before.

He stood there looking at her, with cold speculation.

In a way it unnerved her. Not that she was frightened. He seemed quite decent in his own way, and harmless; but he made her feel uncomfortable. If he had said something rude she would have preferred it. It would have been no more than she would have expected of him. But instead, this quiet contemptuous look. Yes, that was it. The thing began to take on definition in her mind. How dare he; the insolence!

'Well, what are you waiting for?' she said, because she felt she had to break the tension somehow.

'I am sorry I made you waste a whole cigarette,' he said.

She laughed a little nervously. 'It's nothing,' she said, feeling a fool.

'There's plenty more where that came from, eh?' he asked.

'I suppose so.'

This won't do, she thought, quickly. She had no intention of standing at a street corner jawing with—well, with a black man. There was something indecent about it. Why doesn't he move on? As though he had read her thoughts he said:

'This is the street, lady. It's public.'

Well, anyway, she didn't have to answer him. She could snub him quietly, the way she should have properly done from the start.

'It's a good thing you're a woman,' he said.

'And if I were a man?'

'As man to man maybe I'd give you something to think about,' he said, still in that quiet, even voice.

In America they lynch them for less than this, she thought.

'This isn't America,' he said. 'I can see you are an American.

In this country there are only men and women. You'll learn about it.' She could only humour him. Find out what his ideas were about this question, anyway. It would be something to talk about back home. Suddenly she was intrigued.

'So in this country there are only men and women, eh?'

'That's right. So to speak there is only you an' me, only there are hundreds and thousands of us. We seem to get along somehow without lynchings and burnings and all that.'

'Do you really think that all men are created equal?'

'It don't seem to me there is any sense in that. The facts show it ain't so. Look at you an' me, for instance. But that isn't to say you're not a woman, the same way as I am a man. You see what I mean?'

'I can't say I do.'

'You will though, if you stop here long enough.'

She threw a quick glance in his direction.

The man laughed.

'I don't mean what you're thinking,' he said. 'You're not my type of woman. You don't have anything to fear under that heading.'

'Oh!'

'You're waiting for the bus, I take it. Well, that's it coming now. Thanks for the light.'

'Don't mention it,' she said, with a nervous sort of giggle.

He made no attempt to move along as the bus came up. He stood there quietly aloof, as though in the consciousness of a male strength and pride that was justly his. There was something about him that was at once challenging and disturbing. He had shaken her supreme confidence in some important sense.

As the bus moved off she was conscious of his eyes' quiet scrutiny, without the interruption of artificial barriers, in the sense of dispassionate appraisement, as between man and woman, any man, any woman.

She fought resolutely against the very natural desire to turn her head and take a last look at him. Perhaps she was thinking about what the people on the bus might think. And perhaps it was just as well that she did not see him bend forward with that swift hungry movement, retrieving from the gutter the half-smoked cigarette she had thrown away.

THE RETURN OF YEN-TCHIN-KING

Lafcadio Hearn

Before me ran, as a herald runneth, the Leader of the Moon;
And the Spirit of the Wind followed after me,—quickening
his flight.

—Li-Sao

In the thirty-eighth chapter of the holy book, *Kan-ing-p'ien*, wherein the Recompense of Immortality is considered, may be found the legend of Yen-Tchin-King. A thousand years have passed since the passing of the good Tchin-King; for it was in the period of the greatness of Thang that he lived and died.

Now, in those days when Yen-Tchin-King was Supreme Judge of one of the Six August Tribunals, one Li-hi-lié, a soldier mighty for evil, lifted the black banner of revolt, and drew after him, as a tide of destruction, the millions of the northern provinces. And learning of these things, and knowing also that Hi-lié was the most ferocious of men, who respected nothing on earth save fearlessness, the Son of Heaven commanded Tchin-King that he should visit Hi-lié and strive to recall the rebel to duty, and read unto the people who followed after him in revolt the Emperor's letter of reproof and warning. For Tchin-King was famed throughout the provinces for his wisdom, his rectitude, and his fearlessness; and the Son of Heaven believed that if Hi-lié would listen to the words of any living man steadfast in loyalty and virtue, he would listen to the words of Tchin-King. So Tchin-King arrayed himself in his robes of office, and set his house in order; and, having embraced his wife and his children, mounted his horse and rode away alone to the roaring camp of the rebels, bearing the Emperor's letter in his bosom. 'I shall return; fear not!' were his last words to the grey servant who watched him from the terrace as he rode.

◆

And Tchin-King at last descended from his horse, and entered into the rebel camp, and, passing through that huge gathering of war, stood in the presence of Hi-lié. High sat the rebel among his chiefs, encircled by the wave-lightning of swords and the thunders of ten thousand gongs: above him undulated the silken folds of the Black Dragon, while a vast fire rose bickering before him. Also Tchin-King saw that the tongues of that fire were licking human bones, and that skulls of men lay blackening among the ashes. Yet he was not afraid to look upon the fire, nor into the eyes of Hi-lié; but drawing from his bosom the roll of perfumed yellow silk upon which the words of the Emperor were written, and kissing it, he made ready to read, while the multitude became silent. Then, in a strong, clear voice he began:—

'*The words of the Celestial and August, the Son of Heaven, the Divine Ko-Tsu-Tchin-Yao-ti, unto the rebel Li-Hi-lié and those that follow him.*'

And a roar went up like the roar of the sea,—a roar of rage, and the hideous battle-moan, like the moan of a forest in storm,—'Hoo! hoo-oo-oo-oo!'—and the sword-lightnings brake loose, and the thunder of the gongs moved the ground beneath the messenger's feet. But Hi-lié waved his gilded wand, and again there was silence. 'Nay!' spake the rebel chief; 'let the dog bark!' So Tchin-King spake on:—

'*Knowest thou not, O most rash and foolish of men, that thou leadest the people only into the mouth of the Dragon of Destruction? Knowest thou not, also, that the people of my kingdom are the first-born of the Master of Heaven? So it hath been written that he who doth needlessly subject the people to wounds and death shall not be suffered by Heaven to live! Thou who wouldst subvert those laws founded by the wise,—those laws in obedience to which may happiness and prosperity alone be found,—thou art committing the greatest of all crimes,—the crime that is never forgiven!*

'*O my people, think not that I your Emperor, I your Father, seek your destruction. I desire only your happiness, your prosperity, your greatness; let not your folly provoke the severity of your Celestial Parent. Follow not after madness and blind rage; hearken rather to the wise words of my messenger.*'

'*Hoo! hoo-oo-oo-oo-oo!*' roared the people, gathering fury. '*Hoo! hoo-oo-oo-oo!*'—till the mountains rolled back the cry like the rolling of a typhoon; and once more the pealing of the gongs paralyzed voice and hearing. Then Tchin-King, looking at Hi-lié, saw that he laughed, and that the words of the letter would not again be listened to. Therefore he read on to the end without looking about him, resolved to perform his mission in so far as lay in his power. And having read all, he would have given the letter to Hi-lié; but Hi-lié would not extend his hand to take it. Therefore Tchin-King replaced it in his bosom, and folding his arms, looked Hi-lié calmly in the face, and waited. Again Hi-lié waved his gilded wand; and the roaring ceased, and the booming of the gongs, until nothing save the fluttering of the Dragon-banner could be heard. Then spake Hi-lié, with an evil smile,—

'Tchin-King, O son of a dog! if thou dost not now take the oath of fealty, and bow thyself before me, and salute me with the salutation of Emperors,—even with the *luh-kao*, the triple prostration,—into that fire thou shalt be thrown.'

But Tchin-King, turning his back upon the usurper, bowed himself a moment in worship to Heaven and Earth; and then rising suddenly, ere any man could lay hand upon him, he leaped into the towering flame, and stood there, with folded arms, like a God.

Then Hi-lié leaped to his feet in amazement, and shouted to his men; and they snatched Tchin-King from the fire, and wrung the flames from his robes with their naked hands, and extolled him, and praised him to his face. And even Hi-lié himself descended from his seat, and spoke fair words to him, saying: 'O Tchin-King, I see thou art indeed a brave man and true, and worthy of all honour; be seated among us, I pray thee, and partake of whatever it is in our power to bestow!'

But Tchin-King, looking upon him unswervingly, replied in a voice clear as the voice of a great bell,—

'Never, O Hi-lié, shall I accept aught from thy hand, save death, so long as thou shalt continue in the path of wrath and folly. And never shall it be said that Tchin-King sat him down among rebels and traitors, among murderers and robbers.'

Then Hi-lié in sudden fury, smote him with his sword; and Tchin-King fell to the earth and died, striving even in his death to bow his head toward the South,—toward the place of the Emperor's palace,—toward the presence of his beloved Master.

◆

Even at the same hour the Son of Heaven, alone in the inner chamber of his palace, became aware of a Shape prostrate before his feet; and when he spake, the Shape arose and stood before him, and he saw that it was Tchin-King. And the Emperor would have questioned him; yet ere he could question, the familiar voice spake, saying:

'Son of Heaven, the mission confided to me I have performed; and thy command hath been accomplished to the extent of thy humble servant's feeble power. But even now must I depart, that I may enter the service of another Master.'

And looking, the Emperor perceived that the Golden Tigers

upon the wall were visible through the form of Tchin-King; and a strange coldness, like a winter wind, passed through the chamber; and the figure faded out. Then the Emperor knew that the Master of whom his faithful servant had spoken was none other than the Master of Heaven.

Also at the same hour the grey servant of Tchin-King's house beheld him passing through the apartments, smiling as he was wont to smile when he saw that all things were as he desired. 'Is it well with thee, my lord?' questioned the aged man. And a voice answered him: 'It is well'; but the presence of Tchin-King had passed away before the answer came.

◆

So the armies of the Son of Heaven strove with the rebels. But the land was soaked with blood and blackened with fire; and the corpses of whole populations were carried by the rivers to feed the fishes of the sea; and still the war prevailed through many a long red year. Then came to aid the Son of Heaven the hordes that dwell in the desolations of the West and North,—horsemen born, a nation of wild archers, each mighty to bend a two-hundred-pound bow until the ears should meet. And as a whirlwind they came against rebellion, raining raven-feathered arrows in a storm of death; and they prevailed against Hi-lié and his people. Then those that survived destruction and defeat submitted, and promised allegiance; and once more was the law of righteousness restored. But Tchin-King had been dead for many summers.

And the Son of Heaven sent word to his victorious generals that they should bring back with them the bones of his faithful servant, to be laid with honour in a mausoleum erected by imperial decree. So the generals of the Celestial and August sought after the nameless grave and found it, and had the earth taken up, and made ready to remove the coffin.

But the coffin crumbled into dust before their eyes; for the worms had gnawed it, and the hungry earth had devoured its substance, leaving only a phantom shell that vanished at touch of the light. And lo! as it vanished, all beheld lying there the perfect form and features of the good Tchin-King. Corruption had not touched him, nor had the worms disturbed his rest, nor had the bloom of life departed from his face. And he seemed to dream only,—comely to see as upon the morning of his bridal, and smiling as the holy images smile, with eyelids closed, in the twilight of the great pagodas.

Then spoke a priest, standing by the grave: 'O my children, this is indeed a Sign from the Master of Heaven; in such wise do the Powers Celestial preserve them that are chosen to be numbered with the Immortals. Death may not prevail over them, neither may corruption come nigh them. Verily the blessed Tchin-King hath taken his place among the divinities of Heaven!'

Then they bore Tchin-King back to his native place, and laid him with highest honours in the mausoleum which the Emperor had commanded; and there he sleeps, incorruptible forever, arrayed in his robes of state. Upon his tomb are sculptured the emblems of his greatness and his wisdom and his virtue, and the signs of his office, and the Four Precious Things: and the monsters which are holy symbols mount giant guard in stone about it; and the weird Dogs of Fo keep watch before it, as before the temples of the gods.

VANKA

Anton Chekhov

Nine-year-old Vanka Zhukov, who had been apprentice to the shoemaker Aliakhin for three months, did not go to bed the night before Christmas. He waited till the master and mistress and the assistants had gone out to an early church-service, to procure from his employer's cupboard a small phial of ink and a penholder with a rusty nib; then, spreading a crumpled sheet of paper in front of him, he began to write.

Before, however, deciding to make the first letter, he looked furtively at the door and at the window, glanced several times at the sombre ikon, on either side of which stretched shelves full of lasts, and heaved a heartrending sigh. The sheet of paper was spread on a bench, and he himself was on his knees in front of it.

'Dear Grandfather Konstantin Makarych,' he wrote, 'I am writing you a letter. I wish you a Happy Christmas and all God's holy best. I have no mamma or papa, you are all I have.'

Vanka gave a look towards the window in which shone the reflection of his candle, and vividly pictured to himself his grandfather, Konstantin Makarych, who was night-watchman at Messrs. Zhivarev. He was a small, lean, unusually lively and active old man of sixty-five, always smiling and blear-eyed. All day he slept in the servants' kitchen or trifled with the cooks. At night, enveloped in an ample sheep-skin coat, he strayed round the domain tapping with his cudgel. Behind him, each hanging its head, walked the old bitch Kashtanka, and the dog Viun, so named because of his black coat and long body and his resemblance to a loach. Viun was an unusually civil and friendly dog, looking as kindly at a stranger as at his masters, but he was not to be trusted. Beneath his deference and humbleness was hid the most inquisitorial maliciousness. No one knew better than he how to sneak up and take a bite at a leg, or slip into the larder or steal a *muzhik*'s chicken. More than once they had nearly broken his hind-legs, twice he had been hung up, every week he was nearly flogged to death, but he always recovered.

At this moment, for certain, Vanka's grandfather must be standing at the gate, blinking his eyes at the bright red windows of the village church, stamping his feet in their high-felt boots, and jesting with the people in the yard; his cudgel will be hanging from his belt, he will be hugging himself with cold, giving a little dry, old man's cough, and at times pinching a servant-girl or a cook.

'Won't we take some snuff?' he asks, holding out his snuff-box to the women. The women take a pinch of snuff, and sneeze.

The old man goes into indescribable ecstasies, breaks into loud laughter, and cries:

'Off with it, it will freeze to your nose!'

He gives his snuff to the dogs, too. Kashtanka sneezes, twitches her nose, and walks away offended. Viun deferentially refuses to sniff and wags his tail. It is glorious weather, not a breath of wind, clear, and frosty; it is a dark eight, but the whole village, its white roofs and streaks of smoke from the chimneys, the trees silvered with hoar-frost, and the snowdrifts, you can see it all. The sky scintillates with bright twinkling stars, and the Milky Way stands out so clearly that it looks as if it had been polished and rubbed over with snow for the holidays...

Vanka sighs, dips his pen in the ink, and continues to write:

'Last night I got a thrashing, my master dragged me by my hair into the yard, and belaboured me with a shoe-maker's stirrup, because, while I was rocking his brat in its cradle, I unfortunately fell asleep. And during the week, my mistress told me to clean a herring, and I began by its tail, so she took the herring and stuck its snout into my face. The assistants tease me, send me to the tavern for vodka, make me steal the master's cucumbers, and the master beats me with whatever is handy. Food there is none; in the morning it's bread, at dinner gruel, and in the evening bread again. As for tea or sour-cabbage soup, the master and the mistress themselves guzzle that. They make me sleep in the vestibule, and when their brat cries, I don't sleep at all, but have to rock the cradle. Dear Grandpapa, for Heaven's sake, take me away from here, home to our village, I can't bear this any more... I bow to the ground to you, and will pray to God for ever and ever, take me from here or I shall die...'

The corners of Vanka's mouth went down, he rubbed his eyes with his dirty fist, and sobbed.

'I'll grate your tobacco for you,' he continued, 'I'll pray to God for you, and if there is anything wrong, then flog me like the grey goat. And if you really think I shan't find work, then I'll ask the manager, for Christ's sake, to let me clean the boots, or I'll go instead of Fedya as underherdsman. Dear Grandpapa, I can't bear this any more, it'll kill me... I wanted to run away to our village, but I have no boots, and I was afraid of the frost, and when I grow up I'll look after you, no one shall harm you, and when you die I'll pray for the repose of your soul, just like I do for mamma Pelagueya.

'As for Moscow, it is a large town, there are all gentlemen's houses, lots of horses, no sheep, and the dogs are not vicious. The children don't come round at Christmas with a star, no one is allowed to sing in the choir, and once I saw in a shop window hooks on a line and fishing rods, all for sale, and for every kind of fish, awfully convenient. And there was one hook which would catch a sheat-fish weighing a pound. And there are shops with guns, like the master's, and I am sure they must cost 100 rubles each. And in the meat-shops there are woodcocks, partridges, and hares, but who shot them or where they come from, the shopman won't say.

'Dear Grandpapa, and when the masters give a Christmas tree, take a golden walnut and hide it in my green box. Ask the young lady, Olga Ignatyevna, for it, say it's for Vanka.'

Vanka sighed convulsively, and again stared at the window. He remembered that his grandfather always went to the forest for the Christmas tree, and took his grandson with him. What happy times! The frost crackled, his grandfather crackled, and as they both did, Vanka did the same. Then before cutting down the Christmas tree his grandfather smoked his pipe, took a long pinch of snuff, and made fun of poor frozen little Vanka... The young fir trees, wrapt in hoar-frost, stood motionless, waiting for which of them would die. Suddenly a hare springing from somewhere would dart over the snowdrift... His grandfather could not help shouting:

'Catch it, catch it, catch it! Ah, short-tailed devil!'

When the tree was down, his grandfather dragged it to the master's house, and there they set about decorating it. The young lady, Olga Ignatyevna, Vanka's great friend, busied herself most about it. When little Vanka's mother, Pelagueya, was still alive, and was servant-woman in the house, Olga Ignatyevna used to stuff him with sugar-candy, and, having nothing to do, taught him to read, write, count up to one hundred, and even to dance the quadrille. When Pelagueya died, they placed the orphan Vanka in the kitchen with his grandfather, and from the kitchen he was sent to Moscow to Aliakhin, the shoemaker.

'Come quick, dear Grandpapa,' continued Vanka, 'I beseech you for Christ's sake take me from here. Have pity on a poor orphan, for here they beat me, and I am frightfully hungry, and so sad that I can't tell you, I cry all the time. The other day the master hit me on the head with a last; I fell to the ground, and only just returned to life. My life is a misfortune, worse than any dog's... I send greetings to Aliona, to one-eyed Tegor, and the coachman, and don't let any one have my mouth-organ. I remain, your grandson, Ivan Zhukov, dear Grandpapa, do come.'

Vanka folded his sheet of paper in four, and put it into an envelope purchased the night before for a kopek. He thought a little, dipped the pen into the ink, and wrote the address:

'The village, to my grandfather.' He then scratched his head, thought again, and added: 'Konstantin Makarych.' Pleased at not having been interfered with in his writing, he put on his cap, and, without putting on his sheep-skin coat, ran out in his shirt-sleeves into the street.

The shopman at the poulterer's, from whom he had inquired the night before, had told him that letters were to be put into post-boxes, and from there they were conveyed over the whole earth in mail troikas by drunken post-boys and to the sound of bells. Vanka ran to the first post-box and slipped his precious letter into the slit.

An hour afterwards, lulled by hope, he was sleeping soundly. In his dreams he saw a stove, by the stove his grandfather sitting with his legs dangling down, barefooted, and reading a letter to the cooks, and Viun walking round the stove wagging his tail.

HOW A MUZHIK FED TWO OFFICIALS

M. Y. *Saltykov-Shchedrin*

Once upon a time there were two officials. They were both empty-headed, and so they found themselves one day suddenly transported to an uninhabited isle, as if on a magic carpet.

They had passed their whole life in a Government Department, where records were kept; had been born there, bred there, grown old there, and consequently hadn't the least understanding for anything outside of the Department; and the only words they knew were: 'With assurances of the highest esteem, I am your humble servant.'

But the Department was abolished, and as the services of the two officials were no longer needed, they were given their freedom. So the retired officials migrated to Podyacheskaya Street in St Petersburg. Each had his own home, his own cook and his pension.

Waking up on the uninhabited isle, they found themselves lying under the same cover. At first, of course, they couldn't understand what had happened to them, and they spoke as if nothing extraordinary had taken place.

'What a peculiar dream I had last night, Your Excellency,' said the one official. 'It seemed to me as if I were on an uninhabited isle.'

Scarcely had he uttered the words, when he jumped to his feet. The other official also jumped up.

'Good Lord, what does this mean! Where are we?' they cried out in astonishment.

They felt each other to make sure that they were no longer

dreaming, and finally convinced themselves of the sad reality.

Before them stretched the ocean, and behind them was a little spot of earth, beyond which the ocean stretched again. They began to cry—the first time since their Department had been shut down.

They looked at each other, and each noticed that the other was clad in nothing but his night shirt with his order hanging about his neck.

'We really should be having our coffee now,' observed the one official. Then he bethought himself again of the strange situation he was in and a second time fell to weeping.

'What are we going to do now?' he sobbed. 'Even supposing we were to draw up a report, what good would that do?'

'You know what, your Excellency,' replied the other official, 'you go to the east and I will go to the west. Toward evening we will come back here again and, perhaps, we shall have found something.'

They started to ascertain which was the east and which was the west. They recalled that the head of their Department had once said to them, 'If you want to know where the east is, then turn your face to the north, and the east will be on your right.' But when they tried to find out which was the north, they turned to the right and to the left and looked around on all sides. Having spent their whole life in the Department of Records, their efforts were all in vain.

'To my mind, your Excellency, the best thing to do would be for you to go to the right and me to go to the left,' said one official, who had served not only in the Department of Records, but had also been teacher of handwriting in the School for Reserves, and so was a little bit cleverer.

So said, so done. The one official went to the right. He came upon trees, bearing all sorts of fruits. Gladly would he have plucked an apple, but they all hung so high that he would have been obliged to climb up. He tried to climb up in vain. All he succeeded in doing was tearing his night shirt. Then he struck upon a brook. It was swarming with fish.

'Wouldn't it be wonderful if we had all this fish in Podyacheskaya Street!' he thought, and his mouth watered. Then he entered woods and found partridges, grouse and hares.

'Good Lord, what an abundance of food!' he cried. His hunger was going up tremendously.

But he had to return to the appointed spot with empty hands. He found the other official waiting for him.

'Well, Your Excellency, how went it? Did you find anything?'

'Nothing but an old number of the *Moscow Gazette*, not another thing.'

The officials lay down to sleep again, but their empty stomachs gave them no rest. They were partly robbed of their sleep by the thought of who was now enjoying their pension, and partly by the recollection of the fruit, fishes, partridges, grouse and hares that they had seen during the day.

'The human pabulum in its original form flies, swims and grows on trees. Who would have thought it Your Excellency?' said the one official.

'To be sure,' rejoined the other official. 'I, too, must admit that I had imagined that our breakfast rolls, came into the world just as they appear on the table.'

'From which it is to be deduced that if we want to eat a pheasant, we must catch it first, kill it, pull its feathers and roast it. But how's that to be done?'

'Yes, how's that to be done?' repeated the other official.

They turned silent and tried again to fall asleep, but their hunger scared sleep away. Before their eyes swarmed flocks of pheasants and ducks, herds of porklings, and they were all so juicy, done so tenderly and garnished so deliciously with olives, capers and pickles.

'I believe I could devour my own boots now,' said the one official.

'Gloves, are not bad either, especially if they have been born quite mellow,' said the other official.

The two officials stared at each other fixedly. In their glances gleamed an evil-boding fire, their teeth chattered and a dull groaning issued from their breasts. Slowly they crept upon each other and suddenly they burst into a fearful frenzy. There was a yelling and groaning, the rags flew about, and the official who had been teacher of handwriting bit off his colleague's order and swallowed it. However, the sight of blood brought them both back to their senses.

'God help us!' they cried at the same time. 'We certainly don't mean to eat each other up. How could we have come to such a pass as this? What evil genius is making sport of us?'

'We must, by all means, entertain each other to pass the time away, otherwise there will be murder and death,' said the one official.

'You begin,' said the other.

'Can you explain why it is that the sun first rises and then sets? Why isn't it the reverse?'

'Aren't you a funny man, your Excellency? You get up first, then you go to your office and work there, and at night you lie down to sleep.'

'But why can't one assume the opposite, that is, that one goes to bed, sees all sorts of dream figures, and then gets up?'

'Well, yes, certainly. But when I was still an official, I always thought this way: "Now it is dawn, then it will be day, then will come supper, and finally will come the time to go to bed."'

The word 'supper' recalled that incident in the day's doings, and the thought of it made both officials melancholy, so that the conversation came to a halt.

'A doctor once told me that human beings can sustain

themselves for a long time on their own juices,' the one official began again.

'What does that mean?'

'It is quite simple. You see, one's own juices generate other juices, and these in their turn still other juices, and so it goes on until finally all the juices are consumed.'

'And then what happens?'

'Then food has to be taken into the system again.'

'The devil!'

No matter what topic the officials chose, the conversation invariably reverted to the subject of eating; which only increased their appetite more and more. So they decided to give up talking altogether, and, recollecting the *Moscow Gazette* that the one of them had found, they picked it up and began to read eagerly.

BANQUET GIVEN BY THE MAYOR

'The table was set for one hundred persons. The magnificence of it exceeded all expectations. The remotest provinces were represented at this feast of the gods by the costliest gifts. The golden sturgeon from Sheksna and the silver pheasant from the Caucasian woods held a rendezvous with strawberries so seldom to be had in our latitude in winter...'

'The devil! For God's sake, stop reading, Your Excellency. Couldn't you find something else to read about?' cried the other official in sheer desperation. He snatched the paper from his colleague's hands, and started to read something else.

'Our correspondent in Tula informs us that yesterday a sturgeon was found in the Upa (an event which even the oldest inhabitants cannot recall, and all the more remarkable since they recognized the former police captain in this sturgeon). This was made the occasion for giving a banquet in the club. The prime cause of the banquet was served in a large wooden platter garnished with vinegar pickles. A bunch of parsley stuck out of its mouth. Doctor P——who acted as toast-master saw to it that everybody present got a piece of the sturgeon. The sauces to go with it were unusually varied and delicate—'

'Permit me, Your Excellency, it seems to me you are not so careful either in the selection of reading matter,' interrupted the first official, who secured the *Gazette* again and started to read:

'One of the oldest inhabitants of Viatka has discovered a new and highly original recipe for fish soup; A live codfish (*lota vulgaris*) is taken and beaten with a rod until its liver swells up with anger...'

The officials' heads drooped. Whatever their eyes fell upon had something to do with eating. Even their own thoughts were fatal. No matter how much they tried to keep their minds off beefsteak and the like, it was all in vain; their fancy returned invariably, with irresistible force, back to that for which they were so painfully yearning.

Suddenly an inspiration came to the official who had once taught handwriting.

'I have it!' he cried delightedly. 'What do you say to this, Your Excellency? What do you say to our finding a muzhik?'

'A muzhik, Your Excellency? What sort of a muzhik?'

'Why a plain ordinary muzhik. A muzhik like all other muzhiks. He would get the breakfast rolls for us right away, and he could also catch partridges and fish for us.'

'Hm, a muzhik. But where are we to fetch one from, if there is no muzhik here?'

'Why shouldn't there be a muzhik here? There are muzhiks everywhere. All one has to do is hunt for them. There certainly must be a muzhik hiding here somewhere so as to get out of working.'

This thought so cheered the officials that they instantly

jumped up to go in search of a muzhik.

For a long while they wandered about on the island without the desired result, until finally a concentrated smell of black bread and old sheep skin assailed their nostrils and guided them in the right direction. There under a tree was a colossal muzhik lying fast asleep with his hands under his head. It was clear that to escape his duty to work he had impudently withdrawn to this island. The indignation of the officials knew no bounds.

'What, lying asleep here you lazy-bones you!' they raged at him, 'It is nothing to you that there are two officials here who are fairly perishing of hunger. Up, forward, march, work.'

The muzhik rose and looked at the two severe gentlemen standing in front of him. His first thought was to make his escape, but the officials held him fast.

He had to submit to his fate. He had to work.

First he climbed up on a tree and plucked several dozen of the finest apples for the officials. He kept a rotten one for himself. Then he turned up the earth and dug out some potatoes. Next he started a fire with two bits of wood that he rubbed against each other. Out of his own hair he made a snare and caught partridges. Over the fire, by this time burning brightly, he cooked so many kinds of food that the question arose in the officials' minds whether they shouldn't give some to this idler.

Beholding the efforts of the muzhik, they rejoiced in their hearts. They had already forgotten how the day before they had nearly been perishing of hunger, and all they thought of now was: 'What a good thing it is to be an official. Nothing bad can ever happen to an official.'

'Are you satisfied, gentlemen?' the lazy muzhik asked.

'Yes, we appreciate your industry,' replied the officials.

'Then you will permit me to rest a little?'

'Go take a little rest, but first make a good strong cord.'

The muzhik gathered wild hemp stalks, laid them in water,

beat them and broke them, and toward evening a good stout cord was ready. The officials took the cord and bound the muzhik to a tree, so that he should not run away. Then they laid themselves to sleep.

Thus day after day passed, and the muzhik became so skilful that he could actually cook soup for the officials in his bare hands. The officials had become round and well-fed and happy. It rejoiced them that here they needn't spend any money and that in the meanwhile their pensions were accumulating in St Petersburg.

'What is your opinion, Your Excellency,' one said to the other after breakfast one day, 'is the Story of the Tower of Babel true? Don't you think it is simply an allegory?'

'By no means, Your Excellency, I think it was something that really happened. What other explanation is there for the existence of so many different languages on earth?'

'Then the Flood must really have taken place, too?'

'Certainly, else; how would you explain the existence of Antediluvian animals? Besides, the *Moscow Gazette* says—'

They made search for the old number of the *Moscow Gazette*, seated themselves in the shade, and read the whole sheet from beginning to end. They read of festivities in Moscow, Tula, Penza and Riazan, and strangely enough felt no discomfort at the description of the delicacies served.

There is no saying how long this life might have lasted. Finally, however, it began to bore the officials. They often thought of their cooks in St Petersburg, and even shed a few tears in secret.

'I wonder how it looks in Podyacheskaya Street now, Your Excellency,' one of them said to the other.

'Oh, don't remind me of it, your Excellency. I am pining away with homesickness.'

'It is very nice here. There is really no fault to be found with this place, but the lamb longs for its mother sheep. And it is a pity, too, for the beautiful uniforms.'

'Yes, indeed, a uniform of the fourth class is no joke. The gold embroidery alone is enough to make one dizzy.'

Now they began to importune the muzhik to find some way of getting them back to Podyacheskaya Street, and strange to say, the muzhik even knew where Podyacheskaya Street was. He had once drunk beer and mead there, and as the saying goes, everything had run down his beard, alas, but nothing into his mouth. The officials rejoiced and said: 'We are officials from Podyacheskaya Street.'

'And I am one of those men—do you remember?—who sit on a scaffolding hung by ropes from the roofs and paint the outside walls. I am one of those who crawl about on the roofs like flies. That is what I am,' replied the muzhik.

The muzhik now pondered long and heavily on how to give great pleasure to his officials, who had been so gracious to him, the lazy-bones, and had not scorned his work. And he actually succeeded in constructing a ship. It was not really a ship, but still it was a vessel, that would carry them across the ocean close to Podyacheskaya Street.

'Now, take care, you dog, that you don't drown us,' said the officials, when they saw the raft rising and falling on the waves.

'Don't be afraid. We muzhiks are used to this,' said the muzhik, making all the preparations for the journey. He gathered swan's-down and made a couch for his two officials, then he crossed himself and rowed off from shore.

How frightened the officials were on the way, how seasick they were during the storms, how they scolded the coarse muzhik for his idleness, can neither be told nor described. The muzhik, however, just kept rowing on and fed his officials on herring. At last, they caught sight of dear old Mother Neva. Soon they were in the glorious Catherine Canal, and then, oh joy! they struck the grand Podyacheskaya Street. When the cooks saw their officials so well-fed, round and so happy, they rejoiced immensely. The officials drank coffee and rolls, then put on their uniforms and drove to the Pension Bureau. How much money they collected there is another thing that can neither be told nor described. Nor was the muzhik forgotten. The officials sent a glass of whiskey out to him and five kopeks. Now, Muzhik, rejoice.

MISERY

Anton Chekhov

The twilight of evening. Big flakes of wet snow are whirling lazily about the street lamps, which have just been lighted, and lying in a thin soft layer on roofs, horses' backs, shoulders, caps. Iona Potapov, the sledge-driver, is all white like a ghost. He sits on the box without stirring, bent as double as the living body can be bent. If a regular snowdrift fell on him it seems as though even then he would not think it necessary to shake it off... His little mare is white and motionless too. Her stillness, the angularity of her lines, and the stick-like straightness of her legs make her look like a halfpenny gingerbread horse. She is probably lost in thought. Anyone who has been torn away from the plough, from the familiar grey landscapes, and cast into this slough, full of monstrous lights, of unceasing uproar and hurrying people, is bound to think.

It is a long time since Iona and his nag have budged. They came out of the yard before dinnertime and not a single fare yet. But now the shades of evening are falling on the town. The pale light of the street lamps changes to a vivid colour, and the bustle of the street grows noisier.

'Sledge to Vyborgskaya!' Iona hears. 'Sledge!'

Iona starts, and through his snow-plastered eyelashes sees an officer in a military overcoat with a hood over his head.

'To Vyborgskaya,' repeats the officer. 'Are you asleep? To Vyborgskaya!'

In token of assent Iona gives a tug at the reins which sends cakes of snow flying from the horse's back and shoulders. The officer gets into the sledge. The sledge-driver clicks to the horse, cranes his neck like a swan, rises in his seat, and more from habit than necessity brandishes his whip. The mare cranes her neck, too, crooks her stick-like legs, and hesitatingly sets off...

'Where are you shoving, you devil?' Iona immediately hears shouts from the dark mass shifting to and fro before him. 'Where the devil are you going? Keep to the r-right!'

'You don't know how to drive! Keep to the right,' says the officer angrily.

A coachman driving a carriage swears at him; a pedestrian crossing the road and brushing the horse's nose with his shoulder looks at him angrily and shakes the snow off his sleeve. Iona fidgets on the box as though he were sitting on thorns, jerks his elbows, and turns his eyes about like one possessed as though he did not know where he was or why he was there.

'What rascals they all are!' says the officer jocosely. 'They are simply doing their best to run up against you or fall under the horse's feet. They must be doing it on purpose.'

Iona looks as his fare and moves his lips... Apparently he means to say something, but nothing comes but a sniff.

'What?' inquires the officer.

Iona gives a wry smile, and straining his throat, brings out huskily: 'My son...er...my son died this week, sir.'

'H'm! What did he die of?'

Iona turns his whole body round to his fare, and says:

'Who can tell! It must have been from fever... He lay three days in the hospital and then he died... God's will.'

'Turn round, you devil!' comes out of the darkness. 'Have you gone cracked, you old dog? Look where you are going!'

'Drive on! drive on!...' says the officer. 'We shan't get there till to-morrow going on like this. Hurry up!'

The sledge-driver cranes his neck again, rises in his seat, and with heavy grace swings his whip. Several times he looks round at the officer, but the latter keeps his eyes shut and is apparently disinclined to listen. Putting his fare down at Vyborgskaya, Iona stops by a restaurant, and again sits huddled up on the box... Again the wet snow paints him and his horse white. One hour passes, and then another...

Three young men, two tall and thin, one short and hunchbacked, come up, railing at each other and loudly stamping on the pavement with their goloshes.

'Cabby, to the Police Bridge!' the hunchback cries in a cracked voice. 'The three of us,... twenty kopecks!'

Iona tugs at the reins and clicks to his horse. Twenty kopecks is not a fair price, but he has no thoughts for that. Whether it is a rouble or whether it is five kopecks does not matter to him now so long as he has a fare... The three young men, shoving each other and using bad language, go up to the sledge, and all three try to sit down at once. The question remains to be settled: Which are to sit down and which one is to stand? After a long altercation, ill-temper, and abuse, they come to the conclusion that the hunchback must stand because he is the shortest.

'Well, drive on,' says the hunchback in his cracked voice, settling himself and breathing down Iona's neck. 'Cut along! What a cap you've got, my friend! You wouldn't find a worse one in all Petersburg...'

'He-he!... he-he!...' laughs Iona. 'It's nothing to boast of!'

'Well, then, nothing to boast of, drive on! Are you going to drive like this all the way? Eh? Shall I give you one in the neck?'

'My head aches,' says one of the tall ones. 'At the Dukmasovs' yesterday Vaska and I drank four bottles of brandy between us.'

'I can't make out why you talk such stuff,' says the other tall one angrily. 'You lie like a brute.'

'Strike me dead, it's the truth!...'

'It's about as true as that a louse coughs.'

'He-he!' grins Iona. 'Me-er-ry gentlemen!'

'Tfoo! the devil take you!' cries the hunchback indignantly. 'Will you get on, you old plague, or won't you? Is that the way to drive? Give her one with the whip. Hang it all, give it her well.'

Iona feels behind his back the jolting person and quivering voice of the hunchback. He hears abuse addressed to him, he sees people, and the feeling of loneliness begins little by little to be less heavy on his heart. The hunchback swears at him, till he chokes over some elaborately whimsical string of epithets and is overpowered by his cough. His tall companions begin talking of a certain Nadyezhda Petrovna. Iona looks round at them. Waiting till there is a brief pause, he looks round once more and says:

'This week...er...my...er...son died!'

'We shall all die,...' says the hunchback with a sigh, wiping his lips after coughing. 'Come, drive on! drive on! My friends, I simply cannot stand crawling like this! When will he get us there?'

'Well, you give him a little encouragement...one in the neck!'

'Do you hear, you old plague? I'll make you smart. If one stands on ceremony with fellows like you one may as well walk. Do you hear, you old dragon? Or don't you care a hang what we say?'

And Iona hears rather than feels a slap on the back of his neck.

'He-he!...' he laughs. 'Merry gentlemen... God give you health!'

'Cabman, are you married?' asks one of the tall ones.

'I? He he! Me-er-ry gentlemen. The only wife for me now is the damp earth... He-ho-ho!... The grave that is!... Here my son's dead and I am alive... It's a strange thing, death has come in at the wrong door... Instead of coming for me it went for my son...'

And Iona turns round to tell them how his son died, but at that point the hunchback gives a faint sigh and announces that, thank God! they have arrived at last. After taking his twenty kopecks, Iona gazes for a long while after the revellers, who disappear into a dark entry. Again he is alone and again there is silence for him... The misery which has been for a brief space eased comes back again and tears his heart more cruelly than ever. With a look of anxiety and suffering Iona's eyes stray restlessly among the crowds moving to and fro on both sides of the street: can he not find among those thousands someone who will listen to him? But the crowds flit by heedless of him and his misery... His misery is immense, beyond all bounds. If Iona's heart were to burst and his misery to flow out, it would flood the whole world, it seems, but yet it is not seen. It has found a hiding-place in such an insignificant shell that one would not have found it with a candle by daylight...

Iona sees a house-porter with a parcel and makes up his mind to address him.

'What time will it be, friend?' he asks.

'Going on for ten... Why have you stopped here? Drive on!'

Iona drives a few paces away, bends himself double, and gives himself up to his misery. He feels it is no good to appeal to people. But before five minutes have passed he draws himself up, shakes his head as though he feels a sharp pain, and tugs at the reins... He can bear it no longer.

'Back to the yard!' he thinks. 'To the yard!'

And his little mare, as though she knew his thoughts, falls to trotting. An hour and a half later Iona is sitting by a big dirty stove. On the stove, on the floor, and on the benches are people snoring. The air is full of smells and stuffiness. Iona looks at the sleeping figures, scratches himself, and regrets that he has come home so early...

'I have not earned enough to pay for the oats, even,' he thinks. 'That's why I am so miserable. A man who knows how to do his work,...who has had enough to eat, and whose horse has had enough to eat, is always at ease...'

In one of the corners a young cabman gets up, clears his

throat sleepily, and makes for the water-bucket.

'Want a drink?' Iona asks him.

'Seems so.'

'May it do you good... But my son is dead, mate... Do you hear? This week in the hospital... It's a queer business...'

Iona looks to see the effect produced by his words, but he sees nothing. The young man has covered his head over and is already asleep. The old man sighs and scratches himself... Just as the young man had been thirsty for water, he thirsts for speech. His son will soon have been dead a week, and he has not really talked to anybody yet... He wants to talk of it properly, with deliberation... He wants to tell how his son was taken ill, how he suffered, what he said before he died, how he died... He wants to describe the funeral, and how he went to the hospital to get his son's clothes. He still has his daughter Anisya in the country....And he wants to talk about her too... Yes, he has plenty to talk about now. His listener ought to sigh and exclaim and lament... It would be even better to talk to women. Though they are silly creatures, they blubber at the first word.

'Let's go out and have a look at the mare,' Iona thinks. 'There is always time for sleep... You'll have sleep enough, no fear...'

He puts on his coat and goes into the stables where his mare is standing. He thinks about oats, about hay, about the weather... He cannot think about his son when he is alone... To talk about him with someone is possible, but to think of him and picture him is insufferable anguish...

'Are you munching?' Iona asks his mare, seeing her shining eyes. 'There, munch away, munch away... Since we have not earned enough for oats, we will eat hay... Yes,... I have grown too old to drive... My son ought to be driving, not I... He was a real cabman... He ought to have lived...'

Iona is silent for a while, and then he goes on:

'That's how it is, old girl... Kuzma Ionitch is gone... He

said good-by to me... He went and died for no reason... Now, suppose you had a little colt, and you were own mother to that little colt... And all at once that same little colt went and died... You'd be sorry, wouldn't you?...'

The little mare munches, listens, and breathes on her master's hands. Iona is carried away and tells her all about it.

A DREAM OF WILD BEES

Olive Schreiner

A mother sat alone at an open window. Through it came the voices of the children as they played under the acacia-trees, and the breath of the hot afternoon air. In and out of the room flew the bees, the wild bees, with their legs yellow with pollen, going to and from the acacia-trees, droning all the while. She sat on a low chair before the table and darned. She took her work from the great basket that stood before her on the table: some lay on her knee and half covered the book that rested there. She watched the needle go in and out; and the dreary hum of the bees and the noise of the children's voices became a confused murmur in her ears, as she worked slowly and more slowly. Then the bees, the long-legged wasp-like fellows who make no honey, flew closer and closer to her head, droning. Then she grew more and more drowsy, and she laid her hand, with the stocking over it, on the edge of the table, and leaned her head upon it. And the voices of the children outside grew more and more dreamy, came now far, now near; then she did not hear them, but she felt under her heart where the ninth child lay. Bent forward and sleeping there, with the bees flying about her head, she had a weird brain-picture; she thought the bees lengthened and lengthened themselves out and became human creatures and moved round and round her. Then one came to her softly, saying, 'Let me lay my hand upon thy side where the child sleeps. If I shall touch him he shall be as I.'

She asked, 'Who are you?'

And he said, 'I am Health. Whom I touch will have always the red blood dancing in his veins; he will not know weariness nor pain; life will be a long laugh to him.'

'No,' said another, 'let me touch, for I am Wealth. If I touch him material care shall not feed on him. He shall live on the blood and sinews of his fellow-men, if he will; and what his eye lusts for, his hand will have. He shall not know "I want."' And the child lay still like lead.

And another said, 'Let me touch him: I am Fame. The man I touch, I lead to a high hill where all men may see him. When he dies he is not forgotten, his name rings down the centuries, each echoes it on to his fellows. Think—not to be forgotten through the ages!'

And the mother lay breathing steadily, but in the brain-picture they pressed closer to her.

'Let me touch the child,' said one, 'for I am Love. If I touch him he shall not walk through life alone. In the greatest dark, when he puts out his hand he shall find another hand by it. When the world is against him, another shall say, "You and I."' And the child trembled.

But another pressed close and said, 'Let me touch; for I am Talent. I can do all things—that have been done before. I touch the soldier, the statesman, the thinker, and the politicians who succeed; and the writer who is never before his time, and never behind it. If I touch the child he shall not weep for failure.'

About the mother's head the bees were flying, touching her with their long tapering limbs; and, in her brain-picture, out of the shadow of the room came one with sallow face, deep-lined, the cheeks drawn into hollows, and a mouth smiling quiveringly. He stretched out his hand. And the mother drew back, and cried, 'Who are you?' He answered nothing; and she looked up between his eyelids. And she said, 'What can you give the child—health?' And he said, 'The man I touch, there wakes up in his blood a burning fever, that shall lick his blood as fire. The fever that I will give him shall be cured when his life is cured.'

'You give wealth?'

He shook his head. 'The man whom I touch, when he bends to pick up gold, he sees suddenly a light over his head in the sky; while he looks up to see it, the gold slips from between his fingers, or sometimes another passing takes it from them.'

'Fame?'

He answered, 'Likely not. For the man I touch there is a path traced out in the sand by a finger which no man sees. That he must follow. Sometimes it leads almost to the top, and then turns down suddenly into the valley. He must follow it, though none else sees the tracing.'

'Love?'

He said, 'He shall hunger for it—but he shall not find it. When he stretches out his arms to it, and would lay his heart against a thing he loves, then, far off along the horizon he shall see a light play. He must go towards it. The thing he loves will not journey with him; he must travel alone. When he presses somewhat to his burning heart, crying, "Mine, mine, my own!" he shall hear a voice—"Renounce! renounce! This is not thine!"'

'He shall succeed?'

He said, 'He shall fail. When he runs with others they shall reach the goal before him. For strange voices shall call to him and strange lights shall beckon him, and he must wait and listen. And this shall be the strangest: far off across the burning sands where, to other men, there is only the desert's waste, he shall see a blue sea! On that sea the sun shines always, and the water is blue as burning amethyst, and the foam is white on the shore. A great land rises from it, and he shall see upon the mountain-tops burning gold.'

The mother said, 'He shall reach it?'

And he smiled curiously.

She said, 'It is real?'

And he said, 'What *is* real?'

And she looked up between his half-closed eyelids, and said, 'Touch.'

And he leaned forward and laid his hand upon the sleeper, and whispered to it, smiling; and this only she heard—'This shall be thy reward—that the ideal shall be real to thee.'

And the child trembled; but the mother slept on heavily and her brain-picture vanished. But deep within her the antenatal thing that lay here had a dream. In those eyes that had never seen the day, in that half-shaped brain was a sensation of light! Light—that it never had seen. Light—that perhaps it never should see. Light—that existed somewhere!

And already it had its reward: the Ideal was real to it.

URMI: THE STORY OF A QUEEN

Cornelia Sorabji

Five p.m. and Saturday. Without, a cold wet mist, a grey sky, dirty streets; within, the curtains drawn, the cosiest of lounges, the softest of cushions, the fire crackling merrily, the kettle hissing gently—how nice it was to be warm, and sleepy!... Presto! They don't think long about things here. A moment ago that lovely red ball nestled confidingly between the peaks of those moss-covered mountains; now it has dropped, disappeared, gone to rest, leaving only its glorious curtains for us to look upon. Or, is this the entrance to the palace of some deity—into whose presence-chamber the sun has just been ushered? The strong mountains are on guard, and the stars in motion have played the royal anthem.

All here is in darkness, save for that reflection from the west... Softly—our way is through that wooded forest, under those great strong trees that embrace each other in their solitariness. Past the quiet lake, inside the gates. Another palace—large gardens, cool deep verandahs, marble halls, tall statues, Quick! Tarry not—through the courtyard. What is that? Only the sacred tulsi in its accustomed place. Grave men in red uniforms watch the buildings. Pass them by; they question not. At last! A low dark room—there, in that corner, on the bed. Hush! A moan—she is in pain—step gently. Poor thing! Small and sad, and beautiful! What eyes! What hair! What jewels! What lovely, clinging, saffron silk! Who hurt her? Her small hands are clenched—she beats her forehead—she calls on 'Krishna.' Now she rises—listen! She speaks.

'Bukku! Come near me. Are the women there? Send them away. I want you—only you. Listen, Bukku; there is not much time. What means this sickness? Is it death? Feel my hands; they burn. My head—it's like a hot stone, lying out in an April sun. I will not live the night. What say you?'

'Hush! Light of my eyes! My child—my flower, my tender lotus-bud! That will not be, that must not be! Your father is measuring the ground on a long pilgrimage to Benares. You will recover. Have you your amulet? Take hold of it; and see, here's a new charm. My grandmother learnt it of a faqir, and taught it me. It cured the good Akbar once, when he lay dying. The little Gulam went up to the hills this morning, and brought me the healing herb from a far-distant spot. See, too, my bracelets—they are with the priests—they will appease the gods. They were good gold. Nay! my beautiful, you will live many years. My treasure! My precious stone, the worst is past.'

'No! Bukku! you are kind, you love me. You are the only true creature I have beside me. All else are false, and mean me ill. They are like the hooded cobra, they sting me in the grass. Oh, Bukku! I have not loved this royal state. And they love me not here. Would that I were home again, on the cool soft banks of my own river. Remember you, Bukku, how the lotus floated on the water, and the plantain trees spread their green shade over our heads? And my father—my dear kind father— how I read with him, seated on his knee, stories of early times when the world was young; and of the beautiful Sakuntalla, and the poor Nar Jehan; and those verses of Kalidas, when he read them to me—'twas like the little summer brook playing with the pebbles—so pleasing to my ear... It's all over now. He will miss me, my poor old father. And perhaps he, my lord whom I may not name, *perhaps* he will sigh for me, and say, "She was young, and the gods made her beautiful, and—she is dead!" And he will be just a little grieved, and bid them play sad music, and feed poor Brahmins, in my name... Then he will go out, and hunt or shoot, or sit with his councillors, and forget me quite. I've loved him, Bukku. He was good to me, and strong and wise and kind; and when I talked to him of my early days and pastimes, and the things which I loved, he smiled, and said, "It is not so with all my other wives; they know not what to talk about; they have not read your favourite books; they cannot read; they care not what occurs in other lands; they ask me for new jewels and prettier clothes; and they look modest, and sometimes beautiful; and that is all: but you."... And once he praised my wisdom, and said he would I share his throne with him. See! keep you this letter; when they lift me on to the bier, and bear me to the burning ground, and put the torch to these cold limbs, go to him, put *that* in his hand. It's not long; just one line—he will know, and understand...

'And now, Bukku, quick! the child! My strength is failing. Bring him to me—nearer —lift him up. How beautiful he is! His eyes, how large, how dark, how deep! I feel I am looking into a well of light, of sunshine, of clear cool water. His small round arms, how soft they are! He smiles! poor child, he wants me—and I go, whence I return not, unless perchance as some small reptile, or a tree, or a flower.

'I would it were a flower, and that I grew where *he* would touch me, and feel my petals, and say, "I like that flower; it is as pure and fragile as my little Urmi."... But, when I'm gone, take the child, carry it hence. They mean it harm. You have nursed me—nurse it; but *hide* it—hide it safely from them— from Afzul. My father will pay you, and will see to its future. Now, while it is young and helpless, you must love it and care for it. Tell it of me and of its father...but let *them* here think that it is dead. You know what to do; some poor baby you will purchase in the market, will have a prince's end... I will tell you all, Bukku—you shall tell my father. Tell him how they hated me here. You remember, when I came, how they looked at me, and shook their heads, and said a "God forbid!" because I read and wrote? And when the king, our lord, favoured me above them all, and sought my presence, and listened to my words, I heard them whisper. "Bold minx!" they said, "child of the Evil One! She knows what it does not beseem women to know, for she reads and writes as if she were some common clerk. And when she talks to *him*, she lifts her eyes and looks upon his face. How know we that in her distant home she did not break her *purdah*? We hear that her father taught her many things which he learnt of the Feringhee."…

'And my women who loved me, they turned against me. All but you, Bukku, whom they did not dare to touch; but they kept you from me, knowing that you loved me. I was wretched, and wrote my father word that they looked coldly on me. He said, "Try gifts, try gold and jewels." They took them—but it made no change; and I would I'd never left him—but for the king whom I loved—yet him I seldom saw. After the boy came, things were worse. Lying ill here one day behind this heavy curtain, I heard them talk, and Afzul was with them, and he said, "Would that the king had hearkened to my words, and taken to wife the bride whom I had chosen. With this one I have had no commission; and she is the child of the Evil One. See how she has bewitched the king. He praises her looks, and her learning, and her ways; and, now that there is an heir, his regard for her has grown tenfold. We must *remove* her and the boy. Say the word: it shall be done!" And then, Bukku, *his* mother, whom I had tried to love as mine own, said, "You know your work: *do it*. I give you leave: she has come between my son and me!" And Afzul—how he looked! I saw his eye gleam, and he swore an oath by his father's head. He is a terrible man. Shield my boy from him; let him not see his face. It would haunt his baby days—it would make a stain on his mind. Oh! would I were here to protect him! But what power would I have? It would but make matters worse, could I intervene. *You* will care for him, Bukku—you and my father. The king—he cannot; he must think him dead.

'You see *that*... Afzul... did... his work...

'What is this, Bukku? Is it—*death*?

'My eyes grow dim. Call on Krishna. I am falling—hold my hand... The lord my king—would he were here!... My love! I have loved you much; love me a little.'

...Through the open door streamed in the moonlight, and kissed the lovely figure as it lay; from the hills came the weird bark of the jackals; an owl shrieked in the mango grove... What is that? the death-wail? They know, then, that all is over. Is it well with them in the agent's sanctum? in the zenana? in the servants' courtyard? in the king's chamber? Is it well?

Seven p.m.—The fire is low; I am cold. Was it only a dream? Alas! would it were! It was the wail of some poor child in a London street. And it stirred the memory of other sad things in far-distant climes, across the seas... Poor Urmi!

DYJHICON: THE COWARD-HERO

A. G. Seklemian

Dyjhicon was a poor unfortunate fellow who had only two goats and a cow. His wife was an ambitious woman, and annoyed him by her frequent demands.

'I want you to go out and work,' she often said. 'I want you to build a new house, I want to buy myself some new dresses, oxen and sheep, a horse and wagon.'

Dyjhicon, tiring of her endless complaints and scoldings, one day took his great stick and drove the cow out of the house, saying to himself:

'Let me run from this wicked wife to the wilderness and there die.'

This was what the woman wanted. Thus he ran from her and wandered in the wilderness. When he was hungry he milked the cow and drank the milk, and when he was tired he mounted the cow. He was very timid,—a typical coward. The sight of a running rat was enough to make him tremble.

'Eh!' he thought, nevertheless, 'it is better to be torn by wild beasts than to become the slave of a wicked woman.'

One day, as the cow was pasturing on a green meadow and Dyjhicon was lying down lazily, the flies stung him. He cursed his wife and clapped his hands to kill the flies. Then he counted to see how many flies he had killed at one stroke, and lo! they were seven in number. This encouraged him, and he took his knife and carved upon his stick these words:

'I am Dyjhicon; I have killed seven by one stroke of the hand.'

Then he got astride the cow and rode away. After a long journey he came to a green meadow in the centre of which there was a magnificent castle with an orchard around it. He let the cow graze in the meadow and he lay down to sleep. Seven brothers lived in that castle. One of them, seeing Dyjhicon and his cow in the meadow came to find who it was that had ventured to enter their ground. Dyjhicon was sleeping, with his stick standing near him. The man approached and, reading the inscription, was terrified.

'What a hero!' he thought to himself, 'he has killed seven men by one stroke of the hand. He must be a brave man, else he would not dare to sleep here so carelessly. What courage! what boldness! he has come so far without arms, without a horse, without a companion. This man is surely a great hero.'

He went and informed his brothers as to what he had seen; and all the seven brothers came to pay their respects to the unknown hero, and to invite him to their humble home. The cow, being frightened by their approach, began to leap and bellow. Her voice wakened Dyjhicon, who, seeing seven men standing before him, was terrified, and snatching his club, stood aside trembling. The seven brothers thought that he was angry with them, and was trembling on account of his wrath, and that he would kill all of them by one stroke of his stick. Thereupon they began to supplicate him to pardon their rudeness in disturbing his repose. Then they invited him to go with them, saying:

'We are seven brothers and have a great reputation as good fighters in this district. But we shall be entirely invincible, if you will join us and become our elder brother. We will take great pleasure in placing our house and all that belongs to us at the service of such a hero as yourself.'

Hearing this, Dyjhicon ceased trembling, and said:

'Very well, let it be as you say.'

They took him to the castle with great pomp and served

to him a grand banquet, at which all the seven brothers stood before him, folding their arms upon their breasts and awaiting his permission to sit. Dyjhicon was in great alarm, his heart was faint and he had fallen into meditation as to the manner in which he might free himself from this perplexing situation. The seven brothers thought that he was not only a very brave hero, but was also such a great sage, that he did not care even to look at their faces. They began to cough in a low voice to draw his attention. On account of his internal fear Dyjhicon suddenly shook his head. The seven brothers took this as a permission to sit. After the banquet they said to him:

'My lord, where have you left your horse, arms and servants? Will you command us to go and bring them?'

'Horse and arms are necessary for timid men,' said Dyjhicon; 'I have never had need of them. I use horse and arms only when I fight a great battle. As to servants, I never need them; all men are my servants. You see, I have come so far having only a cow and my stick. Dyjhicon is my name; I have killed seven by one stroke of the hand.'

Their esteem and admiration for Dyjhicon increased every day, and at last they were so much fascinated by his alleged bravery that they gave him in marriage their only sister, who was a very beautiful maiden. Dyjhicon knew that he was unworthy, but he could not refuse this gift.

'Eh!' he said, 'I will do you the favour of marrying her since you entreat me so earnestly.'

They brought costly garments, and putting them on Dyjhicon, made him a handsome bridegroom. They had a splendid wedding festival which was reported in all neighbouring countries. The four princes of the neighbouring countries had asked the hand of the maiden in marriage, and all of them had been refused. Now hearing that the maiden was given in marriage to a stranger, the four princes waged war against the seven brothers. Dyjhicon, hearing this, was stricken with fear, and longed that the earth might open its mouth and swallow him. He thought to run away, but there were no means of escaping. While he indulged in these sad meditations, the seven brothers came, and bowing down before him, said:

'What is your order, my lord? Will you go fight yourself, or will you have us go first?'

This caused Dyjhicon's heart to melt. He began to tremble in his whole body, and to strike his teeth one against another. The seven brothers thought that it was because of his violent rage, and that in his fury he would destroy whole armies.

'My lord,' they said, finally, 'let us seven brothers go fight them at first, and if we find them hard to conquer we will send you word, that you may come to our assistance.'

'Well, well; do so,' answered Dyjhicon, somewhat relieved.

They went and began the battle. Their neighbouring peoples were in constant terror of the seven brothers, who were famous as brave fighters. Now that they had also a brother-in-law who could kill seven men by one stroke of the hand, their foes were the more afraid of them. But this time the men of the four princes were united, and they fought with unusual zeal and determination. This caused the seven brothers to retreat a little, and they sent to brother Dyjhicon, saying:

'We are in trouble; come to our assistance.'

A fast horse and magnificent arms awaited him. He began to curse the day when he came to that house. But what could he do now? At last he decided to go to the battle-field, cast himself against the swords of the enemy and die; death was preferable to such a disgraceful life. As soon as he mounted the horse, the beast who knew that the rider was inexperienced, ran away like a winged eagle. Dyjhicon could not stop or manage it. The seven brothers thought he was so brave that he left the horse free in order to reach and slaughter the enemy. The horse broke into the line of the enemy, who began to fly, saying:

'Who can stand before this great hero?'

In their hurry to retreat they began to slaughter one another. Dyjhicon, who had never been on horseback before, was so much afraid that he thought he was already lost. As the horse was running through the forest, he threw his arms around an oak tree and embraced it, letting the horse go from under him. The tree happened to be rotten and was rooted out when he took hold of it. This caused a great panic among the enemy, who ran away exclaiming:

'Aha! he has pulled up by the roots an enormous oak, and now he means to batter us into pieces with it. Who can stand before this strong warrior?'

So crying as they ran away, they slaughtered one another. Thereupon, the seven brothers came and embracing the feet of their heroic brother-in-law, exclaimed:

'What magnificent courage! What a great victory!'

With these words they brought Dyjhicon home with great pomp and glory. The four princes who waged the war, being greatly humiliated, sued for reconciliation, and in order to gain Dyjhicon's favour, each of them sent him as a present one thousand ewes with their lambs, ten mares with their colts, and other costly offerings.

Thus the greatest coward became the greatest hero.

SALMAN AND ROSTOM

A. G. Seklemian

Salman was a strong and mighty man, He was as large as a hill, as powerful as a giant, and a terrible tyrant. He lived in one corner of the world, but his fame spread terror over all the earth. He had a horse of lightning, and his arms were as strong as iron. He assaulted men in their peaceful habitations, and took tribute from them; none could refuse to pay him tribute, else he would slaughter and destroy the people. In another portion of the earth there was another strong brigand, called Chal, who had a son named Rostom. This Rostom was a huge man, as large as a mountain, and greatly celebrated for his extraordinary strength and bravery. It was only the land of this Chal which did not pay tribute to Salman.

One day Chal mounted his horse and started, saying: 'Let me go and see what kind of a man Salman is.'

After a long journey he met a huge man mounted on a horse swift as lightning; the staff of his spear was as thick as a man's waist. Chal did not know that this was Salman himself; but nevertheless he prepared his spear for battle. To his surprise, the horseman gave spur to his horse and passed by Chal without even looking at his face. Upon this Chal was offended, and threw his spear after the horseman. Salman turned back, seized Chal, whom he bound under the belly of his horse, and galloped until he came to a tent pitched by a gurgling spring. He dismounted, nailed Chal's ear to the tent's beam, and lay down to sleep. Chal was almost mad with rage; he gnashed his teeth and muttered to himself:

'He did not speak a word to me, he did not tell me his name. I wish I might know who he is.'

Salman soon waked, and asked:

'Fellow, who are you?'

'I am from Chal's country,' answered Chal. He was so much afraid that he did not say that he was Chal himself.

'Ah!' exclaimed Salman, releasing Chal's ear, 'why did you not tell me before? Go and bid Rostom, Chal's son, come hither that we may measure swords. There cannot be two men of equal strength; the world must know who is the stronger champion. I am Salman.'

Chal returned to his house and sighed deeply. Rostom, hearing him sighing, said:

'How now, father? You are Chal and I am Rostom, your son, and yet you sigh! Nay, you must tell me your grief.'

Chal told him of his meeting with Salman, and the latter's challenge to Rostom. Rostom took with him his cousin Vyjhan, and both disguised themselves, assuming the habit of pilgrims. Rostom kissed his white-hoofed horse on both eyes and said to his father:

'When I am in trouble my horse will know it and will beat the ground with his feet. Then bind my arms upon his back and set him free; he will come and find me.'

Vyjhan, who accompanied Rostom on his journey, was far from being a common mortal. He had a wonderful voice; if he cried in the East his voice would be heard in the West. After traveling for a long time, Rostom and Vyjhan came to a city and encamped upon a meadow outside the town. Rostom was sleeping, when Vyjhan heard a terrible uproar in the city and went there to inquire the cause of the trouble. Some of the people were running like chased deer, some were tearing their hair, some beating their breasts, and all were weeping and wailing.

'Why, what is the matter?' asked Vyjhan.

'Salman has come, demanding seven years' tribute that is in arrears,' the people answered.

Soon they collected the amount; but the question now arose, by whom they should send the tribute, because Salman would take away the man by whom the tribute was sent, and kill him.

'Give it to me, I will take it,' said Vyjhan.

Soon Rostom heard in his sleep Vyjhan's shrill voice, saying: 'Help, Rostom! Salman is carrying me away.'

Rostom got up and learned from the people what had happened, and lo! his white-hoofed horse came running and stood before him. Immediately Rostom jumped on the back of his horse, which galloped away and soon reached Salman's tent. Salman, having nailed Vyjhan's ear to the tent beam, came out to meet Rostom. Then and there took place a duel the most terrible that has ever been recorded in the history of the world. Bows and arrows, spears and swords were cut into pieces. Finally they came near one another, seized each other, and both were entangled in each other's hair.

Up to the present time they have not yet conquered one another, but are still struggling. Now and then they pull and shake each other so violently that the earth quakes, and that is what men call an earthquake; and Vyjhan's voice is still heard deeply from afar.